A.K.A.
A cosmic fable

'It will be a hit . . . it is a delight . . . Dr Rob
Swigart has learned the trade of satire. He knows
when to prick and when to stab. There are a
number of nasty CIA types in A.K.A. and
Swigart pins them meticulously down to the
tuna-fish sandwiches, sadism, white socks and
bubblegum shoes . . . Everything, and most near
everyone, comes together in the close of A.K.A.
I got the feeling I'd been there, myself. Swigart
makes it both ludicrous and believable through
the writer's equivalent of gene splicing . . . This
artist, miles ahead, has given us a mutant fable
for the 8os.'

San Francisco Bay Guardian

'The plot of Swigart's novel runs through a mad
melange of space technology, desert-spa health
clubs, underground film-making, and government
intrigue, all of which is smothered by a thick layer
of good-time sex. The plot weaves its way through
the workings of energy cells, adrenalin glands,
and termites – all linked together in an answer to
the world's problems . . . If fiction wants to be
fun, it had better keep up with the competition
of movies and TV. In this league, A.K.A. does
nicely.'

Chicago Sunday Times

Rob Swigart

A.K.A.
A COSMIC fAblE

MAGNUM BOOKS
Methuen Paperbacks Ltd

A Magnum Book

A.K.A. A Cosmic Fable
ISBN O 417 03990 5

First published 1978
by Houghton Mifflin Company Inc., New York
Magnum edition published 1979

Magnum Books are published
by Methuen Paperbacks Ltd
11 New Fetter Lane, London EC4P 4EE

Made and printed in Great Britain
by Richard Clay (The Chaucer Press) Ltd,
Bungay, Suffolk

This is Jane's book

Acknowledgments

Special thanks must go to many who contributed in one way or another to this fable: Sharon and especially Jack Erwin; Bill and Louise Winter, who gave August his vitiligo, among other things; Grandma Kaiser, who stitched Jonah's rabbit suit, and Jonah's parents, Peter and Judy Steinhart; my friend Tom Hecker; Diane and Michael Flaherty; Buff Bradley, the Zen Baptist, and Susan; Michael Murphy, who loaned me Reich; Patti Harris, who made the shirts; and Doc Burgert, who has the ripest laugh west of Chicago . . .

Electronic Prologue

. . . the reader, like the writer himself, will not be able to escape the feeling that the investigation of the orgasm, *the Cinderella of the natural sciences*, has led us far into deeply stirring secrets of nature.

– Wilhelm Reich, *The Function of the Orgasm*

A Place Setting

THE DIRECTOR LEANED BACK in his swivel chair and stared out at the blistering smelter of late June in Washington. What was being forged out there? He swiveled around and pressed a button.

"Computer? Team A reports Avery Augenblaue's return. What do they mean?"

"They mean he is returning, Mr. Director."

"Yes. But where is he returning from?"

"Intergalactic space. He's been gone for ten years and is due to return today."

"Where is he landing?"

"Kankakee, Illinois. Augenblaue AeroSpace facility."

"I seem to remember something about the launch. What happened then?"

"He took off in the *A.K.A. Monastic*, and there was a riot in the stands."

"The stands?"

"Affirmative. Press corps, relatives, representatives of foreign governments, government officials. The President."

"Oh, God. The President. That's when he disappeared?"

"I perceive query in your tone. Affirmative."

"Didn't we have any control?"

"Augenblaue AeroSpace is private industry. Government has no control."

"But surely there were laws? Laws that were broken?"

"None to cover what happened."

"Will he return?"

"In seven minutes, twenty-three seconds. According to Dr. Ambrose Merkin, head of Augenblaue AeroSpace research."

"What will be the effect on the world of this return, which my agents think significant enough to be reported to me directly? And to the President, Most Secret?"

"The effect will be enormous, but unknown. There are, throughout the world, over one billion members of the AKA Clubs. All of them are waiting for Avery's return. Statistical predictions for various eventualities indicate skews in several significant directions."

"For instance?"

"Should, for example, Avery *not* return, a Sino-Soviet War: 87 percent probability. Northern California, Oregon, and the southern half of Washington certain to attempt secession from the Union."

"OK, OK. There will be effects. What should we do?"

"Beep."

"No answer?"

"I cannot answer that, Mr. Director. I am only a machine incapable of giving judgment. You will have to decide for yourself."

"The President is on my ass about this. I have to tell him something. I need more data. Give me more data."

"Beep."

"No answer?"

"You did not ask a question, and the command was too imprecise."

"Very well. I'll look into it. Terminate program."

"Program terminated. Good night, Mr. Director."

Oh, boy, thought the Director, leaning back in his chair again. He locked his hands behind his head and stared out at the sun dipping like a stale doughnut into the sour coffee of the Potomac. Oh, boy.

PART I / TEN YEARS

The social ramble ain't restful.

– Leroy R. 'Satchel' Paige

1 / Humble Pie

"YOU LOOK FAMILIAR," said Ambrose Merkin. "I can't quite place you, but I'd swear I've seen you somewhere before."

"I used to be in the navy." Constantine Hubble had tightly curled blond hair and finely chiseled if somewhat bland features.

"Oh, well, never mind. What can I do for you?" Ambrose leaned back in his chair. He had large gray muttonchop whiskers and a pair of heavy, black-framed glasses pushed up on top of his head. He rubbed the bridge of his nose wearily.

"My name is Hubble. I'm a special investigator for the Department. We are trying to track down Avery Augenblaue, who, it seems, is missing. As you know, the tenth annual AKA convention starts tomorrow, and if Avery doesn't show up there are liable to be riots. If he does show up, for that matter, there are liable to be, uh, disturbances. So we must locate him. Considering the edgy and divisive state of the country at this time, the President feels that national security is involved. You understand."

"Yes. I'm familiar with national security," said Ambrose. "But I'm afraid I can't help you. I haven't seen Mr. Augenblaue since he brought the *Monastic* back from intergalactic space."

"I see," said Hubble. He sat straight in his chair, his strangely undersized porkpie hat squarely in his lap. "Perhaps you could recall for me the last time you saw him? That may provide some clue to his whereabouts."

"Certainly," said Dr. Merkin, showing his large teeth, behind which clicked the dwindling remains of a lemon-flavored throat lozenge. "He returned, as I'm sure you're aware, two months ago Friday, in the late afternoon. We were expecting him since the ship had been programmed for reentry on that day, though because of the lapse of ten years we couldn't be precise about the time. The Lorentz-Fitzgerald contraction equations, as developed from Einstein's Special Relativity Theory, in which motion is contracted by a factor of $\sqrt{1-v^2/c^2}$, showed some anomaly in time relative to motion that could not be entirely worked out beforehand by computer, though as it happened we were remarkably accurate. You could refer to my paper, 'Some Lorentz-Fitzgerald Anomalies in the Augenblaue Intergalactic Flight: The Orgone Side Effect,' which was published last year in the *Astrophysical Journal*. It predicted a deviation of 1.9×10^{-12} nanoseconds, which, as I indicated, was remarkably accurate."

"Yes, yes, Dr. Merkin. But my question concerned Mr. Augenblaue. It is imperative that we find him before the AKA Club convention starts."

"Sorry. Where was I?" Ambrose stroked his muttonchops and sucked at the last of the lemon lozenge. "Yes. The return. Well, Mr. Augenblaue landed at the Augenblaue AeroSpace complex out at Kankakee at 4:47:32 P.M. It was truly lousy weather, I remember. Unseasonably cold and windy for June, with a kind of bitter cold rain. Wind out of the northwest at twenty-five gusting to forty. Knots, that is. Four-tenths of an inch of precipitation, mostly as rain or small hailstones. Really vicious weather."

"I'm sure everyone in the world remembers that day and what the weather was like. It was the day he returned from *out there*, the day he arrived with the truth about *The* Blue Light. There's no doubt that everyone remembers that it was raining in Kankakee." Hubble seemed to be a bit enraptured with his memory, but he brought himself up short.

"But what we're investigating, Dr. Merkin, is what occurred after Mr. Augenblaue landed. Please continue. Time is getting short."

"Right. Sorry, again." Ambrose leaned back in his chair and sighed. He glanced out his office window in the Augenblaue AeroSpace Research Facility building in suburban Evanston, Illinois. His window afforded him a view across Lake Shore Drive of Lake Michigan. "It certainly is a hot day," he remarked at last. "Not at all like the day Avery returned."

Hubble had no time to waste looking out the window. Besides, he already knew that the sun was shining, that it was hot and humid, and that the lake simmered like broth. "Please, Dr. Merkin."

"Uh, well. Avery opened the hatch of his ship and stepped out. He was wearing, let me get this right, not his pearl gray jumpsuit, the one he left in, but a regular business suit. Yes, I remember distinctly, it was a yellow and brown broad check suit, ten years out of date, of course — very narrow lapels — and an orange silk choker. He looked very handsome at the hatch of the *Monastic*, enabling us to snap lovely publicity photos. Just a second, I have a few here."

Dr. Merkin leaped from his chair and rummaged in a file cabinet behind his desk.

"Now where the hell are those pictures?" he muttered, tossing papers over his shoulder. He grabbed a second handful of papers and tossed them too, and then another, until the air between himself and Hubble was filled with fluttering white pages seesawing through the air like falling leaves. "I stored them in this drawer. Goddam." He slammed the drawer closed.

"Dr. Merkin, it's not necessary to show . . ." Special investigator Hubble started to speak, but Ambrose opened another drawer and began hurling papers over his shoulder again.

"Aha!" he shouted as the last papers settled to the floor. His desk was littered with scraps and sheets of paper covered with penciled notes and equations. "Got 'em!" he shouted triumphantly.

He handed Hubble three glossy eight-by-ten color pictures of Avery saluting from the hatch of the *Monastic*. "There!" he said. "A yellow and brown broad check business suit. And an orange silk choker."

"Dr. Merkin, really. I think you are dissembling. We are wasting valuable time." Hubble's voice had grown very tense.

"Mr. Hubble, these are *historic* photos! These pictures of Mr. Augenblaue will go down in history; pictures of the man who went *out there* and saw *The* Blue Light! What he wore when he landed is *important!* You are the *first* person to see these photos outside of the staff here at Augenblaue AeroSpace. You should be *honored!*" Ambrose settled in his chair, smiling thinly.

Constantine Hubble attempted to collect himself. The tightness in his voice spread to his features; his face looked as if it were being pinched by a million fingers. A thin whistle parted his lips and fled into a sigh.

"Doc-tor Mer-kin, please. We. Are. In. A. Hurry." A stratospheric voice.

"Right!" said Dr. Merkin with sudden vigor. "Let's get down to business. Well, Avery climbed from the hatch. A technician had rolled an aluminum ladder up to the spacecraft, which as you know is shaped something like a dumpling, or perhaps a bagel, with a door on the side. All on fins, you understand. Notice the tops of the fins in this photo here. He came down the ladder, waving and smiling and looking remarkably fit and youthful, as if he hadn't aged a bit. That was an effect of the Lorentz-Fitzgerald contraction. Only a month or so had passed for Avery, although to us it was ten years, so he actually hadn't aged much at all. Nevertheless, we were surprised that he looked so young. I said to my assistant, Dr. Rath, 'Ben,' I said, 'it is remarkable to see him looking so young, don't you think? Even though he's been away only a month, his time, it is surprising that he hasn't aged more.' And how do you suppose Dr. Rath responded?"

Ambrose leaned forward, gazing directly into Hubble's darkening eyes.

"No," Hubble answered weakly. "I've no idea. And furthermore," his voice rose, "*I don't care!*" Hubble's heated words half lifted him from his chair.

Ambrose remained unruffled. " 'It certainly is remarkable, Ambrose.' Those were his very words."

A peculiar keening sound started low in the back of Hubble's throat, and as it swelled in volume it filled the room.

"Well." The scientist backed up in his narrative. "Avery descended the ladder, waving and smiling. When he reached the ground he paused for a moment, taking it all in. The AeroSpace complex hasn't changed drastically in ten years, but there were one or two new buildings at the periphery of the field. He had a clear view of them because the stands built for the launch had been torn down. Except, of course, for that maroon fencing with the, uh, missing President's profile on it. That's a national monument. But, to continue, Avery is very involved in the company. Not like some chairmen of the board, who don't participate in the day-to-day workings of the company. Avery was very interested, even that day, after being away for ten years. He was checking out the field, and it was clear that he was *involved*."

This interview was not going well for Connie Hubble; somewhere he had lost the initiative, had lost control of it. It had taken him a long time to get past all the secretaries for an appointment with the Augenblaue AeroSpace research director. He had spent almost an hour with Merkin and hadn't learned anything yet. Jesus, he though, this guy Merkin is off the wall. Or else that's some kind of *dummy* sitting in his chair, jabbering away.

"After he had paused at the bottom of the ladder for a few seconds, or was it longer? It might have been several minutes, now that I reconsider it. Yes, even as much as two minutes. He walked over and shook my hand. 'Good to see you again, Ambrose,' he greeted me. The small group of technicians and media people around us gave a loud cheer for him. They all belong to AKA, so they, I should say, *we*, felt privileged to be with him."

"What happened next?" Hubble asked. He was slumped in his chair, watching Ambrose through slitted eyelids.

"Then his wife drove him home, of course. It was a long drive back to Evanston, and his wife was throwing a welcome home party for him."

Ambrose displayed his large teeth and wide, innocent eyes.

"Ahhhhh," whispered Constantine Hubble.

2 / Intergalactic Pudding

"WHAT'S IT LIKE out there?" Avery already knew pretty much what it was like out there. It was like nothing.

"Well, if you mean out *there*" — Ambrose Merkin gave a little twitch of his hand, toward the heavens — "it's like nothing." Dr. Merkin was Avery's director of research. "Or at least almost nothing."

"Sounds nice," said Avery. All around them the sounds of

rivets, liquid oxygen hissing through pipes, intense pressures, purposeful work, painted the background — the white noise of industry. Muted voices wavered through the misted air.

"If you like that sort of thing," said Dr. Merkin. He gave another twitch to his left hand, a flipper twitch. He was leaning over the railing of the catwalk 227 feet above the assembly floor of the Augenblaue AeroSpace facility at Kankakee, Illinois. "I wouldn't like it myself. No girls."

"Ah," said Avery. He smiled. "No girls. I leave Sunday." This was Friday.

"How long did you say you'd be gone?" Kay, his wife, asked him when he got home.

"About ten years, all together. I think. Well, I know. Actually." They were standing in the vestibule of their house in suburban Chicago. She was arranging flowers for Avery's bon voyage party the following night.

"The bluebells look nice, don't you think, dear?"

Kay had peculiar orange hair that stood up straight until, fatigued, it fell over backward. Avery's cosmetics division had tried without success to duplicate that hair. No one understood why. Avery was the only person in the world who found her hair attractive. At the moment it clashed nastily with the delicately washed blues of the original Japanese woodblock print behind her head, "Autumn Moon at Ishiyama," by Hiroshige. The flowers, too, seemed a vulgar display beside the subtle sky and lake in the print.

"The bluebells look nice." Avery sighed. He was about to grab his wife's ass, which bunched and unbunched sinuously under her silk frock like a giant sea anemone, when the butler, August, emerged from the solarium and walked across the parquet and through the double doors into the dining room. He was carrying a silver tray stacked high with place cards.

Avery's hand continued upward to scratch feebly at his furrowed forehead. "Ah," he said. "Ah, who's coming? To the party." His momentary lust quite died.

"Well. The General and his wife. The Governor and the former Governor . . ."

"Is that wise?" Avery murmured.

"Well, it should liven things up. The President can't come, but he's sending the Secretary of State."

"Oh, him," said Avery.

"Yes. And Dr. Merkin and his new wife. She was a Ballinger, I believe. And the Sparrows."

"Birds?"

"No, no," Kay said impatiently, without a smile. "The people. He's in frozen foods. He's bringing his wife, his mother and his niece, so we have an extra woman. I understand the niece is, uh, overweight. Do you suppose it would be all right to pair her off with your brother Nelson? After all, he's also fat."

"Ah, yes. Sparrow Frozen Peas. I'm sure Nelson will do fine for the Sparrow niece."

Kay's buttocks bunched and unbunched across the parquet to the dining room. She carried a huge spray of goldenrod, to which Avery was intensely allergic. He sneezed.

"And" — she paused to look back at him dragging along behind her — "of course the Countess is coming."

"Of course."

Avery's daughters, six and eight, tumbled from the solarium. "Come look at Freddie, come look at Freddie," shouted Alicia Katherine, the oldest. "He's mating with the tortoise, with Arthur!" Alicia Katherine kept the rabbits; Angela Kismet kept the turtle. She didn't like bunnies.

"Who's Freddie?" Kay asked through her lemon-sucking lips.

"Freddie's the Dutch gray. Come see. Daddy, come see, Freddie's mating with Arthur."

"That certainly is interesting, pumpkin," said Avery. Both his daughters had their mother's stiff orange hair and amoebic freckles. "I should certainly like to see that."

The animal cages were mounted on a large three-tiered trolley so the girls could wheel their pets from room to room. Besides the five rabbits there was Arthur, the Galápagos tortoise; two boa constrictors, small and unnamed as yet; a coatimundi named Pecker; a cage with a fluid population of gerbils whose patriarch was named Pee Pee; and on top a revolting parrot in midmolt named Fats.

Freddie, the Dutch gray, was in the cage with Arthur, who weighed fifty-three pounds, but Freddie was no longer humping. He was lying on his side gasping painfully for breath, utterly spent. Arthur was munching sedately on a cabbage leaf. He looked very wise and serene.

"Don't you think he looks wise 'n' serene, Daddy?" asked Angela Kismet with a lewd wink Avery wasn't sure he had seen.

"Why, uh, yes, I think he does." He was about to leave when Freddie suddenly leaped up and went back to work, vainly stabbing at Arthur's vast shell.

"Oh, goody," said Angela Kismet. "I just love reptiles. They're cool."

"That they are," said Avery. Arthur finished his cabbage leaf and began another.

"Wow!" Alicia Katherine was excited. "Do you think they'll mix — a hopping turtle or a rabbit with a shell?"

Silently August entered the solarium. He was a movie version of a cadaver, slightly green with opaque eyes and hair that lay submissively on his damp cranium.

"Mrs. Augenblaue would like to speak with you in the dining room, sir. And she wishes the children to return their pets to their rooms." His voice seemed to be coming from underground. Not British, Avery had thought. No, Central Europe somewhere. But Kay simply doted on him.

August crept away, and Avery returned to the dining room. "What is it, dear?" he asked, and sneezed again. The sideboard was covered with vases of goldenrod.

"The Countess just called. She's coming over this afternoon to help me prepare for the party. Just try to be nice."

"Who are you bringing to the party?" Avery asked the Countess when she swept into the room like an errant breeze.

"I'm bringing an Able-bodied Seaman, a charming man I met at the Waldorf last month. A most charming man."

"Of course," said the Countess at the party, preening her downy bosom with a hand dazzlingly jeweled; she was looking across the noisy room at her sailor, who leaned against the bar with a drink in his hand and a surly expression on his perfect face. The party was in full swing, and dinner was about to be served. She was talking to the former Governor's wife, who was shaped like a bowl of pretzels.

"Of course," the Countess repeated, "I love him for his *rank*."

"Hmm," said the former Governor's wife. Her mouth steadily chewed an hors d'oeuvre, so the "Hmm" was muted.

"I realize," said the Countess in a conspiratorial whisper, "that he's not really our sort of people. Not our sort at all, no. But he fucks like a maniac."

The former Governor's wife swallowed her hors d'oeuvre. "That's nice," she said.

The party was a great success, rotating as it did around the Secretary of State, with the two frigid poles of the Governor and the former Governor to maintain separation. The Countess was invited to the children's room to witness the mating of Freddie and Arthur, but things were quiet.

Mr. Sparrow lost his wife to Avery's brother Nelson and went home with his mother and his niece. It was rumored in his neighborhood that strange things went on at his house, very peculiar things. But it was a well-bred neighborhood with quiet estates and the rumor stayed local.

Avery hugged his two exquisite children to himself and whispered that he would go away, but not to worry please, that he would be back, and that even gone he would look over them, and they said Sure, not certain then how long ten years really was, and he turned gruffly from the room.

He left the next day for intergalactic space, where he would tumble through the silence far from stars and girls, listening to Mozart on his tape deck and thinking of himself as one small raisin adrift in the intergalactic pudding.

When he returned the former Governor had lost his wife and was married to the Countess. There was no trace of the Able-bodied Seaman.

3 / Frozen Daiquiris

AVERY'S MIDDLE NAME WAS Krupp, which connected him, distantly but distinctly, to the German Krupps, who spent the nineteenth century and half of the twentieth manufacturing steel and ordance for anyone who wanted those things. Almost everyone wanted them, so the Krupps got rich.

Avery suppressed his middle name, but he was in rockets after the war. He was also visibly in petrochemicals, cosmetics and detergents. But mainly he was in rockets. Tiny rockets the size of knitting needles, carrying small explosive heads that could blow the kneecap off an enemy soldier or disable a tank. Medium-sized rockets to carry satellites the size of golf balls into orbit, where they would roll around the cosmic fairway looking for other satellites. Eventually he abandoned military rockets but maintained his interest in rocketry. The result was the large rocket that would hurtle him into his self-imposed exile in intergalactic space, where he would be far from girls.

The vehicle Avery would travel in was not a rocket by conventional standards since Ambrose Merkin had developed the Merkin Drive for it. The *A.K.A. Monastic* flew entirely on orgone power alone.

The orgone was a little blue ball of sexual energy that zipped invisibly around the firmament in total disorder until Dr. Merkin figured out how to control it.

The press was very excited by the launch. The stands around the small concrete launching pad were packed with reporters. The networks sent their top anchor men to cover the takeoff.

"Well, Larry, the countdown is proceeding smoothly, and it's ten minutes to launch. In the meantime we have a special report on the revolutionary new Merkin Drive from Dick Peters, who is with Dr. Merkin in his laboratory."

"Thank you, Walter. Well, Dr. Merkin, we understand that this new drive you have developed for Augenblaue AeroSpace runs entirely on sexual energy alone. Is that correct?"

"Well, Dick. Ah, you don't mind if I call you Dick, do you? Good. Well, it does not run on sexual energy exactly, but rather on orgones, which as you may know were postulated by Dr. Wilhelm Reich some time ago, but which were not proved to exist until quite recently." Dr. Merkin waved his hand toward a complex device standing on the floor behind him. "This electrogravitic device captures, as we say, free-floating orgones and channels them into a coherent stream, rather like a laser. The energy is enormous; it will have no difficulty propelling Mr. Augenblaue into intergalactic space."

"Well, that's just fantastic, Dr. Merkin. Now, in your test runs of this new spacecraft, have you . . ."

"There have been no test runs. This will be the first flight of the *Monastic*." Dr. Merkin wagged his head in a quick summary gesture.

"But what about side effects or unknown dangers? Surely it is customary to test a new process or device first?"

"Yes, usually. But Mr. Augenblaue was in something of a hurry, and he and I are both quite certain that the device will work satisfactorily. There may be some side effects, but Mr. Augenblaue is quite prepared for them."

At five minutes to launch Avery sat in his comfortable launch chair, which would double as bed and couch in intergalactic space. He was watching programs about him on all three networks. Other screens showed him views of the crowd in the stands. Avery was looking forward to liftoff. Dr. Merkin had assured him of an exciting show.

There was a hold at two minutes because one of the CBS microwave transmitters went out and a new one had to be rushed into place. Ordinarily that would have been tough luck for CBS, but this was not an ordinary launch.

Avery glanced at his number seven screen while the hold was in effect, and he saw Kay's vibrant orange hair blazing in the special VIP box. She was having a party. His brother Nelson stood by Mrs. Sparrow. Mr. Sparrow's mother and his niece Dudee were there as well, but there was no sign of Mr. Sparrow himself. The Countess held hands with her Able-bodied Seaman, whose torso was plastered with a dazzling white T-shirt that gave the writhing play of his perfect chest muscles star billing.

Avery noticed that the President had made it today, and the Secretary of State. Kay directed August to serve the frozen daiquiris, her head near his, so they looked like a candle flame and its snuffer together. Avery caught the word "historic" from his monitors and glanced back at Walter.

"This is a historic event in man's perennial quest for the farthest frontier. Here, today, a man will launch his frail craft and vulnerable body for the first time into intergalactic space, out beyond the plane of the galaxy toward the Magellanic clouds. Before Man has even reached the nearest stars, Avery

Augenblaue, director of all the various and powerful Augenblaue enterprises, will himself fly into the unimaginably vast emptiness of space beyond the stars.

"And what is the purpose of this trip, you may ask. Dick Peters asked one of Mr. Augenblaue's aides that question — Why should a man of such wealth and power as Avery Augenblaue want to take an unproved spacecraft with a revolutionary new drive that has never even been tested before into the void between galaxies, a place where there are neither stars nor planets nor air to breathe, nor anyone to talk to, a voyage that could take as long as *ten years*, as we reckon time, without companion or repair station should anything go wrong?

"The aide replied, 'Because it's there.' We have heard those words before in answer to similar questions. It seems, at times, the only answer; that Man's curiosity, his fervent seeking for an answer to the great riddle of existence —"

"Excuse me, Walter, but the countdown is starting again. Our technical difficulties have been resolved."

"Uh, right. Thank you, Dick."

The six-screen monitor in the VIP box displayed a tiny Walter looking serious, but no one was watching. Dog-day August's feet whispered from guest to guest, dispensing violet frozen daiquiris. The President, his formal profile bent to the mouth of his press secretary, glanced up, saw the red light on the television camera aimed his way, and immediately turned his outstanding left profile toward it so that his determined lantern jaw was outlined neatly against the maroon fencing behind him for the world to admire.

The public address system announced one minute and counting, and an expectant hush oozed slowly down the sides of the stands, smothering conversation in a sticky glue of sweaty anticipation. Even Kay could feel the damp at her aggressively deodorized armpits. One minute.

As the seconds ticked away, the press corps in the stands, and the important visitors, and the party in the VIP box, and the Secret Service agents scattered through the crowd, and three spies for Soviet Russia, and three spies for Red China, and seven spies for Guatemala, and fourteen Israeli agents — including one on loan to the Egyptians, who couldn't afford to send one of their own — and assorted other special interests, including a well-dressed executive from an aircraft firm with a wallet full of money who kept trying to buy information from an ABC technician, all rose to their feet in an agony of silent waiting.

The crowd became one being, unified by a single purpose — well-dressed women and well-groomed men, reporters of a hundred newspapers and syndicated services, *Time, Newsweek, U.S. News & World Report, Fortune, Gay Sunshine, Rolling Stone, Mother Earth News, Reuters, Playboy, Viva, Hustler, Field and Stream, Good Housekeeping, The Watchtower, Farm Quarterly, Pravda, Asahi, Screw.* The silence deepened and intensified and began to layer, deepest at the bottom of this small stadium around the ship, where the most important people seemed to absorb into their silence even the stray sounds of the outside world, the rasp of breeze, the chirp of a bird, the distant whine of engines; then another layer like shellac across the middle of the stands; then at the top of the stands where the breeze did wisp unnoticed the hair of those unfortunates who were unable to obtain seats closer to the launch.

Into the glutinous silence the terse numbers of the countdown fell like pebbles into tar, vanishing one by one without a trace. At last the final five seconds arrived — four, three, two, one, zero — and the crowded stands took one long collective breath, expecting a roar of sound or a violent blast from the gold-painted bagel shape of the *A.K.A. Monastic* down below, but instead, for several seconds, nothing whatsoever happened.

In the groin of the ship the countless free-zapping orgones were beginning to align themselves at right angles to the base of the craft. As they danced into plac, they were packed tighter and tighter into the magnetic bottle of the engine. Then carefully controlled pressure was leaked from the vents below. A watery blue light wavered between the legs of the spaceship. Avery watched in delight as the faces of the crowd, and particularly on his number seven screen the faces of Kay and her friends, registered first anticipation, then confusion, cynicism and contempt, renewed anticipation, then amazement as the blue light intensified beneath him.

It was all proceeding in complete silence. The ship began to bob gently up and down as the pressure increased; faster and

faster the silent bobbing continued until with incredible sud-
denness a column of blue light shot into the air higher than the
eye could follow it, a blue geyser supporting Avery's golden
bagel, which disappeared into the intergalactic void without a
peep.

The vast column danced and sparkled bluely in the exact
center of the stadium, and the crowd remained standing, breath
held, waiting for something to happen.

The *A.K.A. Monastic* had vanished, the pillar of light, sparkling
and popping before their eyes, the proof of its existence. And all
those zillions of coherent orgones in that column of light had
nowhere to go once the ship they had propelled was gone. With
nothing to push against they could do naught but zing and sing
in their infinite column for those endless moments before losing
their coherence and rapidly dispersing.

They scattered into the incredulous crowd in the stands, infus-
ing everyone with a rush of sexual energy so massive that the
sounds of tearing clothes and sexual frenzy were truly awful in
the memories of the survivors.

4 / Tapioca

"OH, MY GOD. Oh, my God. Oooh!"

There were satisfactory quantities of orgones in the mauve
bedroom where Kay Augenblaue and her Balkan butler August
thrashed and coupled like galvanic earthworms, an impression
that was compounded by the strange earthy odors August gave
off, odors damp, and dark, and pouched in secret sins.

"Oh, my God," said Kay, and her long crimson fingernails
plowed eight parallel furrows through the topsoil of August's
back from the neck to the hillocks of his buttocks, which
clenched like two deflated basketballs and plunged suddenly
downward, sending into Kay's plumbing the sensations of an
electronic Roto-Rooter.

She had been reaching behind her for another violet frozen
daiquiri when the wave of orgone power washed across the

stands, and what she grabbed instead in that terrible moment was August's powerful organ, suddenly charged with such an angry longing that even her awful orange hair and his cadaverous reek could not keep them apart.

The only person stationary for any length of time, in fact after the orgone column collapsed into the crowd was the President, who thought the blue light emanated from the television cameras, so he turned his magnificent left profile to the camera. The light was so intense that it imprinted the image of that profile onto the maroon fence behind him, which was subsequently declared a national monument.

Kay and August had become inseparable in the two months since the launch, "a launch of more than a spaceship," as one columnist put it. They had slithered together through a trough of sexual oils from the stands to the Augenblaue mansion and through the vestibule and across the parquet and up the carpeted spiral of the staircase and down the hall to the master suite, where their two sinuous bodies continued to writhe in a seemingly unfulfillable frenzy of desire, leaving behind them a damp and slippery trail that caused the cook, jogging across the parquet, to slip and dislocate her elbow.

Kay's hair was spread out on the satin pillow like a dollop of dried ketchup, emitting every now and then from the tip of one of her livid orange hairs a thin pinprick of blue light that floated away from the bed to be lost in the glare from the enormous skylight above them. The sun rose slowly over the lip of this skylight, pouring into the room a mellow golden light that contended mightily with the damp-earth smells and pallid colors of the two frantically humping bodies. Gradually its heat produced a thick syrup of exhaustion that embalmed the two on the bed into something resembling sleep. It also engendered in the furrows of August's back the seeds of a bumper harvest of infection.

The sun moved across the skylight and set on the other side. At last they stirred, limp and scarred veterans of the First Orgone War. "Oh, my God," said Kay again, stirring. This time her voice was flat and tired.

"Yes, madam," said August in a toneless voice.

"This can't go on," said Kay. "It just can't go on. We've been at it for two months now and it's killing me. That son of a bitch

Avery is responsible for it. He *knew* what would happen. He *knew*. My God! I mean, the President and Mr. Sparrow's mother, for Christ's sake! They haven't been seen since. The President is missing! Only the Countess was lucky enough to end up with the right person. And the Secretary of State! Oh, God, how can I ever face those people again?"

"Yes, madam," August repeated. He was about to add something reassuring, but the pain in his back was beginning to penetrate his exhaustion, so he twitched instead.

Kay got up and limped across the room to the dresser. She peered at herself in the gilt mirror; her eyes, she noticed, looked like a double-vision version of Crater Lake in a storm. Her groin felt as if it had been under construction for years. Her mouth was filled with the flavors of mold and rust. Her joints ached. From certain angles she thought she could see the faint blue flush of unspent orgones, and when she sniffed she thought there was the faintest trace of ozone in the air around her.

"I hate sex," she said, lifting the corner of her upper lip delicately with the very tip of the fingernail on the fourth finger of her left hand and staring closely at her teeth, which were outlined in red — either lipstick or blood.

"I've always hated sex," she said, and looked as though she were about to spit at the mirror when she heard glass shattering. She spun around to see her eight-year-old Alicia Katherine Augenblaue fall through the skylight onto the soggy purple satin sheets. She bounced once on the Beautyrest mattress, and August, still lying face down to air his painful back, bounced once in response. As he connected with the mattress again, a sliver of skylight glass pinned a fold of his flesh firmly to the bed.

"Wow!" said Alicia Katherine. "That was better than watching Freddie try to mate with Arthur!"

"Oh, for God's sake," said Kay. "Look what you've done to the skylight. Your father will be furious. He used to love lying there looking up at the stars."

"Oh, Mommy, really. You'd think we couldn't afford to have it replaced." Ally Kate pouted a bit.

"Yes. Well, you run along now. August and I have business to take care of."

"I guess so." Ally grinned. "Well, I'll be seeing you, August." She bounced off the mattress and ran to the door.

The bounce sent a terrible wave of pain through August's left side and increased his already pronounced pallor.

"Yes, Miss Ally," he said through clenched teeth. His hand crept down to remove the splinter of glass, but he couldn't figure out how to do it without increasing the pain. Kay poked reluctantly at the glass a time or two, but August howled in such mournful agony that finally she had to call the fire department.

"I think that should do it," said the plain man in the crew cut after he had removed the glass, bandaged the butler's side, and sprayed his back with anesthetic.

"Thank you very much," said Kay, slipping a folded bill into the man's jacket pocket. "By the way, what is your name, in case we need you again?"

"Harker, ma'am. Jonathon Harker." His voice was bland and humble, a kind of aural tapioca, neutral and unassuming. His short hair was the color of tapioca, his eyes two gobs of tapioca, and he gave off a faint aroma of tapioca. He looked as though library paste ran through his veins.

He lingered. He looked blandly around the room, at the pile of broken glass on the floor and bed, at the jagged teeth of the skylight, at the soggy satin sheets, at August's naked and bloody form, at Kay's tired eyes and faint blue glow, at the mauve walls and gilt mirror and violet carpeting and the elaborate, carved New Zealand headboard. He took the folded bill from his pocket and put it on the dresser.

"I couldn't take that, ma'am. Not ethical." His lukewarm tapioca voice drowsily evaporated in the room.

"I will have to make a report, though," he said, "so I'll have to ask how all this happened."

His tone was so mild that Kay didn't understand what he was asking her. She was distracted as well by something that was going on in her lean body. A buzzing. A high whine. A minute pure tone of reactivated orgones coruscating down her flaccid epidermis under the purple housedress she had put on. There was something about this man. Something about him.

"Ma'am," he urged. "Will you tell me what happened?"

I know, thought Kay. Something about his blandness. I must have that blandness. I must *bathe* myself in that blandness.

"What?" she asked faintly, her body leaning toward Mr. Harker. "What did you say?"

Her hands rose slightly in the air. She wanted to plunge her hands into that tapioca smoothness, to scoop it up by the double handfuls and smear it all over her face.

She edged toward him like a sleepwalker.

"What happened here?" he repeated, automatically backing up as she invaded his body space. She had a desire to rip off her dress and bellyflop into all that soothing blandness. She wanted, as her fingernails began to unsheathe and arch out, to grab Mr. Harker and rip his clothes off him and fuck him inside out.

At that moment August groaned. He had tried to sit up, and a monstrous pain stabbed through his side. There was, after all, he remembered, a jagged hole in his side. He deserved a groan.

It was such a horrible underground chain-rattling crypt-haunting ghoulish beyond-the-grave groan, however, that Kay, deflected from her advance on Jonathon Harker, shrieked into Harker's startled face, "You wanna know what happened? I'll tell you what happened. This man here was sleeping peacefully in this bed when suddenly someone fell through the skylight onto him. A burglar, I guess. Ripped his back like that and pinned him to the bed. It was terrible."

Kay ran out of steam, her body slumping as if it had softened in the sun.

"I see," said Mr. Harker, jotting notes in his notebook. "Did the burglar steal anything?"

"What burglar? Oh, that burglar. No, he just ran away."

After Harker left Kay said, "God, I hate sex. I wish I could take pills to stop myself. I hate it."

5 / Onion Dip

IF THE MOON HAD BEEN settled, A. K. Akley would have built a house there. He had a place picked out, on the western slopes of Mount Hadley overlooking the Palus Putredinis — the Marsh of Decay. It was nice on the moon, very quiet, and the weather or lack of it predictable. The sun rose and set every two weeks. Up there he would weigh only twenty-five pounds.

But the moon wasn't settled, so A. K. Akley built his house in Hawaii instead, where he was president of the Akley Republican Furniture Company, "Furniture for the Silent Majority." He built his house in Ka Lae because it was as close as he could get to the moon. Ka Lae was the southernmost point in the United States. The Polynesians who lived there gave the name Ka Lae to the white man, who gave them syphilis and Christianity in return. The name meant "South Cape," but that was not what attracted A. K. Akley to the spot. What attracted him was that it was completely sterile.

Mauna Loa, the local volcano, a nasty goddess with an evil temper, periodically spread a thick layer of molten lava over Ka Lae, and every time she did, the highway department had to chisel out a new road. Nothing grew there and there was no fresh water. Like the moon, A. K. always said. Like the moon. Except of course there was air to breathe and an agreeable ocean to swim in. And the days were shorter.

"I like it here," A. K. said to the florid, sweaty man beside him. "I own most of the land around here, so no neighbors. Of course, there is that development down the road — you may have spotted it on your way in. No? Well, people seem darn disappointed when they get to their new homes. Darn disappointed. Most of them come all the way from California. You ever been to California? No? Well. Milpitas, I've got a big warehouse in Milpitas."

The florid man's name was Ed Sox, and he'd come for a job interview. He mopped his perspiring brow with a large red bandana.

"I see you're looking at my swimming pool," A. K. said, gesturing toward the swimming pool.

Ed, who had not been looking at the swimming pool, looked at it. It appeared to be filled with fine white sand.

"We hauled that sand in by truck. Every grain of it. And before that by boat. Doesn't even come from this island. From Oahu."

"Huh?"

"Oahu. The sand comes from Waikiki. You know, surfing, lissome wahines, hula-hula."

"Oh." Ed had traveled all the way from Tulsa, Oklahoma,

where he ran a furniture business of his own, Ed's Acres, a retail outlet that advertised mainly on late-night television. Now that he was here he was confused.

For one thing, Mr. Akley had not asked his name or interviewed him for a job, although Mr. Akley had personally called him in Tulsa and asked him to fly out to Hawaii. Mr. Akley had mentioned that he'd seen Ed on television advertising his furniture.

"I think you gotta big future in the manufacturing end of the furniture business, Ed," Mr. Akley had told him.

"Whaddya mean?"

"Well." A. K.'s voice was a tinsel ghost through the wires and microwave relays of A.T.&T. "You're selling Akley Republican Furniture there in Tulsa on TV. I was sitting in my motel room in Tahlequah, Oklahoma, watching the late movie called *Stranger in My Arms* with June Allyson, Jeff Chandler, Sandra Dee, Charles Coburn and Mary Astor, when your commercial was shown. You jumped up and down on a couch made by Akley Republican Furniture. You're a large man, Mr. Sox, and the couch held up.

"I thought to myself, Now there's a man who makes Akley Republican Furniture look *good*, and a man who makes Akley Republican Furniture look *good* is a man that Akley Republican Furniture *needs!*"

And there he was, visiting Mr. Akley at his fabulous vacation home in Ka Lae on the big island of Hawaii at the southernmost point in the United States, and Mr. Akley didn't remember the phone call.

Ed stared at the swimming pool full of sand. Was that a clue? A diving board stretched out over one end of the pool.

"I don't unnerstand," said Ed. "Why fill the pool with sand?"

"I figured you might ask that," Mr. Akley said, leaning back in his deck chair and taking a long sip of his pineapple punch. Ed was sure he had just made a mistake.

"It's really very simple," A.K. went on. "Sand requires no pumps to circulate, no chlorine to disinfect it, no refilling to replace evaporation. Sand, in other words, *eliminates maintenance!*"

"Oh."

"But we're not here to talk about me," said Mr. Akley, putting down his drink. "So, Mr., ah, what can I do for you?"

"Beg pardon?"

"I asked what I could do for you. You're here at my home in Hawaii admiring my pool and I'm wondering what I can do for you. I get very few visitors, very few. This place is a bit remote, you know, yes, and I haven't had any visitors for weeks. Weeks. Until you. At least, that's what the staff tells me, though I can't really be certain. None of them speaks English. Not one. And I don't speak whatever it is they speak, so. Maybe they just turn everyone away. They could do that. I'd never know. Then again, they are supposed to turn everyone away. That's their job. But I can't tell them that, can I? Eh? I mean, they don't speak any English. As I said. You don't look so good."

"Uh," said Ed. He was beginning to perspire quite freely. His face was fat and red and glistening, and his short-sleeved Hawaiian shirt his wife, Betsy Sue, had given him for the trip was too tight, especially under the arms. The shirt was decorated with large heliotrope pineapples. "Uh."

He stared doggedly at the sand-filled swimming pool, trying to make sense of what Mr. Akley had told him. Mr. Akley politely gazed at him. Finally Ed said, "You invited me."

"I did?" A. K. was incredulous. "How extraordinary. I don't ordinarily invite people out here. I ordinarily don't like people. Why did I ask you out here?"

"Well, you said Akley Republican Furniture needed me."

"I did? How odd. Very odd indeed. What did I say we needed you *for*, if I may ask? That is, if you don't mind answering, Mr., ah, what did you say your name was?"

"Sox. Ed Sox. From Tulsa, Oklahoma?"

The midafternoon sun was blinding, the sky almost white with heat. It was so bright, in fact, that Ed couldn't pinpoint the sun overhead.

"How do you spell that? Soaks, did you say? A very peculiar name, if you don't mind my saying so. Yes, a funny name." Mr. Akley smiled over the lip of his pineapple punch.

"Not Soaks. Sox. As in Argyle."

"Ah, I see. As in Argyle. Do you spell that with a *y* or with an *i*?"

"Spell what?" The universe was beginning to close in on Ed Sox.

"Argyle."

"Why do you need to spell Argyle?"

"Look, Mr. Argyle, I don't have time for this. If you're going to waste my time, then I'll thank you to leave."

"No, no. You don't understand. My name is Sox. Ed Sox."

"Oh, well, why didn't you say so in the first place. If you can't be more cooperative I'm afraid there's no room in our organization for you. Let's take a walk."

Without a backward glance, Mr. Akley jumped up and strode off down a path hewn through the black lava. Ed heaved himself out of his deck chair and padded dutifully after him. They passed the swimming pool and skirted a huge outcropping of lava. The house, with its vast expanses of glass wall and fanciful cupolas and wrought-iron balconies, was out of sight. There was nothing to see but lava, and light, and an ocean so dazzling that it revealed nothing.

"I had to get you away from the staff," Mr. Akley whispered. "There are spies everywhere."

He draped his arm around Ed's shoulders, drawing him into his confidence. A feeling of privilege flushed through Ed's sweating bulk.

"As you know, Ed" — and the first name made Mr. Akley and Ed buddies forever — "Akley Republican Furniture is made for the Silent Majority, for all those wonderful people who *love America*. Akley Republican Furniture appears in every important motel chain in the United States. Akley Republican Furniture *is* America, the essence of America, the spirit of free enterprise, the soul of capitalism.

"Do you realize what the real secret of Akley Republican is, Ed?" Akley's voice dropped to a hoarse croak so conspiratorial that Ed had to lean forward to hear; his large ear, with it's tiny explosions of coarse hair, hovered inches from A. K.'s mouth.

"The secret of this company is, *Make cheap and sell dear!* Do you understand what that means, Ed? It means that Akley Republican Furniture makes CRAP! Frankly, Ed," A. K. continued, "if you brush against one of our coffee tables it topples over sideways like a slaughtered steer: its legs collapse, the screws pull out of the bottom, if you catch my meaning. The stuff is simply no damn good. But people love it, they gobble it up, we can't manufacture it fast enough. It's really amazing what people will buy."

Ed was feeling confused again. His home in Tulsa was filled with Akley Republican Furniture. To him, it was elegant, durable furniture. The plastic veneer finish was easy to clean and stood up under the most intense abuse. Ed loved Akley Republican Furniture. So did his wife.

"Ed," said Mr. Akley, guiding Ed by the shoulders, "there's just one other thing you should know about our furniture."

"What's that?"

"Bugs."

"Huh?"

"Bugs. Termites. Well" — and Mr. Akley expansively waved his hand — "you'll find out all about that. I hope you don't mind my little test, Ed, but frankly, we need a man who can think on his feet, a man ready for anything. This is a very competitive business, Ed. I'm happy to say I think we've found our man in you, Ed. Yes, I do. You're hired. Go home and get ready to move to Milpitas, California."

"Why, thank you, Mr. Akley."

"Now there's just one thing I don't quite understand, Ed. Just one thing." He looked quizzically at Ed.

"What's that, Mr. Akley?"

"I just don't understand how the hell you jumped up and down on that couch without collapsing it."

"Oh." Ed smiled sunnily. "That's easy. I *believe* in Akley Republican Furniture. That's all."

6 / Frozen Peas

SIGISMUND SPARROW HAD LOST his wife to Avery's brother Nelson at the dinner party the night before the launch. His mother had apparently disappeared, along with the President. None of them, in the three months since that historic launch into intergalactic space, had been seen again.

So he was left to rattle around in his enormous mansion with his niece Dudee, who had taken it into her mind to go on a crash diet, to progress, she said, from one hunger to another, from food to sex. She hoped to become a radiant sylph. Sigismund didn't believe it; he barely noticed her eventual departure. He had lost the two people nearest and dearest to him and was in a profound depression.

The day of Dudee's return from the Crystal Grape, a diet ranch near Needles, California, Sig was standing forlornly in his chromium kitchen. At the ranch, Dudee had eaten nothing but nuts and roots, three weeks' worth of nuts and roots; she had ridden electric bicycles at seventy-five miles per hour for three hours a day; she had been forced to swim underwater in a tank full of cosmetic mud; she had had her cream-puff body pummeled by towel boys with rippling muscles. She returned on a rainy Sunday evening with a suitcase full of sex manuals and velvet ropes.

Sigismund, captain of the world's vastest frozen food empire, was glumly opening a package of Sparrow Frozen Knockwurst and Sauerkraut Dinner. It was the last package in his enormous freezer. He hadn't left the Sparrow mansion for over three weeks, but at irregular intervals he had opened up another packet of food and eaten it, sometimes without bothering to heat it up first. He hardly noticed, in his bleak and bereft depression, that he was eating ice.

He leaned against the spackled Formica countertop, staring morosely at the frozen knockwurst that lay petrified in its abstract nest of sauerkraut. Even my niece, he was thinking, feeling sorry for himself, has gone off to that fat farm in southern California. Even little Dudee. The self-pity was a triangular fin circling the sinking life raft in his head.

Around him the kitchen hummed a monotonous melody, a melancholy song; the refrigerator hummed, the freezer hummed, the fluorescents hummed on and on, and all the chrome glistened and glinted back at him his dismal reflection, his hangdog face, his pouchy eyes and tired paunch, his coarse, disordered mop of light brown hair. His eyes began to water and blear as he stared at the knockwurst. Even little Dudee gone away, and poor Siggy all alone.

He shrugged and carried the cardboard carton to the stove, where he dropped it, cardboard and all, into a pot of boiling water. Poor me.

The cardboard melted to paste. The knockwurst turned from ice-rimed gray to hot steamy gray and bobbed gently in a boiling glue of cardboard and sauerkraut while the apex of the Sparrow corporate pyramid peered at Boyle's Law in action.

At the same time a sleek yellow taxi rolled through the rainy downtown Chicago streets, bearing Dudee, now truly little, toward her Uncle Sig with the biggest surprise of his life.

Just as he sat down to eat at the counter of his chrome kitchen next to the window smeared with rain, so that looking through it he recognized his own beagle-pup self in double-exposure over a watery world of empty lawn, that taxi rolled yellow and smooth up his driveway and deposited a brand-new Dudee, willow tall and whiplash tough and totally strange, before his front door. She let herself in, dropped her two cases of manuals and ropes in the hallway, and bounded through the house to surprise her sad Uncle Sig at his pathetic dinner.

"Uncle Sig," she shouted, banging through the swinging kitchen door. "Uncle Sig, it's me, I'm back, and, boy, have I got some stuff to show you!"

"Oh, hi," said the chairman of the board, scarcely recognizing her or caring who she was. His eyes flickered once at her and dropped back to his plate, but she was shrugging out of her rain-wet coat and underneath was a clinging double-knit bag full of apples and pears and nectarines and soft juicy melons, and his eyes flickered up again.

"Who're you?" he asked.

"Dudee, back from the Crystal Grape," she said, and her nipples buzzed braless under the double-knit. She swung her head, and her hair, which had been snarled and dull when she left, now glistened warmly under the faintly blue fluorescents, a rich chestnut cascade over her collar.

"Dudee?" asked Uncle Sig, his voice like a chipped plate.

"Yep, me, Dudee. Wow, Uncle Sig, this place sure is a mess. You're a mess." She observed that he was wearing the same pale blue shirt he wore the day she left, though now the buttons were gone and twenty-one nights of sleepless thrashing had taken their toll in wrinkles. It hung open to his waist, so his soft torso drooped in the kitchen glare.

She noticed his plate. "My God, what's that?"

"Frozen knockwurst."

"My God. You didn't even take it out of the package!"

"I didn't?"

"No. Come on," she said, ripping what was left of his shirt off his grimy form and leading him, incredulous, out of the kitchen and up to the master bedroom. She left him sitting dazed on the pale green settee while she filled the huge sunken tub with steamy water and four handfuls of bubble bath. And she changed into a surf-white Turkish bath towel. In the bathroom she peeled from his listless body his smelly pants and shorts.

She released her towel and hauled him into the shower, where she soaped and scrubbed and rinsed him like an elephant in the zoo. He was passive and bewildered.

Then she took him into the sunken bath and washed his greasy hair and slid her amazing new body all over his and fondled him, and the final "poor me" drifted like a jellyfish through the murky tidal basin of his mind and shredded and floated away forever.

Her otter body, browned all over by the hot Needles sun, appeared and submerged in the soapy waters. Sigismund's abandoned banana rose with it, and later he found himself spread-eagle on the bedroom carpet looking down at it and thinking of the knockwurst he almost ate for dinner.

Dudee took from her suitcase long loops of crimson velvet rope and tied his wrists to the feet of the king-sized bed, and his ankles to the knobs of the bathroom and bedroom doors, and while he lay there helpless, she:

brushed her long chestnut hair all up and down his bubbled and soap-slick body;

nibbled on his nose, his eyelids, his ears, his cheeks and chin;

nibbled on his soapy toes and giggled;

sucked on his soapy toes and sighed;

licked his kneecaps, first one, then the other;

swung around and planted her knees on either side of his head and inched them into his ears so he couldn't hear and wagged in his face, just out of reach of his lips or tongue, the glistening invitation of her desire;

tickled his little jewels and laughed;

whispered into his ear the longest string of dirty words he had ever heard, without a pause for breath;

flicked her marshmallow-soft tongue into his ear and slopped it around with a deafening slurp that made his aching groin quiver;

plopped herself down on his ice-hard knockwurst and rode up and down with her gorgeous breasts and nipples like bullets banging on his face like hail until he got bigger and bigger, then blew up and passed out.

"What happened?" he asked two hours later, when he woke up to find Dudee massaging his genitals back to life.

"You're the king of frozen foods," she said, "and we've just begun!"

7 / Chop Suey

THE DAY AVERY RETURNED from ten years in intergalactic space there were 312,005 dinner parties in the continental United States. There were also 4967 homocides that day.

The welcome-home party that Kay gave for Avery was the only one of those 312,005 dinner parties to include a homocide. That day.

Avery hadn't changed a bit; he was still medium tall and magnetic, with glacial blue eyes and bushy black hair. He was pink and glowed with health and vigor.

Of course, time moved differently in intergalactic space, and he had only aged a month.

Kay had aged a little, but not much. Her buttocks still bunched and unbunched under her watered silk in a way that made Avery's fingers itch. Her ghastly orange hair still stood straight up and then fell over like yarrow sticks. The Chinese ambassador once mentioned to the Countess that one could tell the future from Kay's hair if one only knew how to read it.

The only noticeable change in Kay, really, came from her ten years of milking August's molten dong with all her pursed and avid orifices: she smelled faintly but distinctly of damp earth and ozone. Avery pretended not to notice.

"Hello, dear," she greeted him at the door. The guests, lined up in the vestibule, applauded. Over their heads hung a large silk banner that Kay had had woven. It had taken eighteen months to weave it, so elaborate was the design. It read: WELCOME HOME, AVERY.

He kissed her on her downy freckled cheek. He read the banner, "Welcome Home, Avery." The guests applauded again.

Avery noticed that the banner covered the spot where "Autumn Moon at Ishiyama" had hung over the table where her vulgar bluebells had flaunted themselves for his bon voyage party. He sighed.

Kay twined her arm in his and, smiling broadly, led him past the line of guests. "You remember the Secretary of State, don't you, dear?" Avery shook hands with the Secretary of State, who had attended his going-away party. There was a bit more gray in his hair, but he still radiated confidence.

"How are you, Avery?" he asked. "How was intergalactic space?"

"Very peaceful," said Avery. "Like a month's vacation."

"The Department would like a debriefing. At your convenience, of course."

"Of course," said Avery, leaving the Secretary of State to guess whether that meant of course he'd give a debriefing or of course it would be at his convenience.

"And the Countess," said Kay, "And her husband, the former Governor. Now Secretary of the Army."

"Nice to see you again, Countess. Mr. Secretary," said Avery. The Countess preened.

"Call me Bob," said the Secretary of the Army.

"OK, Bob," said Avery.

"Mr. Sparrow and niece Dudee."

Mr. Sparrow wore purple-tinted, square, rimless glasses and a ruffled violet shirt with an aquamarine formal bow tie. His dinner jacket was also aquamarine, with a navy blue satin collar. His black satin formal trousers flared over two-tone shoes made from two different kinds of leather, alligator and baby kangaroo. His brown hair curled extravagantly over his collar. He was sleek and tanned and fit and radiated a sense of well-being.

"You're certainly looking fit, Sigismund. Life seems to be agreeing with you."

Avery noticed Dudee, and his eyes flickered rapidly for a moment. Her dress, he was sure, had no back, and almost no front, and what there was was almost transparent. Every male compass needle in the room was oriented toward her magnetic north. "And Dudee," Avery said, "you've changed!"

"Not really," Dudee answered with a smile, and her husky tone covered Avery with a thin layer of musk-scented oil.

A tug on his arm led him to the next guest, and the next, and so on down the room, after which the guests retired to the solarium for drinks and Avery went upstairs to freshen up.

At the top of the graceful curve of the staircase his two daughters waited impatiently to welcome Daddy home. Alicia Katherine was now eighteen and so stunning that Dudee faded from Avery's memory. Her orange hair had darkened and softly framed her face.

Angela Kismet was wearing a suit. "Daddy," she exclaimed, and Avery realized that she too, in a quieter way, was a ravishing androgynous beauty. "Daddy, we have something to tell you. It's very important."

"Not now," said Kay, still clamped onto Avery's arm, an orange-haired pipe wrench. "Daddy's very tired and needs a bath."

"But Daddy, it's *really* important." Angela's lower lip peeked shyly out and quivered a moment.

"You can talk to Daddy later," said Kay, a brittle edge fronting her voice. " Right now he's busy."

She steered Avery by the children and down the hall to the master suite, a complex warren of bedrooms, bathrooms, saunas, steam rooms, massage rooms, dressing rooms and parlors. The vast master bedroom with its mauve and violet and gilt, its enormous skylight, its triple bed and satin sheets — all were just the same as when he'd left. Avery grinned at the door, taking it all in, thinking it over.

"Oh, Avery, it's good to have you home," Kay breathed, showing her vulpine smile. She rested her head on Avery's shoulder for a moment.

"It's nice to be home, Kay," said Avery, still grinning in a way that appeared a little simple to his wife. Some unknown effect of intergalactic space? His shoes sank into the violet carpet and rose gently with each step. His nose twitched along her trail of ozone and earth.

When she led him through the mirrored dressing room she

blushed. Oh, the things those mirrors had seen these past ten years. It was not a pretty blush, but Avery didn't notice.

"Now, Avery," she said, her voice a power saw hitting a nail. "You just take your time. The guests will be fine."

She led him on through the massage room and into the cedar and cherrywood sauna and steam room. Here, with her buttocks clenching nervously, she removed Avery's travel-weary clothing. Though those clenching muscles gave Avery a tingling in his groin, he submitted, strangely passive, to the undressing, grinning.

"Ah, Avery, you really look just the same. You haven't changed a bit." She sounded as if she were grinding glass somewhere in her throat.

"Well," said Avery, smiling foolishly, "it's only been a month. For me, that is."

"Your bath is drawn." She nudged him into the steam room. "The steam is just the way you like it." She closed the door behind him and sprinted back through the massage room and the mirrored dressing room, where her image blasted back at her a zillion times her frenzied eyes, red-lined teeth, sickly hair and outsized freckles. She ripped open a closet door and dragged out a half-asphyxiated August.

He was wearing a rubber diving suit, complete with hood and goggles. Around his waist was a belt with attachments containing a long diver's knife, a hatchet, and a .38-caliber revolver. He gasped painfully for several impatient minutes while Kay hopped anxiously from foot to foot and the air filled slowly with the smells of decay.

"For God's sake, hurry up," she hissed. "He won't stay in there forever."

Downstairs the Secretary of State was sipping his favorite drink, Southern Comfort and Dr Pepper. "I hope we're going to get some explanation of that episode with the, ah, orgones ten years ago at the launch," he commented to Sig Sparrow. He wished Mr. Sparrow's eyes were not hidden behind those tinted glasses. He hated talking to someone without being able to see his eyes. Eyes revealed a lot about people. When talking to the Arabs, for instance, he always watched their eyes carefully.

"Yes, indeed," Mr. Sparrow answered with a smile. "That was

quite a show. I'm sorry I wasn't there." His left hand, resting on Dudee's bare back, began to drift, and his pinky slid into the top of her dress. She hopped slightly and giggled.

Avery sang in the bath. Wreathes of steam wandered vagrant and wraithlike through the air around him. The visibility was nearly zero, especially down at floor level, where the sunken tub shone dully, its marble sides visible only as icebergs in fog.

"Blow the man down." Avery sang heartily, soaping under his arms. "Blow, blow, blow the man down." Drops of condensation fell from his eyelashes.

"Blow ye winds, ay oh!" sang Avery, and a rubbery figure crept into the steam behind him, closely followed by another.

"High ho," sang Avery, "blow the man down," and the figure closest to him smashed the hatchet against his head with a sickening splat.

"Oh, my God! What the fuck!" Avery screamed.

Next, the figure plunged his diving knife into Avery's chest. "Oooohhh. Oh. Aaaaargh," moaned Avery, as Technicolor blood dyed the bath water.

Bang. Bang. Bang. Bang. Bang. Bang. August emptied the .38 into the still form in the tub.

"Ahhhhhhhh," Avery shuddered. "Guh," he added, then was silent.

"Quick," hissed Kay, "let's get out of here." She groped toward the door, followed by August's squishy frogman's feet.

When they had gone, Avery said, "Gee, I hope I didn't overdo it."

8 / Fish Fry

WHEN ED SOX BOUNDED into his tract home just south of Tulsa, Oklahoma, he hugged his tiny wife to his Hawaiian shirt, where her red nose and button eyes were crushed against a livid pineapple. It was as if the futile drilling for the oil of prosperity in the crumbly shale of cheap furniture had produced an unexpected gusher for Mr. and Mrs. Sox.

"My gosh," said Ed, finally freeing his wife, "it was strange, but baby, we got it made."

"Yes, dear," said Betsy Sue, removing his size fourteen shoes and rubbing his fat feet. His toes overlapped.

"No more Grand Opening Going Out of Business sales. No more jumping up and down on couches on the late show. No more warehouse fires or factory rejects!"

"Yes, dear," she repeated, and she went to the kitchen to bring him a cold beer. She was an Okmulgee sorghum farmer's daughter who had never met a traveling salesman until she was introduced to Ed Sox at a Reformed Baptist fish fry one sweltering July Sunday. Ed was not so heavy then, nor Betsy Sue so thin; they diverged after marriage.

She poured the icy beer into a Tulsa Gushers glass and set it on the table beside the AkleyLounger.

Ed pulled the lever that tilted him backward, shot the footrest into place, leaned his head back, and drained the beer.

"Ahhh," he said, and belched. Betsy Sue was back at work on his feet. "Baby, we're really gonna go places now! We're gonna *move*. Get rich."

"That's wonderful, Ed," she said as she ground her burry knuckles into the soft fishbelly undersides of his feet. Content, he flipped the switch that turned on the massage unit in his AkleyLounger. It was the finest automated AkleyLounger, the top of the line. Hard rubber rollers inside the chair kneaded his back and bottom.

"Oh, Jesus," he moaned. "That's sure nice."

"Don't talk like that, Ed. Don't take the Lord's name in vain like that," said Betsy Sue. But she began to massage Ed's massive calves with her wiry farmer's fingers, and Ed's head lolled back on the headrest.

"OK, baby, but gosh darn it, that feels good." The rollers in the seat moved back and forth, smoothing and soothing the butter of his butt.

"I know, Ed," said Betsy Sue, kneading his legs with her horny hands. Somewhere inside her a ticking began. She worked her firm rodent fingers around his knees, and he giggled, faintly. Very faintly.

Ed's eyes sank back into their pouches and his hairy arms dropped down on either side of the chair, which seemed to have closed up around him like a giant hand, squeezing and stroking him, back and forth, back and forth. Betsy Sue was now up to his thighs, astraddle her husband's massive knees on the rocking AkleyLounger. Suddenly the vibration unit cut in, and the oscillations of the hundred-cycle vibrator combined with the rolling action of the massage unit. Inside Betsy Sue the ticking grew louder, and she slapped and pummeled Ed's thighs through his chino pants. She could feel the vibrations of the chair in her own thighs where they rested on Ed's.

Finally her slapping, skidding, hoof-tough hands hit Ed's solid meat, as she knew they would, and she scrabbled at his fly with a hunger that made the Reformed Baptist minister crouching in her cerebellar cortex wince. Ed's beery breath began to come in shuddering gasps as she released his imprisoned sausage from his Jockey shorts.

"Oh, goshawmighty, baby," he said, his voice humming with vibrations and bobbing with rollers so it came out, "Oooh, *goshawmighty baby*," with a hundred-cycle harmonic.

Betsy Sue's dusty, flowered housedress hiked above her hips as the two of them undulated and vibrated on the AkleyLounger. She rolled her hard red hands around Ed's knobby joint and rolled her white-cotton-pantied sopping crotch around on Ed's pillowy soft thighs, and amid those gray cells the minister put his hands over his eyes and peeked through his fingers. The ticking in her ears was deafening — even Ed could have heard it.

The heating unit in the chair activated and a rosy flush spread over Ed's vast stomach, which was now exposed to view as Betsy Sue's fingers inched their way up the Hawaiian buttons, and the ghastly heliotrope pineapples fell away to either side.

The heat suffused their thighs, and with a terrible Tulsa Gushers cheer he ripped her white cotton panties right off her squirming midsection.

"Oh, Ed," she said, "praise the Lord!" She stuffed his throbbing gob into her ticking stew, and the two of them leaped in time to the rolling, vibrating, warming giant hand of the AkleyLounger. Ed's left hand held on to his wife's housedress while his right hand twirled the controls of the massage unit all the way up. The rollers were a blur of motion on his back and butt, the vibrator reached its peak pitch of violence, and the heater shot up to one hundred degrees. The two of them, bucking and snorting on the chair, fell out of phase with the mechanism, and the entire chair began to rock, the front half leaving the ground and falling back with a thump, then the rear, and Betsy Sue started to pump up and down with a new rhythm that introduced a sideways rocking as well, and all the time she was shouting, "Lord, oh, Lord, oh, praise the Lord!" and the minister in her head curled up like an autumn leaf and blew away.

Through their haze they realized that the doorbell was ringing.

"I'll get it, Ed," said Betsy Sue, smoothing down her dress with her work-rough hands. Ed popped himself back into place and pulled on his pants. Betsy Sue opened the door a sliver and peered out into the afternoon Tulsa sunshine.

"What is it?" she asked.

"Special Delivery for Mr. and Mrs. Sox," responded the familiar voice of their postman, a voice that seemed to come from the center of a half-jelled aspic mold, a voice quivering with a strange kind of delight. Then Ed noticed that the picture window drapes were open.

"I'll take it," said Betsy Sue, and she signed for and brought the letter in.

Ed ripped it open and pulled out the contents, a glossy brochure and a handwritten note. The note said, "Thought you and your wife might be interested in a couple of weeks at this place. It's on me." It was signed "A. K. Akley."

Ed unfolded the brochure and looked at the glorious color photographs.

"What is it?" Betsy Sue stood on her toes and craned over his hairy arms.

"Mr. Akley wants us to go to someplace called the Crystal Grape," said Ed. "It's a place for getting fit. There's a gift certificate enclosed." Ed's voice sounded abstracted. Betsy Sue hopped up and down to get a good look at the brochure Ed seemed be to be *ogling*.

The photographs showed what appeared to be acres and acres of young, beautiful women, all of them stark naked, lying beside an olympic swimming pool.

"Lookit that," murmured Ed. "Wall-to-wall pussy."

That was no way for a Reformed Baptist to talk.

9 / Iced Pop

ANGELA KISMET AND Alicia Katherine both loved their blue-eyed daddy who went away for ten years; they outgrew their tortoise and hare missing him, they outgrew Frankenstein missing him. In his absence they endured field hockey and religion and they smashed head-on into puberty, while all that time their orange-haired mommy wavered and guttered in her mauve bedroom like a badly made candle. August the Balkan butler snuffled from room to room in his crepe-soled shoes looking more pale and wan each passing day.

"You be Daddy and I'll be Mommy," Ally Kate instructed her little sister one Chicago winter day when the wind blustered around the house and burst down the chimney with a dismal pop. A stiff crust of snow covered the lawn with thin blades of powder slicing over it before the wind, as though God were peeling a crystal grape with a paring knife.

"OK," said Angela Kismet, who saw nothing amiss in that suggestion. They were lounging in their room, which was decorated in American Pubescent Girl Equestrienne: photographs of horses, bits and fragments of horse tack nailed to the walls, and by the bed a leather hassock covered with brands.

"Right," said Ally Kate. She shrugged out of her jeans and sweater and into her first formal gown, which she had worn to the tenth-grade Christmas prom.

Her orange hair had darkened (as her father would notice a couple of years later) into a glistening chestnut and framed her gorgeous sixteen-year-old face like an antique frame around an Old Master's madonna. Her freckles had diminished as she grew and now were a scatter of wildflowers across her face and the meadow of her breast. She had left at that tenth-grade prom a dozen adolescent boys with aching hearts and all the symptoms of emphysema.

While the Chef of DNA had made a perfect soufflé of Ally's ingredients, he had whipped in his bowl of hormones a stranger confection of Angela Kismet, for she had grown tall and slim and clean of limb, with her daddy's ice blue eyes and an eagerness to be her daddy's horse.

The sisters played at Mommy and Daddy often, Angela usually playing Daddy. Now, suddenly, in an agony of tangled hormones and body hair, they found themselves in love, so Angela Kismet put on a suit and tie and they danced together amid the trophies and bridles and paintings of chestnuts and bays, dapples and grays. Appaloosas and Arabians that thronged the walls. When they danced, fourteen-year-old Angela led with a loosening in her thighs that was strange to her, though less strange to her older sister, who for the last four years had felt those same sensations, ever since she had plunged at twelve into the bathtub full of mixed emotions referred to in her hygiene manual as the First Period. Oh, she felt it was a time when dark and smoky substances began to swirl through that numb, uninteresting area between her knees and waist. Now Angela felt those stirrings, and oddly enough they were the stirrings of power.

"You dance divinely," Angela remarked. She always said that when they danced, as they had watched the grownups do so often from the landing at the top of the sweeping staircase, but this time a peculiar hinge somewhere in her throat refused to open smoothly. The whole phrase sounded like rust, and Angela blushed above her knotted tie.

"So do you," Ally said, dropping her head onto her sister's shoulder. The rust and blush had sent a tingle through her hidden silks and folds; someone down there seemed to want to talk in private to her sister and urged her pelvic arch forward to whisper through dress and trouser some secrets of the blood, secrets so forbidden and exciting that the two girls pretended it wasn't happening and talked of horses, equitation, and dressage.

"You gonna ride on Sunday in the show?" Angela asked in her improbable voice. She cleared her throat with the sound of a claw hammer removing a rusty nail.

"I don't know yet. Are you?" Ally's voice was a plate of plastic pears, perfect-looking but false.

"Well, I might," said Angela, recognizing through a haze of shame and humiliation how boring this conversation was, and how they had had the same conversation the day before, about how the Arabian stallion had pranced and cantered in the pasture when the roan mare joined him, and that reminded her not to dwell on the gentle tuggings she felt below where her sister's sex whispered to her own, and they bumped coyly together while they danced.

"In that case," Ally murmured silkily into Angela's ear, "I'll ride too," and Angela swirled her around in a smooth fandango that sharply caught the backs of Ally's knees on the branded hassock and tossed her backward onto it. They laughed and decided to watch TV for a time, Angela's arm around Ally's shoulders the way Mommy sometimes sat with August.

But the spell was broken and Angela couldn't concentrate, so she asked, for the millionth time, "When is Daddy coming home?"

Ally pursed her perfect lips and frowned, adding in her head, "Two years, four months and sixteen days."

"How long's he been gone?"

"Seven years, seven months and twelve days."

"Do you think he'll recognize us when he gets back?"

"Of course. Daddy wouldn't forget us. We're very special to him. You know that."

The doorbell rang. "Maybe that's him, home early," Ally said. It was another of their games, whenever the doorbell rang, so they changed into their jeans and sweaters and trooped downstairs to answer the door.

August was already there, unfailingly polite and efficient. He opened the door, and the girls sat on the bottom stair to wait.

"Yes?" said the butler in his underground voice to a man standing at the edge of the wind.

"My name is Joseph Harbin. From the State Department. May I come in? It's very windy out here. And cold."

August opened the door and closed it quietly behind Mr. Harbin, who took off his hat and gloves and stood on the parquet in a slowly growing pool of melting snow. He wore rubbers over his shoes. He took three steps that squeaked loudly, and August said, "Your rubbers, sir."

"Oh, yes. Sorry," said Mr. Harbin. As he was removing them, Kay emerged from the solarium.

"Who is it, August?" she said. Her voice was like wet hemp rope, and her hair followed behind her like a lynch mob as she walked across the hall.

"A gentleman from the State Department, ma'am," said August. He placed the hat and gloves he had taken from Mr. Harbin on the hall table and withdrew. "I'll be going to the store now, ma'am." He gave an unblinking stare at the girls as he went by.

Angela shivered. "Boy, he gets creepier all the time," she said to Ally in a stage whisper.

"Yeah," Ally whispered back, sniffing at the damp-earth smells of August's departing wake.

"What can I do for you, Mr., ah . . . ?"

"Harbin, Mrs. Augenblaue."

"Mr. Harbin."

"The Secretary asked me to drop by while I was in Chicago to ask you once again if you experienced any continued effects from the day of your husband's launch. Some of the people in the stands that day have still not recovered. And of course the President is still missing . . ."

"Mr. Harbin," Kay said in a voice that matched, shade for shade, her ghastly freckled pallor, "I have been over this ground a thousand times with the best scientists and doctors from both the government and my husband's company. Dr. Merkin himself has questioned me at length. I assure you I have had no effects whatsoever from the launch."

"Yes, Mrs. Augenblaue. Please do not be alarmed. This is in the way of a courtesy call, not a formal investigation. The Secretary is naturally concerned and wants to keep in touch with as many people as possible. In case something comes up."

"Mr. Harbin, that was almost eight years ago. I've seen the Secretary several times. I simply do not believe he sent you all the way out here on a day like this simply to ask me that. Unless of course something new *has* come up. I assure you again that I am quite the same as I was."

Ally's whisper was almost audible. "Boy, she's sure lying."

"Yeah," Angela answered.

"No, Mrs. Augenblaue, nothing new has come up, and I'm very sorry to trouble you."

"He's lying too," Angela said.

"That's quite all right, Mr. Harbin. I appreciate the Secretary's concern. Would you care for a drink?"

"Huh?" Joseph Harbin was puzzled. A moment ago she was

cold and unfriendly, now she was offering him a drink. He noticed that her mouth and fingernails were a brilliant crimson. The color created a curious effect with the orange hair, just as Johnny Harker had described it at the briefing: curious. Harker had come to her aid eight years ago, disguised as a fire department rescue worker, when the butler was pinned to the bed. Curious.

But Kay, after her initial rush of hostility toward him, noticed that he was a quiet, unassuming man, very deferential and polite. And that he had short blond hair and a soft, pudding aspect. Like oatmeal, or tapioca. He didn't look dangerous at all. In fact, and she felt that strange lifting in her elbows again and the tugging, magnetic pull toward him under her dress, in fact there was something attractive about him, something that caused the air around her to crackle with ozone smells.

"Do you smell it?" asked Angela in her stage whisper.

"Yeah," Ally whispered back. "I think it's happening again, like that day I crashed through the skylight. It smells like a blown fuse."

"Why, yes, I would like a drink, thank you very much." Together they walked across the foyer and into the solarium. Even without his rubbers on, Mr. Harbin's shoes squeaked on the parquet.

10 / Borborygmi

"BRRRGHUMM. Zzzssetzzzz. Eeeeeeyowwzzzmmmm. Whump. Whump. Whump. Whump. Zzzzz."

The audience in the small theater squirmed uncomfortably under the electronic assault of the soundtrack, a vast descending stomach rumble. On the screen an enormous wave curled in superimposition over the peculiar face of William Lamplighter. The wave was slowed down about sixteen times, so it took a very long time to break. As the first drops began to fall gracefully away from the curling tip of the wave, the soundtrack suddenly, and inexplicably, modulated into a cavatina for two harps by

DuBois, and at the same time a look of such orgasmic rapture spread over Lamplighter's face that every person in the theater was affected.

Lamplighter himself, and his friend Arthur Kadel Accacia, were in the lobby discussing the film when the harp music began, and an audible sigh ran through the audience.

"That's the part that'll get 'em," said Art Accacia, who had not only made the film but also owned the Accacia Kinetoscope Art Theater. He wore faded heliotrope velour bell-bottoms and a dingy sweat shirt with a stylized artist's pallet and the word ART silk-screened on it, front and back.

"Well, it should," said Bill Lamplighter, his voice sounding like a frying pan full of hot gravel. "After all, I went through a lot to get that expression."

He smiled, and the effect was extraordinary. His face was a dictionary of violence, a livid network of scars and welts. The total impression was of someone patched together out of spare parts. There was a rumor, among the small but dedicated underground crowd that frequented the theater, that Lamplighter was over a hundred years old. He looked about forty.

Art smiled too. That had been quite a filming; even Andy Warhol, in *Blow Job*, hadn't been able to capture that fleeting moment with such gut-wrenching intensity.

The harp music segueed into a high F-sharp that warped into a series of layered sine tones, then echoed into a thumping feedback sequence rapidly increasing in tempo and volume as the film progressed to an unrecognizable montage of old pornographic movie fragments in random order. Art and Bill smiled at each other and listened a moment at the swinging doors of the auditorium. They could hear a few well-defined grunts.

"Works every time," said Art. "They don't know what's hitting them."

The two of them strolled across the lobby and out into the cool San Francisco fog. Union Street dropped away below them, and traffic crawled through the gray mist on Polk Street. Bill put a cigarette to his oversize lips and lit it with a small butane lighter. The flame cast a weird, greenish glow over his large, misshapen head.

"I've got to capture that effect sometime," Art said. "Your face lit from below like that."

The audience in the theater didn't know it, of course, but their reactions to the film, called *Bugfuckfour*, were being recorded by infrared photography. Art always used fragments of audience reaction in his films, blurred and solarized and unrecognizable.

Bunny Darlitch, who went to the Accacia Kinetoscope Art Theater every Wednesday night with his girlfriend Reba Hare, never saw himself in the films. Much of the time, though, he was taking notes for his reviews, which appeared on Fridays in the *Boric Acid Weekly*, the underground newspaper for which he wrote.

This week was no exception. He sat in the middle of the crowd with his hat in his lap, scribbling notes on a pad strapped to his knee.

He was, as they say, of two minds: he was writing his review of the film, and he was aware of an odd tide of sexual hunger rising in the audience. This made it difficult to breath.

The film finally ended by running out of the projector, leaving a blazing white rectangle on the screen and the annoying *flap flap* of film slapping the projector. The lights did not come on, but then they seldom did, because Art was usually out for a stroll by this time and only returned to close up the theater when he felt like it.

In Reba's wasted head the end of the film made no impression; she could barely contain herself or her convulsive fingers on Bunny's joint under his hat (a straw boater this week). The ninety-seven people in the theater sat stunned for at least three minutes before anyone moved toward the door, though groans and grunts were distinctly audible from all parts of the room.

"Bunny," Reba whispered at last, breathing into his ear. "Let's go. Come on, for God's sake, let's go!" And Bunny Darlitch, a dimpled marshmallow, dropped his review into the oily pool of his turgid lusts and climbed painfully out of his seat. The two of them, in a kind of hobbling run, crossed the lobby and went out into the night, past Art and Bill, down Polk Street toward the bay, and finally, unable to contain themselves, hurtled into an alley and engaged in a furious pillowy lovemaking on the pavement that left them both covered with tiny bite marks that took a week to fade.

Later that night, seated on a pillow, Bunny wrote his review. "*Bugfuckfour*," he typed, "is a new milestone in the career of

San Francisco's by now best-loved underground filmmaker and poet. Like his first film of three years ago, *Dharma Crapper*, *Bugfuckfour* uses the living image of a Frankenstein face to piece together the transcendence of material and perceptual worlds into a cohesive aesthetic experience of what is surely Tantric in inspiration and effects. The film begins with an extreme close-up of what eventually turns out to be a tooth; very slowly the camera dollies back to reveal lips, then nose and chin, and finally the entire face, which has remained devoid of expression throughout. An annoyingly loud electronic soundtrack, reminiscent of some of the so-called structuralist filmmakers, accompanies this long (49 minute) dolly back. From time to time squirming solarized bodies or contorted faces are momentarily superimposed over the constant image of the face. Then, when the entire head is revealed, though the face still has no expression, a tidal wave breaks in double exposure over it with glacial slowness. (It was shot at about four hundred frames per second.) Just as it breaks, the soundtrack modulates into harp music and the face, in real time, acquires an expression of unspeakable ecstasy.

"The effect on the audience was electrifying. This reviewer was unable to stand up for several minutes after the film had ended. Montage. Collage. Gilded cage. Transsexual universe. Simple image and nonrepresentational sound in a total expressionistic atmosphere of integrated Buddahood and subatomic energies. This is Art Accacia's greatest film to date. We can only guess at what he can do for us in the future."

Reba asked, "Bunny, aren't you coming to bed?"

Art and Bill stood nonchalantly in the fog as a couple walked past them.

"The film was profound, no doubt about that," the man said. "But I must confess it left me a bit mystified." The man was in his fifties, his girl about fifteen.

"It was a fuck film," she said, snapping her gum.

"Now, now, China. It was, ah, erotic. After all, it was called *Bugfuckfour*. That's not what I mean. What I want to know is what the film *meant*." His voice was a bit petulant.

"Aw, Philbrick, the film didn't mean shit. It was a fuck film. You know, pricks . . ."

"Now, China, that's no way for a girl your age to be talking.

Just because you've reached an early sexual maturity is no reason for you to talk like a stevedore. You'll find that too aggressive a vocabulary will be counterproductive in the end. You should allow yourself to blossom slowly into a ripe sexual understanding instead of allowing yourself to be ruled by this anal expulsive compulsion of yours." There was a decidedly professorial tone to his voice.

"Aw shit, Phil, honey, you know you love it when I talk like that. Besides, I'm horny and want you to eat me. Fuck films always do that to me."

"God almighty," said Philbrick, who in truth couldn't stand girls over eighteen. He touted himself as a freaky ex-psychiatrist from New York City who had dropped out to become an artist in San Francisco, a city full of horny girls under eighteen. His only problem was a terrific case of paranoia he had caught from one of his patients, which made it difficult for him to relate. But he was working on it.

"Gooboodoo. Gooboodoo. Gooboodoo," he chanted quietly.

"Shit, Phil, honey," China said as they drifted off into the fog. "You oughta quit that mantra shit. You know it don't do you any good."

11 / Fat Chance

"ARE YOU GOING to the convention this year?" the Countess asked Dudee Sparrow at Avery's welcome home party. "It's supposed to be especially wonderful this year now that he's home again. At least, that's what I hear."

Dudee reached up and fingered her small gold AKA pin where it clung to the meager strapping of her dress. Everyone at the party belonged to the AKA Club, whose members were known as Akaians. The clubs had spread all over the world in the ten years since Avery's blastoff for intergalactic space. The club was a quasi-religion. The Akaians believed in bagel-shaped spaceships and what they called *The* Blue Light. *The* Blue Light was the Answer.

"Of course I'm going," Dudee answered. "It's here in Chicago, at the Argo Palace Hotel, and Avery himself will probably be there, you know." Dudee was a member of the inner circle of the Akaians since her Uncle Sig was president of AKA International.

"Oh, yes." The Countess bobbed up and down in excitement. "He'll not only be there, he'll tell us about *The* Blue Light. He'll tell us what it is, and what it's like *out there!* I can hardly wait. In fact, you don't suppose he might give us a hint tonight, do you? I mean, we were all there at the launch, you know, sort of in on the beginning, as it were, so we've had a bit of personal experience with *The* Blue Light. If that's what *The* Blue Light really is. Maybe we'll get a peek at the truth tonight."

"Maybe."

"Ah," said the Countess to the Secretary of State, who strolled by. "We were discussing the convention."

"We're hoping Avery'll give State a debriefing before the convention. After all, it's still a couple of months away and it would be embarrassing if the world were to learn about *The* Blue Light before the government did. I spoke with Avery about this earlier."

Everyone at the party was talking about *The* Blue Light; it seemed to some people that a bit of it still clung to Avery's wife, Kay, and envy filled those who believed it. It was to be expected; after all, she was the wife of the man who had been *out there.*

Kay was upstairs stripping the soggy wetsuit from August's cadaverous form. As each arm or leg popped from its rubber casing with a wet sucking noise, a puff of damp-earth odor exhaled into the mirrored dressing room. "Jesus, August," Kay said peevishly, "you need a deodorant!"

"I've been sweating. It's not only hot in there but I was nervous. I've never killed anyone before. I can't say I liked it. Ma'am," he added, when Kay gave him a look. They may have screwed like varmints, but she wanted respect. After all, he *was* the butler.

"Yes," she said, peeling away the last section of wetsuit. She should have let him do it himself, for when she saw August's nudity revealed it began to stir more turgid vegetables into the simmering stew of her back burner.

"Goddammit," she said, "I hate sex." She flung herself onto his tired member and began to massage it. "I hate sex," she moaned. "Oh, how I hate it."

"Madam," he said in a voice more sepulchral and weary than before. There was no response from down below. "Perhaps we had better do something about the body. And the guests will be expecting you downstairs."

Gratefully he watched her pull herself together and drop with regret his battered stick.

"You're right, of course," she sighed. "Oh, how I hate it."

They stole silently back through the warren of rooms to the steambath, which they found wide open and empty of both steam and corpse. The tub was dry, though pearls of condensation clung to the wooden walls. The marble glistened, the chrome fixtures glowed. No sign remained of bullets or blood or body. Avery was gone.

"Oh, fuck," said Kay. She left the room. She drew three deep breaths and came back in. The steambath was empty.

"Oh, fuck," she repeated. "August. What the hell happened to Avery?"

She got no answer.

Kay stared at the empty marble half-oyster shell of the tub where only a few moments ago, though it seemed a lifetime or two, she and August had hatcheted and stabbed and shot her husband, detestable Avery, to a well-deserved death. He was dead, dead, dead, no doubt about that. August had split his head open, stabbed him in the chest, and emptied his .38 into Avery, who had groaned and screamed and gurgled in a blood-curdling way, just as he should have. Therefore he was dead-meat stone dead. Ha.

So where the fuck was he? "August, what happened?"

Still no answer. "August?" She groped behind her with her lacquered fingernails and encountered August's clothed body. Her nail caught on his zipper, but he did not move.

"August?" Again, her voice a field mouse under a threshing machine. She spun around to see why he didn't answer.

August stood perfectly straight, at attention. His eyes were wide open, staring, and his mouth hung open, slack. His body, under his butler's uniform, was rigid. He had an expression on his green-tinged face of mild surprise, which fooled Kay for a second. But clearly his expression was deceptive. August was totally catatonic, a cigar store Balkan butler, a department store advertisement for formal clothes, a wooden dummy, a vegetable.

August was useless, leaving Kay on her own.

"Oh, Christ, I suppose I'm on my own now," she said. She carefully steered his stiff-legged body into the west wing hall, where she left him standing against the wall like an antique suit of armor, a new addition to the interior décor. She changed her clothes and rejoined the party.

"Avery's bathing," she informed the Secretary of State. "He'll be down shortly. I hope everyone's having a good time." She passed on to the other guests, attended to the caterers, the hors d'oeuvres, the drinks, pretending that her husband would soon appear.

"He'll be down any minute," she told Sig Sparrow, thinking, dammit, I wish he wouldn't wear those tinted glasses, I can't see his eyes. Sig Sparrow, president of AKA International, said that was nice and that he looked forward to hearing about intergalactic space and *The* Blue Light, and he knew that the whole world was anxious to hear all about it too. Kay agreed, and told the Countess that Avery would be down soon. "He's taking a bath," she said, and the loose parts of her strange orange hair flexed up and down like a bunch of rubber carrots.

"Perhaps he's taking a nap," she mentioned to the Secretary of the Army, who was married to the Countess.

"Call me Bob," he said.

"I don't understand what could be keeping him," Kay told Dudee Sparrow in a voice more and more resembling that of her butler. "But he is very tired from his trip. Perhaps we should go ahead and eat dinner."

During dinner Kay picked at her food. After the last course everyone toasted Avery's empty chair and sang a chorus of "For He's a Jolly Good Fellow" for the first man to sail through intergalactic space and see *The* Blue Light firsthand, the man who had returned with all the answers for a waiting world. At last the party broke up, and they gave each other the AKA Club handshake and went home.

At the top of the stairs sixteen-year-old Angela Kismet waited in her neatly tailored suit and striped silk tie to confide to her daddy the big news she was bursting with, news that she had kept from everyone, including, or rather especially, her mother. The only one to know was Ally Kate, her ripe and gorgeous older sister, best friend and wonderful lover.

Ally Kate sat beside her now, and every time they heard Kay say "He'll be down in a few minutes" or "He's probably taking a short nap," they leaned toward one another and whispered "Bullshit" into each other's ear.

"She's done something bad," said Ally Kate after all the guests had left and the house was silent. Kay had nodded to her daughters and disappeared into the west wing, where August remained impassively against the wall.

"Well, whatever, she's sure as hell lying," Angela responded. "Hey, I haven't seen that creepy August all night."

"You don't suppose they done Daddy in, do you?" Ally Kate probably didn't believe it.

"You mean, *killed* him?"

"Yeah."

"Oh, they better not have. I mean, I'll never get to break the news then."

"Mmmm."

There was a long silence.

"She's not that crazy," said Angela.

"Mmmm."

"Why would they do him in?"

"Well, they've been at it for ten years," said Ally. "Maybe they figured he'd interrupt them or something now that he's back."

"Yeah, but he wouldn't do that. He couldn't stand either of them. That's why he flew into space in the first place. That's why he left, don't you think?"

"You're probably right," Ally said, holding her.

"Well, that's why I'm leaving. Soon's I can," said Angela.

They snuggled closer together, draped their arms around each other, and Ally kissed sweet Angel on the ear, and sweet Angel cupped his sister's breast in his hand and kissed her back and then said sadly, "Oh, Ally, what are we going to do? I was really looking forward to telling Daddy that I was his son, that I'd changed my sex, just for him. And for you, of course."

"If they did something to him," said Ally. "We'll find out about it soon enough. And then we'll get even. We'll track them down and prove it was them. And if they didn't do him in or anything, if he's here, then we'll tell him in the morning. When he wakes up."

"Fat chance," said Angel.

12 / Just Dessert

VIRGE MOSES WAS A VERY happy cop. His wife, Wanita, had recently purchased an entire bedroom suite of Akley Republican Furniture, including an American Heritage fourposter, and since it was to be delivered today, they could try it out tonight, he and Wanita.

He drove slowly through the streets of Cicero, Illinois, in his black and white patrol car, wearing his riot helmet and tinted face protector. Cicero was a tough area, but for a change Virge was not on the lookout for offenders, though usually he managed to run up quite a record for arrests in this neighborhood; junkies, drunks, looters, stickup artists, jaywalkers, muggers, vagrants, armed robbers, psychopaths, rapists, parking meter vandals, domestic arguers, homocidal maniacs, gamblers, con men and disturbers of the peace ran rampant on the streets of Cicero. However, Virge just now had a hard-on for the new fourposter and Wanita's puckered thighs, so he cruised through the rain-swept and chilly streets past narcotics deals, holdups and winos without a glance.

"Som' bitch, man," one of them wheezed. "I ain't never seen Officer Moses drive on by like that!"

As he turned up his street, the car radio (not his police radio, which he had switched off) informed him of the historic landing of the *A.K.A. Monastic*, and that reminded him that he was scheduled for duty at the AKA convention in a couple of months. He was looking forward to that duty, not because he expected any trouble, but because Avery would be there, and he had been *out there* and had seen *The* Blue Light. Virge would be on hand to witness the historic event. That would surely be something to share with his children. He sat in his car until the news was over.

Officer Moses lived on a street of three-story brown houses, all with a small back yard and twelve tiny rooms. The street was straight and flat. Looking in either direction he saw only baroque vistas of identical buildings stretching to a seeming infinity, though today the cold blowing rain obscured the distances and gave the street a slightly homier touch.

Virge had three kids. "It's mine!" "Mine!" "Mine!" blasted him back a foot when he opened the front door. The eight-, nine- and ten-year-old bodies hurtled down the stairs at him and, at the moment before impact, swerved abruptly into the living room, the child in front carrying aloft a huge broken, plastic dump truck.

His helmet on, Virge trudged into the kitchen. He was preoccupied with the American Heritage fourposter and Wanita's dimpled bottom.

"You'll never believe what arrived today," Wanita whispered into his ear after he removed his helmet. She plunged her tongue into his ear, swirling it around wetly, breathing hard. She, too, was eager to try out the fourposter.

"What are those?" he asked when Wanita unwrapped a package on the table. Grandfather Moses on his breathing machine came through loud and clear.

"Satin sheets! Just like advertised in *Playboy!*"

"Oh, boy," said Officer Moses, pulling his wife hard against the silver buckle of his gun belt. In the other room the kids fought over the truck.

Wanita ground her pelvis slowly against her husband's and stroked the outside of his holster with her hand; she continued to tongue his ear.

"You people are *disgusting!*" shrieked Grandma Moses from the kitchen door. "Just disgusting. You used to be a nice boy, Virgil, but you've gotten just disgusting since you married this tramp. Ah ha ha ha ha ha!" she cackled, her wizened face transformed into a livid prune.

Grandma Moses was a bit senile, so Virge and Wanita ignored her, dry-humping each other in the kitchen.

"What the hell haaaaa," Grandfather Moses joined in, trailing off in a dismal wheeze that ended in a racking cough. "Ll's going on?" he finished at last.

"Hello, Dad." Virge blushed, abruptly pushing Wanita away from him. Her buttocks smashed against the kitchen table, and his riot helmet rolled off the table and crashed onto the floor.

"Uhhh, kak, kak, ka-kak-kak," said the father. The breathing machine sighed unattended.

"You better get back to your machine, Dad. It's not good for you to get too excited."

Grandfather Moses looked like a human varicose vein: clotted, dilated, knotted and torturous. By comparison, Grandma Moses was a walking metaphor for health.

"What the hell ahh ahh ahh haa haa ka-kak is going on?" he repeated.

"It's nothing, Dad," Wanita told him. "Mother just came in and called us disgusting. Like she always does."

Grandma Moses was examining the wall next to the kitchen door, chortling calmly to herself. She seemed to have forgotten entirely about the group in the kitchen with her.

"Bang bang bang," shouted little Jimmy. He raced through the kitchen waving his cap pistol, firing it several times. Though it made a satisfactory noise by itself, he still yelled, "Bang!" Dorothy and Virge Junior trailed in hot pursuit, aiming their guns at him. The three of them banged into the back door and ran out into the gray, soggy back yard.

"You kids get back in here this instant!" Wanita shouted. "You wanna catch your death?"

"Aw, Mom." Junior tramped back into the house, leaving a trail of thick, sticky mud behind him. The other two followed.

"Ahhh ha ha ha ha," Grandma cackled. "Those kids are just disgusting." She continued to stare at the wall. This is going to be one of those days, Virge groaned, his lust beginning to melt away.

"Come on up and look at the new bed." Wanita led him out of the kitchen. Grandfather Moses wheezed his way back to his bedroom. He slept in the tiny den, far away from the other bedrooms, so the noise of his breathing machine wouldn't disturb anyone. Grandma Moses continued to cackle at the chipped, off-white paint next to the kitchen door.

The American Heritage fourposter was a dream of spindly Philippine monkeywood and plastic teak veneer draped with thick red velvet and a ruffled flounce. It filled the small bedroom from window to closet leaving barely enough space for the dresser.

"Kinda fills up the room, don't it?" asked Virge with a salacious grin. Wanita folded back the spread to display another set of satin sheets. They were black. Virge gave a low whistle and felt himself bulging against his tight uniform pants. Wanita noticed, and *she* gave a low whistle.

She patted the bed on her way out. "After dinner."

She served corned beef hash for dinner and fruit cocktail for dessert. Grandma Moses prodded the hash with her fork, but before she could open her toothless mouth, all three kids shouted "Disgusting" in unison and collapsed into hysterical, helpless laughter. She snapped her gums together and glared at them. "I don't think that's funny." No one answered.

Virge shoveled enormous gobs of food into his mouth, which he chewed noisily and gulped down. He was in a rush.

"Avery landed today," Grandfather Moses remarked. Virgil didn't answer him, either. "Said on the radio he hadn't changed a bit. All those years in space."

"Mphh," Virge grunted, shoveling in another forkful.

"Said he was going to explain about *The* Blue Light, which has something to do with that riot that occurred when he took off. I mean with the President disappearing and all. What do you think?" Grandfather Moses was eating like a bird.

"You're eating like a bird," Wanita scolded. "Have some more hash."

"You know I don't like corned beef hash," said Grandfather Moses petulantly.

"You haven't coughed once during this meal, Grandpa," said little Jimmy. "You must be feeling better."

"Guess so." The old man grinned. His large ivory false teeth looked very strange in his congealed face.

Grandma Moses dribbled bits of canned pear, grape and peach down her chin and muttered under her breath. Grandfather Moses picked at his dessert. At length everyone was done eating, the dishes were washed, Grandfather Moses was resting in his room, the kids were watching TV, and Grandma Moses was sitting in front of the plastic fire, nodding. Officer Moses and his wife Wanita climbed the narrow stairs again to their fourposter. He carried his riot helmet with the tinted plastic faceplate, and the house settled and creaked around them.

Wanita threw off her clothes and hurled herself onto her back on the new black satin sheets, and Virge slipped his uniform pants and Jockey shorts over his painful erection and prepared to leap on his wife when a piercing scream echoed up the stairs.

"Virgil," Grandma Moses screamed. "Get down here! Your father's having a terrible coughing attack!"

Virge tumbled down the stairs, pulling on his pants, and raced into his father's room. Grandfather Moses was sucking on his breathing machine with a terrible rasping sound.

He looked up at Virge. "Thought I'd give the old bitch a scare." He winked.

13 / Fresh Fruit

THE CHILL RAINS OF Oklahoma blew across the open prairie, and of course the wind came right behind, west to east, but Ed and Betsy Sue Sox packed their new El Dorado and drove head-on into the high-piled clouds. On old Route 66, now Interstate 40, they followed the ancient cattle trail through Oklahoma City, through El Reno, and Clinton and Elk City, Oklahoma, and on to Amarillo, Texas, where they tossed all night on a violent surf of thunder and sex, fitfully lit by livid forks of lightning through their Best Western Motel window.

Next morning they drove on into the freshly washed Texas panhandle dawn in a fever of anticipation. Ed was thinking about his new job as West Coast manager for Akley Republican Furniture, planning in his head the grandest of Grand Opening Sales. Their two weeks at the Crystal Grape had slipped his mind.

But not Betsy's. She had been struck by all those naked women pictured in the brochure at the Crystal Grape. The image had blasted into her retinas and forked in two directions: one, keep

Eddie away from them or them away from Eddie; and two, wow. Since the AkleyLounger episode, when the minister in Betsy Sue's brain was gusted away forever by a concentrated blast of estrogen, Betsy's Reformed Baptist morality was fading and being replaced by lurid photos and half-imagined positions. Wow.

"Are you listening? The brochure says special diets and exercises. Swimming in the Fort Mojave Indian Reservoir. Clean desert air. Treatments." She made him forget his Grand Opening Sale with intimations of wall-to-wall pussy.

"It must be awfully expensive for Mr. Akley to send us there; it's so luxurious in the brochure. Do you suppose it really is? I mean, it all looks so *sinful!*" The word was not dreadful, as it should have been, but somehow *delicious.* Betsy Sue thought about sin all the way from Amarillo to Albuquerque, from Albuquerque to Gallup, and from Gallup to Flagstaff, Arizona, where they had to stop for the night even though they had planned to drive straight through to the Crystal Grape because the weight of all that sin was simply too much for Betsy Sue Sox. They stayed in another Best Western Motel, where they banged up the Akley Republican bed pretty badly. They were charged extra, but Ed didn't mind. He was West Coast manager.

They listened to the car radio from Flagstaff almost to Needles, California. Every station broadcast something about the launch of the *A.K.A. Monastic* from Kankakee, Illinois, and the strange events just after liftoff. Various departments of the federal government were trying to sort it all out. The President had disappeared shortly after the launch. Two months later, now, he was still missing. The Vice President, an avid golfer, kept wandering around muttering "Fore!" and something about "lost in the rough." He was Acting President for the duration of the President's term.

Walter, and various members of the press corps present, were guarded about what had actually happened, but enough innuendoes made their way over the airwaves to give the world the general idea. Rumors were, Walter admitted to Dick Peters a month after the launch, rampant.

The general idea was that what had appeared at first like a riot, a melee of monumental proportions, was quite different from that. When the dust and bluish glare had settled somewhat, there were 2468 naked bodies engaged in furious congress and the (missing) President's profile was indelibly etched on the maroon fence of the VIP box. Some time elapsed before the President's absence was noticed.

Radio station KURB (the Voice of the United Reformed Baptists) informed them that since the launch many clubs had sprung into existence. Some strange people, especially in California, saw tremendous power in the Merkin Orgone Engine, or "the drive," as it was called. These kooks in California felt that Avery Krupp Augenblaue had gone out into intergalactic space for the rest of mankind, and that when he came back he would bring with him the Answer.

"What a load of nonsense," said Ed.

"Yes, Eddie," said Betsy Sue.

"We all know that there's no answer out there. The answer is in the Reformed Baptist Church and in bringing inexpensive furniture to everyone in the world. Once every house is decorated with Akley Republican Furniture, every man, woman and child in the world will have everything he or she needs. Mr. Akley is a very altruistic man, and that is his goal." Ed accepted that as Mr. Akley's goal, but he didn't actually presume that Mr. Akley was as unselfish as all that. Ed was exploring the Power of Positive Thinking.

"Yes, Eddie."

"Just a bunch of kooks out there in California."

"We're moving to California, Eddie."

"Yes, honeypot, I know." Ed reached over and squeezed her thigh. "But we're moving to Milpitas. No kooks there, just the Akley Republican Furniture warehouse and us, and we aren't kooks."

"Oh, Eddie," said Betsy Sue, her round face wreathed in a grin. She slid across the El Dorado's front seat and dropped her rough paw into Eddie's ample lap.

"Now, honeypot," he said with a jolly shake of his belly. "What would the Reformed Baptists think? Besides we're almost there."

He left the Interstate at Topock and drove up the east side of the Fort Mojave Indian Reservoir. Just across from Needles they spotted a sign: THE CRYSTAL GRAPE. It was a discrete sign, a small bronze plaque screwed to a bronzed stainless steel post. Beside it a freshly blacktopped road zipped straight west and disappeared into a stand of giant saguaro cactus.

"This is it," said Ed.

He turned onto the blacktop and drove on toward the cactus under a fierce noonday sun. There were no buildings in sight. Ed drove slowly up the narrow road, and the El Dorado's air conditioner whined in the silence after Betsy switched off the radio, which had begun to repeat the news.

They entered the sudden jagged shade of the cactus; slashes of dense black shadow alternated irregularly with harsh bars of intense light as they passed under the broad spiky arms of the tree-sized plants. The road took a slight turn through the stand, so they had no clear view ahead of them.

"This is a little weird, Eddie," said Betsy Sue, her hand back in the security of his fat lap.

"Sure is, honeypot," he said, slowing even more. It wasn't quite what he had been anticipating. Images of a kind of super Best Western Motel had been dancing in his head, and there didn't seem to be any Best Western Motel around here. Surely they were almost to the lake, and still no sign of the Crystal Grape.

The jagged alternations of light and shade were disturbing and disorienting, but finally the cactus thinned out and a few cabins loomed ahead. White gravel paths connected them, winding among the spikes and thick green columns of the cactus. They came to a clearing, beyond which they could see the glint of blue water. A circular drive brought them to the main building.

A tanned young man in a white suit and cowboy hat was the first and only person around. He was unloading luggage from a limousine parked in front of the entrance.

"Maybe it *is* like a Best Western Motel," Ed murmured. The man in white nodded to them, and Ed noticed a small amethyst grape embroidered on the breast pocket of his jacket. He carried the suitcases up the broad steps and disappeared inside.

"Well," said Eddie, "this is it. I suppose we ought to get out and look around, or register or something."

The heat instantly hammered them flat to the pavement. Never in all the hottest Tulsa heat waves had either of them been subjected to such relentless pounding pressure. It seemed to fall on their heads like a couch-sized bronze anvil, like a downpour of sticky hot fudge, like a collapsing water tower full of boiling sorghum molasses. Ed felt small and helpless and weak; his shirt itched, his shoes were on fire, his pants melted into a nightmare-syrup sucking at his legs. The two of them tottered up the steps in agony and entered the adobe building, minds fogged with sweat and fear, into a lobby of muted light and polished hardwood floors; it was so dim, though blessedly cool, that their glare-blinded eyes couldn't discern anything, so they both jumped at the voice behind them. "Welcome to the Crystal Grape. You must be Mr. and Mrs. Sox. We've been expecting you."

Ed blinked and wiped the sweat from his eyes. Finally he made out the form of a man in a beret, mustache and Vandyke. The man was smiling.

"God almighty, it's hot out there," Ed said.

"Yes, indeed. Yes, indeed. Hundred and thirty today. In the shade. In the *shade*, Mr. Sox. Clean desert air. One of the benefits of the Crystal Grape. I'm sure you'll appreciate the reducing benefits of heat, Mr. Sox. Looking at you, I'm sure of it. Very dry heat, it is. Wonderful. Well, well, well, and how are you today, Mrs. Sox? Well, I hope?"

"Oh, I guess I'll be fine as soon as I catch my breath."

"Fine. Fine. Well. And, ah, here's one of our other guests now, Mr. Sox, Mrs. Sox." His voice was cool oil, soothing and anesthetizing the two of them.

A large young girl moved shyly forward from a dark table where she had evidently been signing the guest register. The suitcases from the limousine stood beside the table.

"Miss Sparrow," said the man with the beret, "this is Mr. and Mrs. Sox, from Tulsa, Oklahoma. Mr. and Mrs. Sox, this is Miss Sparrow, from Chicago. I'm sure you'll both enjoy each other's company during your stay here at the Crystal Grape.

"I am, if I may introduce myself, the owner and operator of the Crystal Grape, Anton Armbruster. But you can call me Keb. Everyone else does, and we want nothing here but to make you feel at home. Mr. Sox, A. K. Akley is an old and dear friend of ours here at the Crystal Grape, and any friend of his is a friend of ours, so again, welcome. Duane will show you to your cabins. Miss Sparrow, Mr. and Mrs. Sox. *Duane!*" he shouted, and seconds later the white-suited young man in the cowboy hat appeared.

"Yes, Keb?"

"Show these good people to their cabins and give them the schedule. Mr. and Mrs. Sox are in Hopi Three, and Miss Sparrow is by herself in Zuñi Nine."

"Yes, sir."

"You know, you've just reminded me of someone, Mr. Armbruster. You look very familiar." Ed squinted in the dim light at Keb's face.

"Call me Keb."

"Uh, Keb. Very familiar."

"I'm quite sure we've never met before, Mr. Sox. I never forget a name or a face. Have a nice day."

14 / Hot Coffee

IT WAS A GOOD THING August went to the store when Kay escorted Joseph Harbin into the solarium because August might have experienced something like jealousy at the way Kay porpoised through Harbin's creamy oatmeal lusts.

"For a person who claims to hate sex all the time, she sure does get into it," Alicia Katherine told fourteen-year-old Angela as they stood at the door of the solarium. The sounds of pounding flesh wafted distinctly from the direction of the couch, backed by the moan of winter wind and the dismal wail of every bleached snowman adrift and lost in the snow.

"Sounds kinda like fun to me," said Angela warmly. "I wish I were a boy, then *we* could do it properly."

"You always wished you were a boy. Why don't you become one? We could run away to California, where you could get it done anonymously, no questions asked. It'd only take a couple of weeks. Besides, California's a very weird place, I hear. It could be interesting."

So as bland and flavorless Joseph Harbin banged their vivid orange mother in the sunless solarium, Ally Kate and Angela Kismet packed their bags, flagged a cab to the airport, and flew to San Francisco, where Angela became Angel in a couple of weeks with practically no trouble at all and felt like a true son to his wandering daddy far away in intergalactic space.

"Look at it, Ally," he said to his sister when he returned to their sublet Nob Hill apartment. "It'll really work, just like it's supposed to."

"And my gosh, Angel, it's so *cute*. It's going to be a lot of fun to play with. Can we play with it now?"

"They say to wait a couple of months, to sort of get used to it. You know, everything's a little different now. But it works. I know it works. So let's stay in San Francisco until we can use it."

It was a foggy night out but cosy in the appartment. The mellow sounds of radio station KAKA-FM filled the living room, whose walls were covered with mandalas and posters of revolutionary leaders of the sixties. A well-worn dartboard with a portrait of President Nixon, disgraced in the early seventies, hung by the door. Pillows were strewn over the floor. Bamboo shades covered the windows, hiding the two from the fog outside.

"How are we doing for money?" Angel asked after making camellia tea. The two of them were seated, naked and cross-legged, on a pillow.

"We're doing okay. Don't worry about it, we've got plenty of traveler's checks. We paid for your operation in advance and still have enough for a couple of months. There's lots to do here in San Francisco." Ally smiled at her new brother.

"Like what?" Angel asked, sipping tea, his fine dark eyebrows lifting quizzically above clear eyes.

"Well, for instance, while you were down there at the clinic I met a very strange man. I'd like you to meet him. He's an artist. I mean, a really terrible artist, but he used to be a psychiatrist. I met him at this coffee house."

"You think he'd be there now?" Angel flashed on foggy San Francisco streets, foghorns wailing over the bay, a warm, steamy coffee house with a poet or two lounging around and maybe some young revolutionaries talking politics. He glanced up at Che Guevara on the wall. Angel had never been to a coffee house, not even when he was a girl, but the idea was certainly appealing; in the old movies they were always interesting places.

"Might be. You want to go?" Ally got up and slid into the blue jeans with the huge sunset embroidered on the seat. Angel put on his new leisure suit and a wide silk tie, and hand in hand they went out into the night to find the Third Eye Coffee House, where artists hung out.

They walked through the swirling winter fog of the city, down streets and up streets, and the ghostly lights wavered soundlessly by them. Their footsteps echoed softly in their newfound world, and they felt as though they were the only people in the universe and they needed no one else, because together they were complete. Ally slid her arm around Angel's waist, and Angel slid his arm around hers. They leaned into one another, walking in step, in long, glorious strides as one. A cooling moisture clung to their eyelids and lips, and they laughed all the way down to the yellow light of the Third Eye Coffee House window. They were alive and in love.

The Third Eye was crowded. Poets, bearded and unbearded, straight and gay, young and old, black and white and yellow and brown, surreal and classical, filled the tables and talked excitedly over cups of cappuccino. Revolutionaries, terrorists, and Young Republicans roamed the room, glaring at members of rival groups. Gurus, Satanists, yogis, swamis, roshis and astrologers chanted or meditated or levitated or smiled seraphically at the crowd.

Philbrick Weevol sat at a table with his girlfriend, China.

"I love it when you eat me," she was saying. "You gotta terrific tongue."

"Really, China, I wish you wouldn't talk like that. You're only a child." He had a pained look on his large brown face.

"Hi, Phil. Can we join you?" Ally asked as she approached his table, leading Angel by the hand.

"Of course, of course." He swung two empty chairs around so they could sit down.

"Aw, shit, Phil, you know you love it when I talk like that," China continued. She had a thin pale face, a thin pale body, and thin, dirty blond hair. She wore a blue workshirt eleven sizes too large that belonged to Philbrick.

"China, this is someone I met a few days ago, a young lady whose name I don't remember, but her brother has just changed his sex, though I can't remember which way. Is this your brother?"

"Yes," Ally answered, squeezing Angel's hand. "His name's Angel, and he's a boy now, and that's a fact."

"I'm sure it is," said Phil with a vacant grin.

"What kind of an artist are you?" Angel asked him. He was looking curiously at China.

"Well," said Phil with a satisfied sigh, "I write poems from time to time. And of course I paint, usually in oils, though of late I've been painting in industrial varnishes. Right now, though, I'm into sculpture; I'm working on a life-sized couch made of maraschino cherries."

"How do you hold them together?" Angel looked intently at him. He didn't seem real.

"Oh, well, I'm baking them. I have a big oven in my studio. I'm calling the sculpture 'Virgin Sofa.' How do you like the title?"

"I don't get it."

"That's just one of his dumb jokes about cherries," said China. "He likes to make dumb jokes about cherries. He likes to fuck little girls with cherries, so he's always making asshole jokes about it. It's a real pain in the ass, if you ask me. Anyway, his goddam couch is going to fall apart, just like that last asshole sculpture he made."

"What was that?" Ally asked.

"A walk-in vagina constructed of marshmallows. Someone almost suffocated in it when it collapsed." China was an overwise and contemptuous teen-ager.

"Sounds weird." Angel couldn't help grinning.

"If you think that's weird, you oughta hear his theory. Hey, Phil old cock, tell these folks about your theory. Phil has this theory about people. He used to be a psychiatrist. Tell 'em your theory, Phil."

"Yeah, tell us about your theory," Ally joined in.

"OK," said Phil, leaning back in his chair. He didn't seem to notice that China was baiting him. A serious, professorial look settled over his wide, halcyon face, a face untroubled by weather of any kind.

"Well," he said in his new tone, "people are descended from plants."

There was a long silence.

"Is that all?" Angel asked at last.

"Yes."

"People are descended from plants?"

"Yes."

"Plants?"

"Yes, plants."

"I may not be old enough to know better, but that sounds silly to me."

"Look," said Phil, getting a little impatient with these kids who couldn't seem to understand his genius. "Most of the time people talk about other people as if they were animals, right? You know: he's a shark, that guy's a real bear, she's a cat, stuff like that."

"OK," said Angel, frowning.

"Well, that's all wrong. People are descended from plants, and that's all there is to it. I wrote the definitive article on the subject, but the psychiatric profession is so backward they won't publish it. One day they will, though. The fact is, everything animal is descended from plants, and plants have personalities, so plant personality elements, plant characteristics, are carried in the DNA from plants to people. I can prove it."

"You mean, there are people who are like trees and mushrooms and stuff like that?" Angel was prepared for anything.

"That's right. China here, for instance, is a quillwort. Quillworts grow in swampy places, hence her pale complexion, and, of course, the sex life of the quillwort is very promiscuous, just like China's. Isn't that right, baby?" He gave her a paternal pat on the head.

"Eat me," she said. "Asshole."

"Some people are angiosperms, some people are palms, some are graminae, or grasses, and so on. It's all very technical, but it's a very neat theory. Unfortunately, on top of not publishing it, I was drummed out of the psychiatric profession because of this theory; some people felt that it didn't reflect a scientific attitude, that it was too far-fetched, that I didn't research it carefully. Nonsense. The truth is that I identified several colleagues according to this taxonomy and they were upset. Envy, of course. Pure envy."

"Of course," said Ally.

"Bullshit," said China.

Ally turned to Angel. "You know who's a fungus?"

"Sure," said Angel, laughing. "August."

15 / Chicken Soup

"Good morning, Mr. Lamplighter," said Dr. Ague. Dr. Ague was the director of the Aldrich K. Ague Biosynthetics Clinic, a modest research facility in the hills above Menlo Park, California. He had a shaved head, blue eyes behind thick glasses, and wore a white smock.

"Good morning, Doctor. I hope I'm not too early." Bill Lamplighter shrugged out of the long black overcoat he always wore, winter and summer, and smiled a hideous smile. The smile was a sharp knife shining in the organic wreckage of his face.

"No indeed, not at all," said Dr. Ague. He bobbed up and down on his toes as though suppressing a bubble of excitement. "Please come right this way."

Lamplighter was Dr. Ague's most notable success. He had not, as was rumored, constructed Bill out of spare parts. No, Lamplighter came to him the way he was, with a face like a coil of hemp rope. Dr. Ague had been working on him at the clinic for some years, finding in huge and hideous William Lamplighter the most unusual and interesting subject he had seen.

"This is, let me see, the eighth year you've been here, isn't that right?" Dr. Ague asked as he led his patient from the muted reception area to the back of the building, through corridors of pleasant pastels and deep pile carpets and into a comfortable room done in cheerful yellows.

"That's right," said Bill, lying down on the examining table in the yellow room. "Eight years."

"And how is the acting business going?" Dr. Ague had a resonant, deep voice, very reassuring, though Lamplighter was in no need of reassurance.

"Going very well. We had the opening of *Bugfuckfour* last night, and it seemed to go over extremely well. Art was very pleased with the reaction."

Dr. Ague rolled up Lamplighter's sleeve. "Aha," he said, "I see. And what's the next film to be called?" He deftly inserted a needle and drew blood from an arm as complexly scarred and twisted as the face.

"*ExtráPosition.*"

"Sounds very interesting. Very interesting. More sex, I suppose?" He squirted the blood he had drawn into a test tube, which he placed in a circular rack and slid into a centrifuge. It started up with a gentle whir.

"Of course. Art wouldn't make a movie without sex." Lamplighter didn't notice the pleased smile on Dr. Ague's face.

The centrifuge gave a quiet beep and began to print out about three feet of computer paper with extraordinary speed.

"*Very* good, Mr. Lamplighter. Very good today," said Dr. Ague, glancing rapidly over the columns of figures. "Truly prodigious levels this year. Truly prodigious. Yes. The treatments should be quite easy this time around."

"That's nice."

"Oh, yes, very simple this year. More and more simple every year, eh, Mr. Lamplighter? You know? Of course you do. And a side effect of all this, an extra benefit as it were, is that you may very well live on indefinitely. But then, you know that as well." Dr. Ague bounced up and down on his toes a moment, his lips pursed over the lists of numbers on his computer print-out. "We have large quantities of PCPA in the blood, Mr. Lamplighter. We are certainly on the right track. How do you feel?" His eyes darted to Bill's ribbed and welted face, which showed no reaction.

"I feel very good, better than usual, more and more *ready*, if you know what I mean . . ."

"Of course, of course," Dr. Ague muttered. "Ready."

"The part that Art felt worked best in *Bugfuckfour*, for example, was the, er, *critical* moment. Just a shot of my face, you understand."

Dr. Ague stood with his back to the floor-to-ceiling windows so his shining shaven head was backlit; it seemed to glow with enthusiasm and impatience. Lamplighter looked past him at the manicured lawn that stretched to a grove of live oak. There were no other buildings in sight. The clinic was very private. The rhododendron hedge tossed gently in the mild winter breeze.

"Well," said the doctor, his face a dark ovoid surrounded by light. "I think we should perform the treatments this time before drawing the other sample, don't you?"

"Whatever you think best." Lamplighter was well paid for being an experimental subject.

"Well, if you'll just remove your clothes, we'll get you ready before I send Nurse Thinger in."

"Nurse Thinger?" Lamplighter asked as he removed his pants.

"Oh, yes," said Dr. Ague. "She's the new research nurse on the staff. I'm sure you'll like her just fine. A very attractive young lady. Well, radiation levels are within proper parameters, Mr. Lamplighter," he went on, looking at a metered instrument.

"Ah, yes," said the doctor. "Nurse Thinger will be quite taken with you, I'm sure." He didn't seem to be joking. "Now, if you'll just step into the irradiation chamber we'll get the more unpleasant parts of the treatment over with."

Lamplighter's body fitted upright into a specially shaped depression in the wall of the small irradiation chamber, and Dr. Ague closed the door. Dim red light filled the room, and parts of William Lamplighter's peculiar body were zapped with rays that tickled and burned and tingled. Ropes of muscle would suddenly coil tightly and as suddenly relax. He smiled and frowned and cried and laughed and fell asleep more than once. When at last the door was opened, he was asleep again.

He woke up on a bed looking at a ceiling of soft gray. He glanced down and saw that he was ready for Nurse Thinger. The door opened and Nurse Thinger came into the room, dressed in white. Unlike her predecessor, Lamplighter noted with relief, she was not chewing gum. He was ready.

"Well, well, well, Mr. Lamplighter, and how are we today?" Nurse Thinger asked in a breathy, pear-shaped and well-trained voice. She moved busily about the room, checking the cabinet against the wall, adjusting the shades, and dimming the lights.

"We're just fine, Nurse Thinger," said Lamplighter in a voice like a dustpan full of ceramic lobsters falling down an elevator shaft.

Her back was to him. "Would you prefer me to be dressed or undressed?" she asked in her professional voice, the voice of science itself, objective, brisk, detached and breathy. This was pure routine.

"Oh, it doesn't really matter. Undressed, I suppose." Lamplighter, too, was engaged in the pursuit of knowledge, and besides, he had made a number of films by now and had seen everything.

Nurse Thinger had not seen everything, so when she dropped her white starched uniform, neatly folded, over the straight-backed chair beside the cabinet, stepped clinically out of her underwear, and turned, bobbing gelatinously, to her subject, she was not really prepared.

"Well, then," she said as she turned, "perhaps we should get start*eeeeeee*. Oh, my God." She staggered backward, her beautiful rump (Lamplighter noticed) crashing as softly as an elastic bag full of marshmallows against the cabinet. She leaped forward as though she had been zapped with a cattle prod.

"Jesus Christ," she whispered, her eyes wide with fascination. Then the eyes rolled up into her head, two whites shone in the dim light for a moment, and breasts, chin and eyes all sank slowly from Lamplighter's sight beside the bed.

"Oh, dear," he said, leaning over to look down at her somewhat overstated but gorgeous body, splayed on the deep wall-to-wall carpeting. She moaned and twitched her hands and feet briefly. Her eyes snapped open and rolled around out of focus. She licked her lips. She closed her eyes and squeezed them shut. She opened them again and licked her lips. She saw Lamplighter's scarred face looking down at her with mild concern.

"Oh, Christ," she said softly, but she did not pass out again. "I'm very sorry, Mr. Lamplighter. You startled me. I wasn't quite prepared for that. I mean, my God." She shuddered once and slowly began to pull herself together. As she sat up, her terrific breasts bobbed gently.

Bill had a strange feeling in his throat. Love?

"I'm supposed to work on *that?*" she asked in a low voice.

Love, thought Bill. Definitely love.

"That's all right," he told her. "It must have been a shock, the first time."

Nurse Thinger hauled herself up by the edge of the bed and looked at it again.

"But it's *beautiful!* I've never seen anything like it."

"It's an implant," Bill told her modestly. He didn't want to take all the credit. "Dr. Ague's work."

"I think he's a genius," said Nurse Thinger. "May I touch it?"

"Oh, of course," said Bill. He inexplicably felt shy. I've never felt like this, he thought. Shy. It must be love.

"Holy cow," said Nurse Thinger, and her soft, professional hand trembled as it slid along Lamplighter's length.

They were getting to know each other, and in the next room Dr. Ague was reeling from wall to wall in helpless, delighted laughter, his high scientific pate shining with excitement.

16 / Cream Cheese

DUDEE SPARROW, WILLOW supple in her peekaboo blouse, was out on the lawn masturbating her dog when Angel and Ally came over the Monday morning following Avery's peculiar welcome home party.

"What are you doing?" Angel asked. Dudee was frowning in concentration.

"Masturbating my dog." Her plump and perfect breasts bobbed coyly in her peekaboo blouse as she pumped.

"Why?" asked Ally.

"Sperm count," said Dudee. An empty bottle lay nearby.

The dog was repulsive. He had an enormously underslung jaw with crooked teeth and a lolling tongue. Vast quantities of drool dripped from the black, wrinkled lips. He looked like a dachshund that had been caught lengthways in a trash compacter, a stubby, off-white bratwurst with loops of loose skin hanging around his middle and bulging, red-rimmed eyes peering pruriently through pouchy lids. At the moment he was lying on his back with a disgusting expression of primal ecstasy on his deformed face.

"Why does he need a sperm count?" Angel asked her. He was fascinated by this process and couldn't tear his eyes away from the long smooth motions of Dudee's hand.

"He's a monorchid," said Dudee.

"What's a monorchid?"

"He's only got one ball and has a low sperm count. We're trying to mate him." She reached for the bottle with her free hand.

"He sure is ugly," said Ally, wrinkling her pretty nose. "What kind of a dog is it? Or is it a kind?"

"English bulldog. They're very rare now." Dudee held her bottle ready without breaking her rhythm.

"I can understand why," Angel said. "It's the ugliest dog I've ever seen. His face looks like someone hit him with a bag of rocks."

"They were very good in the Renaissance for bull baiting," said Dudee. The bulldog's stubby hind end plunged up and down. "Of course, they *are* a bit inbred after all these years. That's why he's a monorchid. We've never been able to mate him; he may be the last of his line, poor thing. But he's purebred. He's registered with the A.K.A."

"A.K.A.?" Ally asked.

"The American Kennel Association. Dogs."

"Wow! Look at that!" Ally exclaimed. Dudee deftly caught every drop in her bottle. "Guh!"

Dudee dropped the dog to cap the bottle with a rubber stopper. "That should do it," she said. The dog, completely relaxed, turned his vacant squashed face to the sky.

"Well, what can I do for you kids?" Dudee rose gracefully from her cross-legged position on the lush lawn and smiled down at Angel and Ally. A flawless blue sky arched over Evanston, all trace of the previous Friday's unseasonable cold and rain swept away by a Pacific high pressure area.

"Daddy's disappeared," said Angel. "We want to find him."

"We wondered if he came by here," Ally added.

"Or if Uncle Sig knew where he might have gone," Angel concluded.

"I haven't seen him since the party the other night when he arrived. He went upstairs to take a bath and so on, but he never came back down. Your mother said he was resting." Dudee smiled, then peered at the contents of the bottle she held.

"Why don't you ask Uncle Sig? I've got to get inside and count this stuff."

"You count it yourself?" Ally found Dudee's preoccupation quite curious.

"Oh, sure," said Dudee, grinning. "It's really very interesting. I kind of enjoy it."

"Mmmm. I suppose so. OK, we'll ask Uncle Sig."

The three of them went into the house, where Dudee directed them to Uncle Sig's study.

"Does Dudee seem a little weird to you?" Ally whispered as they walked through the carpeted hallways.

"A little," Angel answered.

"I mean, why would anyone have a dog that ugly?"

"Status? Anyway, isn't beauty in the eye of the beholder or something?" Angel gave his androgynous grin.

"Oh, I hope not," said Ally.

Uncle Sig, artificially tan and wearing tinted glasses, looked handsome. He sat in his study reading Krafft-Ebing and thinking about his niece Dudee. More and more of late he operated his frozen food empire from his home, where he could keep his eye on his little girl, and almost all the time there danced in his head crimson velvet ropes and musk bubble bath.

"Hello, girls," he greeted them. He wasn't aware of Angel's sex change, though he would have been fascinated. "What can I do for you this fine day?"

"Hello, Uncle Sig," said Ally, speaking for the two of them. "Daddy seems to have disappeared and we were wondering if you had heard from him."

"Disappeared? I know he didn't come down for dinner the other night, but I had no idea he had disappeared. Do you mean he wasn't upstairs all that time?" A fine groove etched its way upward between his sturdy eyebrows, and his dazzling white smile faltered.

"Well, we don't really know that he wasn't upstairs, but we've been waiting for him for three days now and he hasn't shown up."

"I see. Well, surely you asked your mother where he is?"

"Oh, yes, we've asked her, but she doesn't know. She's very vague about it, and we're sort of doubtful, you know." Ally's voice was thin and pleading. "And another thing. August's vanished too."

"August? That cree . . . uh, the butler, you mean?" Sig's frown deepened.

"Yeah."

"The fungus," Angel interjected.

"If Avery's really gone, it could be serious. The convention is only two months away, and there could be trouble if Avery isn't around. An awful lot of true believers will be disappointed. But perhaps he had some pressing business or a personal matter, maybe, to take care of," he finished brightly.

"He would have talked to us first, at least," said Angel. "He knew we had something very important to tell him, and I mean, gosh, we hadn't seen him in *ten years*." His silken lower lip trembled.

"Well, have you phoned Dr. Merkin? He might know something. After all, if Avery were to go anywhere it would probably be to the office."

"We called him this morning. He said he hadn't seen Daddy since he landed at Kankakee Friday afternoon," said Ally, exasperated. Why wasn't Sig more concerned? He was president of the A.K.A. Clubs International. He should be more anxious.

"You're treating us like kids, Uncle Sig," Ally said angrily. "You think we're worrying about our daddy foolishly, don't you? Well, you had better believe this is serious. Avery Augenblaue has disappeared, and we suspect Mommy had something to do with it. Her and August."

"Those are pretty serious charges, girls. What on earth gives you that idea? What's the connection between August and your mother? He's the butler, after all."

"Uh, well." Ally stopped when Angel kicked her. "Well, August has disappeared too," she finished lamely.

"Maybe your father took August with him when he left."

"Uncle Sig, you just don't believe us," said Ally. She turned to go, taking Angel by the hand.

But Uncle Sig did believe them. "Girls," he promised, "I'll look into this. It could be serious, as you say, and it's my job to do what I can for the good of the club. So try not to worry. I have some good friends in the government, especially in the State

Department, and if Avery really has vanished they'll help locate him. OK?"

"Well, OK," said Ally doubtfully. They had no one else to turn to for help. On Friday night they'd made a vow to find out if Kay and August had conspired against Avery, and they were more and more convinced that Avery had been murdered.

Dudee met them at the front door. "Well, did Uncle Sig help out?" She was smiling radiantly.

"Yeah, he promised to help," said Ally.

"Hey, how'd the sperm count go?" Angel asked.

"Low," said Dudee, laughing. "Very low. I'm afraid that poor bastard's the last of his line. Oh, well."

"By the way," Angel asked, "what do you call him?

"Philadelphia." Dudee laughed again.

"Philadelphia?"

"Yes. For cream cheese. And, of course, for brotherly love."

"For brotherly love!" giggled Ally. "Oh, boy!"

17 / Food for Thought

VIRGE WAS JAMMED AWKWARDLY into his pants, so he gave a series of peculiar sideways hops as he puzzled out what to do about Grandfather Moses. The breathing machine hissed and sucked beside the bed, and the old man's face was a gnarled peach pit of hysterical laughter. Grandma Moses was verbally assaulting the door jamb.

"You disgusting old creep!" she shouted at the faded wallpaper beside the door.

"Ah ah ah ah ah hack hack!" Grandfather Moses' laughter gradually turned into a rasping cough that sent him scurrying for the breathing machine in earnest.

"Mom," Virge said, still hopping from foot to foot, trying to juggle himself into his tight police pants. "Mom, you're talking to the wall. Anyway, Dad can't hear you. He's in the middle of an attack."

Grandma Moses paid no attention to Virge, though her voice

sank in volume until she was merely muttering. The words became indistinguishable, a drone of imprecation that hovered in the air like halitosis. The breathing machine wheezed loudly. The white flexible tube was connected by bellows to Grandfather Moses' mouth; he looked as if he were being refueled in flight.

"Damn," Virge muttered. He hopped sideways out of the room and up the stairs to the bedroom and the American Heritage fourposter draped with crimson and covered with black satin sheets. Wanita was lying spread-eagled on the sheet, rotating her marshmallow pelvis and executing bumps at the canopy.

"Ba-*boom*, ba-*boom*," she chanted, and each *boom* blasted her curly mound at the velvet canopy. Virge slammed the door, but she did not interrupt her rhythm. "Ba-*boom*, ba-*boom!*"

Virge tightened miserably inside his pants, which were now twisted through two dimensions. Getting his pants off was a painful operation, but at last he sprang out of them. He rolled his white T-shirt up over his hirsute torso, and his stomach fell two inches, so his navel stared at his erection.

"Ba-*boom*, ba-*boom*. It's a fourposter. Ohhh, my gosh!" She noticed Virge's hard-on. The monkeywood frame creaked dangerously with each thump of her wide behind. The velvet drapes shook, tossing atop the four carved spiral posts like an awning in a storm. "Bring that over here," she directed, changing the ba-*boom* rotation to an up-and-down motion. Thump, thump, thump went the innerspring mattress.

Virge glanced at himself in the mirror over the dresser. Burly torso black with hair, but balding on top. Something ethereal and smooth about the face. It looked like a sissy face to him. Virge had always hated his face. He figured the other cops laughed at his face, and when he was assigned to patrol Cicero he had almost panicked.

He tried scowling at the mirror, knitting his eyebrows together and glaring up through them. He set his mouth in a grim line, thinning his sensual lips. He bunched the muscles at the corners of his jaw. He ground his teeth.

Thump, thump, thump. "Come on, honey. Let's get going," Wanita urged over the creaking of the monkeywood frame.

Christ, thought Virge. I look like I'm inviting someone to kiss me. He snarled at the mirror. It looked to him like an angelic smile. He could feel his desire melting away. He approached the mirror and held his breath to flush his face. He looked like he was blushing.

"Virge, what are you doing?" Wanita's humping pelvis was now crashing against the mattress. Soon even her feet would leave the bed on the upswing. She looked as though she were being vigorously screwed by the Invisible Man. Claude Raines, she imagined. I'm being screwed by Claude Raines. Oh. The movie was on TV last night. Come and get me, Claude. She felt an aching void in her groin. "For God's sake, Virge."

Virge turned and sadly eyed his wife. He had wilted to a shriveled peanut hidden under his sagging belly. No one can believe my face, he thought.

Wanita realized what had happened and stopped her thumping. "Virge, honey, come here." She patted the bed beside her. He sat down.

"Didja arrest anybody today?"

"No." His rosebud lower lip poked out. He stared at his knee.

"Didja arrest anybody yesterday?"

Virge didn't answer.

"Well?"

"Yeah. I arrested somebody."

"Did he resist arrest?" Wanita ran her hand over his hairy back.

Virge knotted his fist. "Yeah, he resisted."

"Didja have to use a little force on him, Virge?" Wanita's pelvis began to rotate again, slowly.

"Had to give him a couple of taps with the club. Punk kid breaking into a parking meter." Virge smiled shyly and shivered as Wanita's fingernail drifted down his spine.

"You dog," she said. "Did he scream?"

"He yelled a little." He jumped when Wanita goosed him as best she could with him sitting beside her on the black satin sheet.

"Was he scared?" Her breathing began to tatter as she envisioned mighty Virge wasting the parking meter punk. Her plump hip grazed Virge's back as it rotated. She reached around and was not surprised to find him as hard as a billy club.

"You didn't hit him with this, did you?" she giggled.

"Are you kidding?" shouted Virge as he whirled around and dived on top of his wife's soft sofa-body. They writhed out of phase for several minutes and the ruffled flounce jiggled in the bedroom light. Wanita's pelvis rotated around and around clockwise and Virge's pumped up and down, so they crashed and bumped at irregular intervals. Wanita emitted sharp little cries, drove her fingernails into Virge's back, and tried to find the solid meat between her legs. Somehow they hadn't connected properly.

The cold rain dashed against the window, which gradually steamed up as the humidity in the small room rose, and deep inside the monkeywood of the bed frame a small colony of almost microscopic termites began to eat their way slowly toward the outside world, digging thread-thin tunnels in the wood. They digested the cellulose they ate, and the resultant waste reacted favorably with the fungus the termites stored in the tunnel walls.

When the tiny members of this termite species, *forniculotermes brevis*, reached the inside of the plastic teak veneer, a new chemical was added to the diet. As debris of the plastic combined with the fungus, traces of a vapor form of the complex organic molecule of p-chlorophenylalanine were released into the termite tunnels.

Virge and Wanita thrashed like two speared pikes on the black satin, breathing heavily and sweating. "In me, dammit, Virge, in me!" Wanita shouted, groping for his stiff joint in the tangle of their bellies. She wanted to stuff the big policeman into her hungry whirlpool.

Virge stabbed blindly, both of them so slippery with sweat and juice she couldn't get a grasp on him. "Damn," he muttered.

Strange things were going on in his head. A row of parking meters seemed to bend over, to purse their violation flags in obscene little bow-mouth invitations. They writhed and winked lewdly, and they all had his face. My face, he thought, I've got to get rid of my face. His body stabbed at Wanita and their bellies slapped.

Meanwhile, *forniculotermes brevis* munched on toward the light, where they would swarm around a new queen, searching for exotic virgin furniture in which to start a new colony.

Suddenly Virge leaped off the bed. Wanita gave a sharp cry of disappointment. "Virge, oh, God, Virge, quick!"

Virge hopped to the dresser and grabbed his riot helmet, which he held in his hands for a moment, panting loudly through his nose and staring at himself in the dresser mirror. His sweet face had a curiously mottled appearance. He sucked in his stomach, glanced down at his slick, powerful erection, and put on his helmet. He buckled the straps under his chin, took one final look at his face in the mirror, and swung down the tinted plastic faceplate. His head now resembled a deformed egg with a blue front.

Then, seizing his hard-on with his right hand, he gave a long-drawn-out karate yell and charged his wife, plunging his spear unerringly into her seething belly.

Her calves clamped behind his knees like cell doors slamming shut, and they pumped each other violently, a one-cylinder engine operating at top efficiency. The bedroom light glinted serenely off the shining white plastic of his helmet as it bobbed above Wanita's wildly tossing hair on the black pillowcase. At the moment they came obliviously into Wanita's darkness, *forniculotermes brevis* chomped through the last millimeters of plastic veneer and began to release into the damp bedroom air minute quantities of p-chlorophenylalanine, or PCPA, the most powerful aphrodisiac known to nature.

18 / Butterscotch Delight

"YOU KNOW, BETSY SUE, that fellow Keb still looks awful familiar to me." Ed and Betsy Sue were lying beside the saltwater pool behind the main building at the Crystal Grape. Nineteen-year-old Dudee Sparrow toasted like a marshmallow on a Styrofoam platter nearby.

Betsy Sue watched slim, tanned Duane Hemp operate a vacuum hose in the pool. He was wearing his Stetson. His white jacket with the embroidered grape on the pocket was draped over the back of a deck chair. He had on a white T-shirt, and to Betsy

Sue the corded muscles of his arms looked as though someone were twirling a lasso inside his biceps.

"Who do you think he looks like?" Betsy Sue asked without taking her eyes off those rippling cords. Duane's pants were tight, too; white and tight except where they flared over his hand-tooled cowboy boots.

"I'm not sure. I can't seem to place him. Maybe it's . . . No, it couldn't be him." Ed was gazing into the middle distance so his eyes could just graze the top of Dudee's naked behind as it roasted in the afternoon desert sun. Dudee had adapted to nudity much faster than either Ed or Betsy Sue, both of whom were enveloped in cavernous swimwear.

Betsy Sue snapped her eyes back up to Duane's biceps, pausing only fractionally at his belt — hand-tooled leather like his boots, with his initials, D.H., embossed on it. Tight pants, she thought. Disgusting. But the arms. Little rodeo riders bucking and jumping around just under the leathery skin as Duane raked the pool with his vacuum.

"Couldn't be who, dear?" Betsy Sue asked after a long silence.

"I was thinking it was . . ." A small ripple moved across Dudee's bare pink buttocks, and Ed thought, Hot damn. Beyond her the other guests of the Crystal Grape were toasting in ranks, as if in a machine that cooks hot dogs in bulk, he thought, all rotating on the grill together, and Betsy Sue and I are about the only ones with the wrapper still on. Ed's suit had huge livid pineapples across the front; it matched the Hawaiian shirt he wore home to Tulsa the week before last.

They'd been there only four days, and already Betsy Sue's one-piece black bathing suit, the one with the flounce, was two sizes too large for her, so that when she turned suddenly the bathing suit followed after, a delayed coriolis effect. She wondered if Duane had noticed her. Hell, she thought, and blushed rather prettily at the word: a Reformed Baptist shouldn't wonder such things.

Ed didn't notice when Duane offhandedly sent a dazzling neon smile Betsy Sue's way.

She shivered inside her suit and looked away. She was sweating and couldn't decide whether to get into the pool or go inside. She was almost due, she knew, for a session with the mudbaths.

Before she could make up her mind a shadow fell across the two of them, and she and Ed both twisted around to look up together.

"Well, well, well, Mr. and Mrs. Sox. And how are you getting along?"

The sun backlit the figure over them so no details were discernable, only the silhouette of the beret and a suggestion of mustache and goatee.

"Oh, we're fine, Mr., uh, Keb. Just fine." Ed had to squint to see anything at all. The sky was a blue-white pot full of simmering skim milk. He realized that he was shining with sweat, and his pineapple bathing suit was very uncomfortable.

"I see you are still wearing your bathing suits. The other guests, as you may have noticed, are no longer wearing them."

Ed shifted uncomfortably. Keb continued, "Of course, you need not let that bother you. Take your time, take your time. But remember that the vitamin D treatments are an important part of the whole course here, and you'll have to shed those hot clothes sometime. Soon. And it's time for your mudbaths, I believe, Mrs. Sox. Duane will escort you to the bathhouse. Duane!" he yelled, and Ed jumped as if stung.

"Yes, Keb?"

"Take Mrs. Sox over to the bathhouse. It's time for her mudbath."

"Yes, Keb." Duane gave Betsy Sue another electric smile, and she willingly scrambled to her feet. Duane's right bicep was tatooed DEATH BEFORE DISHONOR in the claws of an American eagle.

"You realize, Mr. Sox," Keb said after Duane had guided Betsy Sue around the corner, "that the treatments here are not merely cosmetic. That is, we do not only make you *look* better, or *feel* better, we actually *make* you better." Ed still lay in Keb's shadow, peering up at the silhouette against the brazen sun.

"Whaddya mean?" Ed asked. He was feeling strange and small at the bottom of the director's shadow, a fat overturned beetle in a pit of hot sand.

"What do I mean?" Keb echoed. The Vandyke bobbed up and down when Keb talked. "What do I mean?" His voice lowered conspiratorially. "I mean *attitude*, Mr. Sox, *attitude*. People don't have the right attitude. *You* don't have the right attitude. In fact, you're still fighting us here, aren't you, Mr. Sox?"

"No, I . . ."

"Never mind. It doesn't matter at all. We'll make you better. Attitude, that's all it takes." Keb was musing now. His shadow shifted suddenly, and he sat down beside Ed. The sun was so blinding that all Ed saw was a washed-out image. Keb smiled.

"For instance, let me tell you a story." Ed noticed that Keb was still wearing his dark glasses.

"The story is this," Keb nodded. "Charles Brown-Séquard. You've heard of Charles Brown-Séquard?" Ed shook his head. "Well, he was a French physiologist. He announced one day that he had injected himself with testicle extract. Yes, indeed. And this was some time ago, mind you. A man way ahead of his time . . . " Keb trailed off.

"Yes?" Ed asked finally.

"Oh, yes. Well, Dr. Brown-Séquard was seventy-two at the time. He claimed that injecting himself with testicle extract made him feel like a man of thirty. You understand? A man of thirty. Matter of attitude, you see?"

"No, I don't think I do."

"Of course, of course. Pretty obscure, eh? Yes, pretty obscure. You've got it. Certainly. Dr. Brown-Séquard died six years later. Old age. The laughingstock of the medical profession, of course. Tragic."

"Huh?"

"Oh, yes, fell over quite dead. Well, it's all ridiculous, naturally." Keb smiled broadly at Ed.

Maybe it's the heat, thought Ed. I just don't understand.

"You see?" asked Keb, still smiling.

"Uh-uh."

"Well, I mean, after all, testicle extract. It's impossible. That sort of thing could never work. One is reminded of Ignatz Semelweiss. Cut and infected himself to prove that dirty hands were causing childbed fever. Lot of mothers and babies dying of it all over the place at the time. He wanted to prove to everyone that dirty hands were responsible."

"What happened to him?"

"Oh, he died. Childbed fever. Another laughingstock, I'm afraid."

"I really don't seem to follow you."

Ed wanted to return to Dudee's behind and drop this conversation. He stole a quick glance back at her and found himself looking at her breasts. She was sitting up and eavesdropping on Keb's lecture.

"Well, Mr. Sox," he said, "you will, you will. Just remember that it's all a matter of attitude. We make you better. We really do. Diet, of course. And various exercises; the machines; baths. Vitamin D. Don't forget to shed your clothes in the next day or two. All a matter of attitude."

Dudee inhaled deeply and let out a long sigh, and her pink-burned breasts rose and fell, and Ed's eyes rose and fell with them.

There's something strange about this place, he thought. I just don't get it.

"That guy reminds me of someone," he told Dudee after Keb had abruptly jumped to his feet and left. "I can't think who, but he reminds me of someone."

"You know, he seems a little familiar to me, too. I can't place him either." Her nipples nodded in agreement.

Godawmighty, I sure am glad I'm wearing a bathing suit, Ed thought. "What do you suppose he means about attitude?" he said, to keep the conversation going.

"I think he means that to be fit we have to feel fit; we have to believe we're fit. And thin, of course. Something like that, anyway." Dudee giggled. She was losing weight and she knew that made her more attractive. She felt better, too. More sap, more vigor. She missed Uncle Sig back there in Chicago, all alone. I'll surprise him, she thought. Boy, will I surprise him!

She lay on her back so the sun could brown her front.

I'll never be able to take off this bathing suit, Ed conceded.

19 / A Fricassee

"AUGUST. HEY, AUGUST! Oh, damn." Kay's red tongue flicked out to moisten the parched landscape of her upper lip. "Oh, damn. August." She glanced quickly down the corridor, then hissed again into his ear. "August, wake up!"

He had been standing in the hall for twenty-four hours while Kay tried to figure out what to do with his rigid form, catatonic outside her bedroom door.

"August." She tugged at his limp hand, and he oozed forward slightly. She tugged again, and he stepped toward her. Tug by tug, she dragged him from hall to bedroom, where she left him standing for a moment beside the bed. Behind him swirled almost visible eddies of the smells of mold and freshly plowed earth.

She paced back and forth, wringing her hands, crossing and recrossing the trail of August's odors, stirring them into the mauve of the room. Her orange hair bobbed and swayed above her narrow face, a clump of rusty weeds in a vacant lot.

August's mouth sagged open, and at length she noticed a faint keening sound coming from him. As his voice rose in pitch and intensity he tilted forward and toppled onto the bed, his feet hanging straight out over the carpet. His nose sank into the down bedspread and he couldn't breathe. The sound died away, to be replaced by a long silence. Kay watched him anxiously, but nothing further happened.

August had stopped breathing. Kay's hair was motionless, one stiff lock across her forehead like a fresh wound. The shaft of sun from the skylight moved across the bed to touch August's thin, limp hair almost gently. It warmed his bald spot. Kay and August were two odd beetles trapped in the clear, hard substance of that amber light.

My God, he's dead, Kay fretted. Now what am I going to do? Avery's body has disappeared, I don't know how, and now August has left me with his corpse on the bed.

She did not move, though she was slightly off balance, one foot poised for a step toward the bed and butler, her left hand lifted a fraction in a gesture that could have been a questioning or a fending off.

Just as Kay noticed that she was holding her breath, August suddenly emitted a long, shuddering, rasping breath, a horrid gargling sound that shattered the amber silence of the room and sent Kay scurrying toward him then back in dread. It could have been a death rattle.

But no. It was August's response to the rising carbon dioxide levels in his blood, levels that signaled his autonomic nervous system to take a breath *now* or never take one again. In some tiny switchboard in his hindbrain that decision was made, and he arched his damp bald fungus head into the air so his lungs could haul in a couple of liters of much-needed oxygen.

"Christ almighty, August." Kay was furious. "You scared the shit out of me. I thought you were dead."

She began pacing back and forth again, her thin red tongue darting out from time to time to brush her cracked lips.

August hadn't heard her. He arched his back to draw in another breath, sinking forward into the bedspread to exhale, arching his back again. He sounded and looked like a huge, slow-moving bellows with a valve defect, pumping slowly but rhythmically on the bed — up, screech, down, pooh, up, screech, down, pooh — while Kay paced and fumed.

Finally he rolled over and sat up. His eyes, two small, round, gray stones embedded in the pasty, mildewed earth of his face, uncrossed and focused on Kay's orange hair.

"What happened," he said in his hollow voice. It was not a question, nor an exclamation, nor even a statement; it had no inflection, no tone. His tongue quested forth from his mouth, a pale mole testing the limits of its burrow. He stared at the orange hair, following Kay, who hadn't heard him, with his eyes.

"Kay?" he finally asked, his voice drawing out the word as though testing it for bitterness, putting a rising inflection at the end to make it a question.

"Aha," Kay squawked, two dissonant notes. "Aha," she repeated.

"Kay-ay?"

"Well?" she demanded. She slammed her hands onto her hips and glared at August's dim face. "What are we going to do now?"

"I dunno. What happened?" August's breathing was nearly

normal now, though tiny drops of saliva sprayed from his mouth with each word. They looked like spores speeding through the bright beams falling through the skylight.

"What do you remember last?" Kay glowered.

"Serving canapés at the party to welcome home Mr. Augenblaue."

"Oh, for God's sake. Do you remember our plan to kill him?"

"Why would we plan to kill him, ma'am?"

"Don't toy with me, August, or I'll have your ass in a grinder. You know perfectly well why."

"No, ma'am. I can't imagine. He's been a good employer."

"August, for God's sake, he's been gone for *ten years*." Her voice rose an octave.

"Ma'am?"

"Oh, never mind. We've got to do something. Listen: we've been, uh, oh, Christ, uh, you know"—she put her index fingers together — "uh, together, all that time, since the launch."

August looked blank. "Launch?"

"You don't remember the launch?" Disbelief flowed across her face like a graph of the great stock market crash of '29.

"I was serving canapés at the welcome home party. Mr. Augenblaue had been away on a business trip, as I recall, and you threw a party to celebrate his return. The Secretary of State was there, and the Countess, and the President. Or was he? No, I think perhaps he wasn't. Let's see, I was walking from the solarium toward the bar with a large silver tray. Fish fingers, the mushroom and bacon hors d'oeuvres. I offered some to the Countess. Mr. Sparrow was next, with his mother. No, that wasn't his mother . . . Who was that woman next to Mr. Sparrow?" August looked at Kay with the innocent question in his pulpy eyes.

"Oh, for God's sake! August, we've been *fucking* for ten years, ever since Avery went on that 'business trip.' The orgone engine, remember? Oh, I hate sex." She glanced at herself in the mirror over the dresser: orange hair and a livid face.

She began to rip off her clothes. The watered silk gown popped its buttons onto the violet carpet and fell in a rustling heap at her feet. She shinnied out of her pantyhose and hooked her arms behind her back to undo her bra, which fluttered to the floor like a wounded gull.

"There," she shouted in triumph. "Take a good look. Does it look familiar? You've been screwing it for ten years. Oh, Christ!" Kay seldom smoked, but she got a cigarette from the dresser and paced around the room puffing smoke into the air, her round muscular buttocks clenching and unclenching with each step.

August sat stock still on the bed. In his earthy head swirled a confusion of peculiar sexual imagery and strange disciplines, spankings and pain, odd tinglings on the insides of his elbows, bites at his throat and neck, a weird weakness in his belly and knees. Coat hangers and rubber suits hung in the dark closet of his needs, all of which surged in a violent rush to his long but forgotten dong and stiffened it painfully in his butler's drawers. Something about the way those large freckled ass-globes bunched as Kay paced around the bedroom.

"See!" Kay shouted in triumph, pointing. "Your body remembers!" The sight of those tented trousers caught at her throat, and she hurled herself at August's dazzled face and scrabbled at his coat and shirt, and pulled in frustration and rage at his belt, while August remained still, a glutinous fricassee of lust, trepidation and fear.

At last Kay had him stripped and backward on the bed, his steeple rising into the sunlight a moment before she lowered her own sopping needs down on it, bringing darkness and delight. She plunged up and down, letting off little animal noises in her throat, noises like two cats fighting, and August, dazed, stared at the ceiling. His memory was coming back.

"Oh, my God, August," said Kay, stopping to point at his torso with a bewildered expression on her blanched face. "What's *that?*"

"What's what?" August mumbled in a mushroom haze.

"Those spots. What are those spots?" She stabbed her laquered fingernails at places on his body, his arms, his face. "Those spots."

He looked down. All over him were places that had faded to an absolute colorlessness, a more than albino paleness, not white, but *the complete absence of color*. They seemed to glow and were surrounded by dark outlines. August was turning into a polka-dotted dummy.

"I remember the launch!" he yelled.

20 / Fruits and Nuts

IF ANGEL AND ALLY ever had doubts that Angel's new apparatus would work, they were quickly dispelled a couple of months after the operation, when the surgeon gave Angel the go-ahead to test it. They filled their bedroom with mellow music from KAKA-FM, spread cushions on the floor, brewed tea, and rubbed each other silly. They went up and down and in and out in a new and satisfying way and were happy with the changes that had been made.

"It works!" Ally exclaimed.

Angel answered, "Yeah. It felt good when I was a girl, but this is really something. Sometimes it seems to *lead*, you know. Like dancing." The two of them examined it but couldn't find any seams or joints, so skillful and practiced was the surgeon at this operation.

"Let's go back to the Third Eye to tell Phil and China the good news. China at least will be glad to hear about it." Ally gave Angel another little kiss, just there, and pulled on her jeans.

"Phil will be glad to hear, too, you know," Angel said, grinning. "He was a *psychiatrist*, after all. Those guys got dirty minds."

So for the final time they cuddled and walked through the San Francisco fog toward the steamy yellow glow of the Third Eye, where they pushed together through the crowds of sallow poets and burly sculptors and endomorphic gurus and intense revolutionaries in rimless glasses discussing the manufacture of bombs and tourists in tie-dyed jeans and T-shirts with pictures of Mickey Mouse or members of an endangered species or special-interest slogans silk-screened on them. At the table in back Philbrick Weevol sat awash in espresso, his temperate features ajangle with caffeine ($C_8H_{10}N_4O_2 \cdot H_2O$), his left hand in China's lap, his right gripping a stubby pencil.

"Hi, kids," he greeted Angel and Ally. "I've just written a poem about you two. It's called 'Children of Paradise.' Want to hear it?" Without waiting for an answer he began chanting in his insipid voice:

> *O children of paradise*
> *Two teen angels in the San Francisco*
> *Hills who walk together*
> *In the Cosmic Dharmas of Love*
> *In the chill and warm weather*
> *Falling from above*
> *Where Che and Buddha dwell*
> *Without fear or risk, O*
> *Children of paradise*
> *You have us in your spell!*

"Jesus Christ," China muttered, "that sure sounds awful to me."

"Quiet," said Phil, "there's more:

> *O children of paradise*
> *Who together grow and change*
> *Into new vegetables*
> *Or kinds of wood*
> *Or fruits or other edibles*
> *Under the leafy shade of Good*
> *Earth and high blue sky*
> *Into something rare and strange*
> *O children of paradise*
> *We must never ask you why?*
>
> *O children of paradise —*

"Hey, come on, Philbrick, cool it," said China. She had noticed the attentive silence from the tables around them. A ring of faces wavered in the misty air of the coffee house, all watching Phil recite.

Squabby Bunny Darlitch at the next table, squirming slightly from a thousand bites old and new, was riveted to his aesthetic chair. Even phthisic Reba Hare bared her pointed teeth in a house-mouse smile as she nibbled a small piece of cheddar on a Ritz cracker. Bunny furiously scribbled notes in his reporter's steno book and muttered things about "urban folk art" under his breath.

Phil continued:

> O children of paradise
> You are the Cosmic Law!
>
> O children of paradise
> Ivy-twined and lichen-close
> Embryophytes of the Great Wheel
> Without Xylem or Phloem
> O love both tangible and real
> I dedicate this poem
> To your new and terrible penis
> A double-double dose
> Of children of paradise
> Order, Family and Genus!"

"OK, Phil, that's enough, we get the fucking point, for Christ's sake! Phil can't write worth shit, you know, but he really knows how to eat a girl, and that's a fact." China's voice was quite loud in the silence between stanzas, and Phil blushed rather prettily.

> O children of paradise
> O gooey Yin and throbbing Yang . . .

Bunny's notes raced down the steno pages as "Children of Paradise" gathered in length and momentum; it seemed there was nothing to stop Philbrick Weevol now that he was in his stride through the taxonomies of botany and sex. His voice assumed an authority and vibrance China had never heard before. This was Bunny's bread and butter. His column in the *Boric Acid Weekly* had featured events at the Third Eye before, but this was the first time Philbrick Weevol wandered into those avant-garde pages. He would be very pleased.

> A universe of Steady State and Big Bang
> O children of paradise
> You are the root and shoot
>
> O children of paradise
> The great two-sided Fuck . . .

"Bunny," Reba asked in her small mouse voice, "is this a good poem? I have to know. If it isn't, why are you writing it down?" She daintily bit into her Ritz and cheddar.

Bunny's flying ball-point paused for a moment. "It doesn't matter whether it's good or not," he said. "What matters is that it is an authentic expression of the urban milieu, a welling up, as it were, of the cultural unconscious, at least from the coffee house subculture. These people are my readers, and they are interested in what is happening here."

"Oh."

> *Shiva dancing in Buddha's navel*
> *The dance of Cosmic Coitus . . .*

"He sure does like the word 'cosmic' a lot, doesn't he?" Reba squeaked into Bunny's ear.

> *Cannot help but exploit us*
> *O children of paradise . . .*
>
> *The mighty redwood tree . . .*

"It's a lousy poem, isn't it, Bunny?"

> *From Chicago to the coast*
> *O children . . .*

"Yes, Reba, it's a lousy poem."

> *. . . of paradise*
> *You are the everything and all!*

"Well, what do you think?" Phil asked, when he'd finished reading, giving Ally and Angel a broad and balmy smile.

"Uh. Well, it's nice, I think. Don't you think it's nice, Ally?" Angel's smile remained fixed, as though it had been set the night before and allowed to harden.

"Hmmm," said Ally.

"I just wrote it."

"Shows, you asshole." China tugged at his arm. "Now let's get home so you can eat me. Do something you got a talent for, at least."

"We sort of came to say good-bye. Angel and I are going back to Chicago," said Ally.

"You mean, it works?" China asked. She knew they were going home as soon as they had tried out Angel's sex change.

"Better than I ever thought possible," Ally answered with a pleased smile. "I've never done it with a *man* before, but it's fantastic."

"We'll sure miss you kids," Phil told them. "Leave us your address, and I'll send you a copy of the poem."

"We'd like that," said Ally, writing it down. "And if you're ever in Chicago, give us a call."

A leaflet dropped onto the table. An earnest girl wearing a sweater dress and straw boater smiled at them as she passed by with her armload of paper.

EIGHTH ANNUAL LABOR DAY CONVENTION
AKA CLUBS INTERNATIONAL

He'll be back in two years. Are you ready?
He's been *out there*. He's seen *The* Blue Light.
Join AKA and be ready for *The* Blue Light.

"Good-bye, you children of paradise," Philbrick Weevol waved.

"See ya," China said, staring hard at Angel's crotch. It didn't look any different to her.

"Let's go home, Bunny," said Reba. "I'm hungry. I want something to eat."

21 / Heroes

THREE MEN CROUCHED UNDER the forsythia hedge as the twilight gloom gathered over the sultry suburbs of Chicago. It had been an appallingly hot and humid day; the air seemed to be filled with Elmer's Glue. It was a day when everyone's laundry washed itself backward from clean to moldy damp and hot.

The three men in the forsythia bushes perspired freely, their identical Arrow shirts stuck fast to their pudding torsos, their Hart Schaffner and Marx jackets stuck to the shirts. The ties they wore, modest of color and width, were limp, the knots damp and fat under their sweaty chins. They were all intensely uncomfortable.

Before them the driveway's asphalt oozed listlessly down a slight gradient to curl around a small black jockey with a ring in his hand in front of the mansion. The jockey would be very hot to the touch.

If the three men expected sunset to bring them any relief from the heat they were wrong.

"Jesus, it's hot," said Connie Hubble. He had had a bad day, but since the convention started tomorrow he was still on duty.

"We know it's hot. How'd the interview with Merkin go?" The man next to him, unpacking equipment from an aluminum case, talked from the side of his mouth.

"Useless, Joe. Couldn't get a thing from that man. Strange, you know. He talked in formulas or blathered about clothes or the weather. Wasted an hour. I'm beginning to think we'll never find Avery."

The third man had on a pair of earphones. He was holding a large parabolic microphone with a pistol grip pointed at the house. "Shhh," he said. "I'm getting something."

"What is it, Jon?" Joseph Harbin asked.

"Shh."

The gloom deepened without breeze. Some minutes before, a huge orange ball of sun had lowered itself gingerly behind the house like an overweight apoplectic matron settling into a fragile lawn chair. The three men sweated in the silence while a frown of concentration creased Jonathon Harker's forehead. His ears sweated into the padded headset.

"What's going on?" Harbin couldn't stand the waiting any longer.

"She's ordering dinner," Harker hissed back.

"Ordering dinner?" Connie Hubble moaned. "Oh, Christ, ordering dinner. What are we going to do?"

"Take it easy, Connie. We're going to keep the house under

surveillance. You know that. Now keep quiet, please. I want to hear."

Harbin turned to Hubble. "Help me set this thing up, will you?"

They assembled a small tripod and attached the infrared scope to it.

"What'd you bring us?" Harbin asked Hubble when the power cords were connected to the scope and it hummed into life. He glanced into the scope and saw the front door of the house as clearly as if it were still daylight.

"Three hero sandwiches," Hubble answered. "You want yours now?" He started to open another aluminum case.

"Quiet!" Harker hissed. "Oh, God!"

"What is it?"

"*Cervelles au beurre noir*. What the hell is *cervelles au beurre noir?*"

"Yeah, what the hell is that?" Harbin repeated.

"Brains," Connie answered. He had picked up some French in the navy.

"Brains?" Harker lifted one earphone. It was slick with sweat. "They eat brains?"

"Sure," said Connie, unwrapping a large hero sandwich.

"*Navets glacés à brun*," Harker said, listening once again to his earphones. "What's that?" He lifted it away from his ear.

"Turnips."

"Christ," Harbin said. He peered through his scope at the front door, but nothing was moving. "Where's the kitchen?"

"To your left," Hubble said. He took a huge bite from his hero sandwich and a piece of tomato squirted out and stuck to his chin.

"*Aubergines farcies duxelles?*"

"Eggplant." Hubble flicked the tomato from his chin.

"Got it!" Harbin shouted, adjusting his scope. On its screen reddish outlines wavered inside the kitchen. "Two of them in there."

"That would be the cook and Mrs. Augenblaue," Harker told him. "She's ordering dinner."

"We know that, dammit. The question is, why is she ordering such a fancy dinner?" Hubble asked with his mouth full, his perfect pudding face a pale splotch in the gloom.

"People coming for dinner," Harker said. "Quiet now, she's

leaving the kitchen. You can see she's leaving the kitchen, can't you?" He tapped Harbin at the scope.

"Yeah. She's going to the solarium. You remember the solarium?" Harbin clearly remembered the location of the solarium, since Kay had banged his brains out there a couple of years before.

"I remember where the solarium is," Harker answered. He'd been there the day Ally fell through the skylight, ten years before. "Boy, this is a weird family."

"You guys want to eat your sandwiches now?" Hubble asked. It was completely dark, a claustrophobic darkness filled with suffocating vapors. Harbin sneezed, banging his eye against the black lens of the scope.

"Shit!" He rubbed his eye.

"Where are they?" Hubble asked, still eating greedily. Sauce oozed from the edges of his hero; his sweaty hands were slick with it.

"There's another figure in the solarium. Who is it?" Harbin leaned back to the scope.

"I dunno," said Harker, listening intently. "There's no conversation. Just heavy breathing."

"Heavy breathing?" Hubble asked.

"Yeah. Heavy breathing. You know, like an obscene phone call."

"I wish this damn scope had better resolution. All I can see are outlines. What'd you say, Connie?" Harbin tried adjusting the focus.

"I said, 'Heavy breathing?' "

"No, no. I mean before that . . . Maybe if I increase the power," he mumbled, twisting a knob.

"I said, 'You guys want to eat your sandwiches now?' "

"Oh."

"Well, do you?"

"Do I what?" Harbin squinted painfully into the scope. "That's slightly better, but I still can't make out who it is."

"Me either. Just heavy breathing."

"Are you ready for your sandwiches?" Hubble licked sauce off his fingers. He crumpled the paper wrapper and tossed it back into the aluminum case.

"Oh, all right!" Harker said. He ripped off his earphones and threw them down in disgust. "We might as well eat. There's only heavy breathing."

Harbin switched off his scope, and the two of them fell on the heroes Hubble handed them.

"Christ almighty, August," Kay said in the solarium, air-conditioned and blissfully cool, the moment Harker removed his earphones. "We must figure out what happened to Avery and stop screwing around like this. We hacked him to pieces. He's got to be dead, so who moved the body?" Kay jabbered about nothing else but finding Avery.

His strange spotted head nodded agreement, though he wasn't concerned about Avery. His only concern was the terrible need he had for Kay, which was as strong as ever. Small blue blobs of light drifted from the tips of her hair from time to time.

"Oh, hell. Turn on the lights, August. The guests will soon be arriving."

Up on the hill, peering down at Harker, Harbin and Hubble and beyond them at the house, Dr. Ambrose Merkin sucked thoughtfully on a lemon-flavored throat lozenge and tugged gently at his muttonchops.

The man next to him stirred slightly in the dark and grinned. Ambrose could see the white of his teeth.

"Things are coming along," the man said, still smiling.

A car rolled past them and turned down the driveway, passing as well the three crouching agents. Harbin sneezed again. "God-dammit," he muttered. "Forsythia isn't even in bloom."

"Who was that?" Harker asked.

Hubble was holding the night-vision binoculars. "Sparrow," he answered, checking the retreating license plate. "Frozen foods."

Kay straightened her smile to greet her guests.

"Yes, indeed, Avery," said Dr. Merkin, watching the car pull up in front of the door. "Things are coming along just fine."

22 / Clam Chowder

"YOU KNOW, DUANE, I've never seen you without your hat." Betsy Sue Sox's small red face, now lightly tanned, a golden delicious apple with a friendly smile, looked up at Keb's assistant with wide eyes.

"No, ma'am." Duane did not return her smile, but focused, whipcord clean and rawhide tough, straight ahead.

He has curly hair, Betsy Sue assumed, staring at the nape of his neck under his Stetson. With a little gray in it. "Why don't you ever take off your hat?"

"No need." Duane opened the door of the bathhouse and ushered her in. "These are your first mudbath treatments, Mrs. Sox?"

"Oh my, yes." She shifted uncomfortably inside the vacuous tent of her black one-piece bathing suit with the flounce. I'll have to buy another suit, she thought. Or go without.

The bathhouse was dark and pleasantly cool after the blazing sun. Duane showed her to the changing room with its flagstone floor, cedar lockers and stacks of huge, aromatic towels. "Through the far door," Duane directed. "Take a towel."

An attendant in white waited for her. The mudbath room was flagstoned as well, with a translucent skylight and a large stone pool filled with mud. Three other guests lounged in the pool, their heads tilted over the edge, towels covering their faces. Occasionally a big bubble rose to the surface in the center of the pool and popped with a solemn noise, releasing a wisp of steam that floated away in the greenish gloom. It was the only sound in the room.

"I'm Rhea, Mrs. Sox," murmured the attendant. "I'll hold your towel. You choose a comfortable place in the pool."

"Is that mud hot?" Betsy Sue whispered, watching another bubble rise and pop open like a ripe melon.

"Not very hot. Not yet. It's really very pleasant."

"How's it going?" Keb asked Duane when he entered the control room. Duane was eyeing a small television monitor on his console.

Betsy Sue in miniature was lowering herself into the mud at the vacant corner of the pool.

"Take a look." Duane nodded at the screen.

Keb watched Betsy Sue sink into the warm mud. "How much weight has she lost?" he asked.

"Twenty." Duane slowly rotated a rheostat.

"Fifteen more and she'll be ready. Run it up to one-twenty."

Duane twisted the knob a bit more and the bubbles appeared more frequently in the center of the pool. "That should open them up," he declared.

The guests were now four clams simmering gently in a chowder. Bubbles rose between their toes to plink softly at the surface. Bubbles ran along the undersides of their legs, tickling them. Bubbles rolled quietly up their backs through the thick mud, and as they rolled they grew hotter and hotter so gradually and imperceptibly that the guests never noticed the rise in temperature. Like clams they softened into the ooze, pores opening to the heat. With towels over their faces they could see nothing but a vague green light, a relaxing light, a sleepy light, and their bodies, once gross and awkward, began to feel the light drifting through them, and they seemed to rise from their seats in the buoyant mud and float in the steam, random and dreamy.

"OK," said Keb. "They seem to be ready."

Duane flipped a toggle switch on his console, and a series of parallel pipes in the bottom of the pool released minute bubbles into the thick goo. These bubbles, infinitesimal quantities of p-chlorophenylalalanine, or PCPA, were absorbed and dissolved into the mud, where the heat spread the substance over everyone bathing there.

Minutes passed, and the bubbles of heat percolated at a gentle musical pace, *plop-plop*, *plop-plop*, while the chemical bubbles raced along bare flesh, soothing and massaging and depositing small quantities of PCPA to be absorbed in the skin.

Rhea sat quietly in her chair in the mud room, reading and smiling to herself. She was reading *The Egyptian Book of the Dead*.

While Duane dreamed of her passive body, Rhea flipped the pages of her book. Time passed. Betsy Sue dreamed of Duane's hair under his hat and the rodeo riders under his biceps and his tight pants that flared over his hand-tooled cowboy boots. As her mind wandered, her feet floated upward in the mud and her hands floated outward, palms down, fingers slightly curled. Tiny effervescing bubbles of PCPA zapped along every nook and cranny of her skin, finding out all her secrets and giving her a few new ones that she would discover later. Somewhere on Mount Olympus, Aphrodite, the goddess of love, was laughing.

"That's enough, Duane," Keb said. "We'll step up the dosage tomorrow; we're just dealing with the subcutaneous material today."

Duane flipped the toggle switch, and the tiny bubbles died away.

But Betsy Sue's skin tingled most strangely; it tingled with desire. The four large limp women had to be hauled from the tub by white-robed Rhea, who helped them to the showers, where cool waters sluiced away all the mud still clinging to them, leaving them pink and young and yearning strangely.

Betsy Sue couldn't believe it.

"Look!" she said to Ed, back again at the pool. "Look at my skin."

Ed noticed that Betsy Sue had neglected to put on her bathing suit, and he was feeling very odd about that.

Dudee Sparrow had been led away to the mudbaths, and Ed was feeling a pang of loss over that, too.

"I'm looking at your skin," he said.

"Does it seem to glow?" she asked, pointing to a spot next to her navel.

"It does seem to glow," he answered. "It seems pinker somehow."

"That's what I thought," said Betsy, smiling. "And it feels so odd. But good."

"In what way does it feel odd?" Ed asked. He was due for the mudbath treatments at five and was apprehensive.

"I can't really describe it. It sort of tingles, or glows; you know what I mean?"

"I can't say that I do."

"Well, it feels like it wants to move away from the rest of me. Like it has a mind of its own." Betsy Sue squirmed a little as she talked.

When a shadow fell over them they glanced up. Ed could make out the beret and beard. Keb all in white, like Duane, towered.

"Well, well, well, Mr. and Mrs. Sox!" He sounded surprised and delighted to see them. "And Mrs. Sox, how did you like our mudbath treatments, eh? Most refreshing, I should think. Yes, indeed, most refreshing. Everyone says so. We have our little secret about them, Mrs. Sox. Only at the Crystal Grape, you know?" He spread his hands as though disclaiming what he was about to say. "Of course, of course. You're going to remind me that other spas have their secrets too. And you would be correct. Quite correct. But we think ours is special. You know what I mean? But of course you do."

"Thank you, uh, Keb. They certainly are most refreshing." Betsy gave a little roll to her hips, and Keb, who noticed, smiled.

Ed, who also noticed, frowned.

"I thought your secret was all a matter of attitude," Ed said.

"And so it is, Mr. Sox, so it is. That, and of course the little secret."

"And what exactly is that secret, Keb?"

"Oh, come now, Mr. Sox," said Keb, wagging a finger. "We couldn't reveal that, now, could we? It is, of course, a combination of many things — temperatures, ingredients, consistency and so forth. Much like other places, though, we have devised our own special proportions. And the secret. Ah, yes. Well, nice talking to you folks." Keb strolled away.

"He looks so familiar," Ed said. "A strange fella, honeypot. A strange fella."

Keb went back to the control room, where he found Duane, his boots resting on the console, reading a magazine, *Arizona Highways*.

"What're you reading, Duane?" Keb asked, rubbing his hands together, a fly washing its feet.

"Poem in here. By some fellow named Philbrick Weevol. A real pretty poem called 'Children of Paradise.' Lot of words I don't understand, like, what's an embryophyte? But it's a real pretty poem."

"I didn't know you liked poetry, Duane. A new side of you, I must say."

"Never read any before," said Duane, thinking about reading this one to Rhea.

Keb peered at the television screen in time to see Rhea put down her book and help Dudee Sparrow into the bath. Rhea placed a towel over Dudee's face and went back to her book.

"What's Rhea reading in there?" he asked.

"Some Egyptian thing," Duane answered, figuring "Throbbing Yang" has *got* to be better than that.

"Well, well, well," said Keb, straightening up and once more rubbing his hands together. "Things do seem to be coming along. That Mrs. Sox was positively glowing. Glowing."

"Yes, sir," said Duane, recrossing his elegantly hand-tooled booted ankles on the console.

23 / An Elephant's Hip

A. K. FLEW IN FROM Hilo on the 3:50 flight. As the airplane sank into a smog layer that made the San Francisco Bay Area look as though it had just been bronzed and was hanging from the cosmic rearview mirror, he turned his nut-tanned face to the man sitting next to him.

"Akley," he said.

"Eh?" The man was reading *Fortune* magazine.

"Akley. Name's Akley. Akley Republican Furniture."

"Oh. Sparrow. Frozen foods."

"Ah, yes. Frozen foods," said A. K., nodding vigorously. "Vacation?"

Sig Sparrow was puzzled. "Vacation?" he mused, nibbling on his lower lip. He glanced over his violet-tinted glasses.

"You vacationing in Hawaii?" A. K. asked. "Live there, myself."

"No, not vacationing," Sig sighed, closing his magazine. "Business."

"Frozen foods?" Akley asked with a genial smile.

"No. AKA Club business." Sig reached up to the lapel of his maroon velveteen Edwardian jacket and fingered the small gold pin there. "I'm the president of AKA International."

"Oh, yes. I see, I see. AKA International. Very interesting, I'm sure. Very interesting. What the hell is AKA International?" he asked so suddenly that Sig Sparrow jumped. *Fortune* slid off his lap onto the floor.

"You don't know what the AKA Clubs are?" he asked. He pushed up his tinted glasses and squinted at Akley.

"Like the Knights of Columbus, I suppose? Or the Rotarians?" Sig shook his head. Everyone had heard of the AKA Clubs.

"Rosicrucians? Wisdom of Ancient Egypt. Pyramids, third eyes, apertures in the forehead, dragon cults, astral projection, telepathy, things like that. I get it." A. K. nodded quickly.

"Not really," Sig said, lowering his glasses. The world turned faintly purple again. "We follow Avery Augenblaue's quest for *The* Blue Light. He's been *out there*, you know, and should be back in a month with the Answer."

"Is that so?" A. K. Akley was not smiling any longer. "Well, let me tell you something. I've never heard of this fellow Augerblow, but the answer you're talking about is not out in some psychotic ectoplasm somewhere, it's right here on this plane with me; it's scattered all over America in every motel room, and in bedrooms and living rooms all over America, too." He leaned back and crossed his arms, glaring at Sig.

"You honestly don't know who Avery K. Augenblaue is?" Sig asked. He picked up his *Fortune* and didn't notice A. K. glaring at him.

"Never heard of him."

"Well, he blasted off for outer space ten years ago. He's been sailing through the intergalactic void ever since, looking for *The* Blue Light. Everyone's heard of him."

"Foolishness," Akley retorted. "Intergalactic space indeed. No answers out there. All right here."

"I don't follow you."

"*Furniture!*" A. K. shouted. "Cheap furniture! Philippine monkeywood. Plastic teak veneer. Let me tell you something, young man . . ."

"I'm no younger than you are," Sig protested, staring hard at the furniture manufacturer. "Older, maybe."

"Nonsense. I have the cargo hold full of furniture on this airplane. I have a warehouse in Milpitas, California, and one in Perth Amboy, New Jersey, and one in Squash, Idaho, and two in Baton Rouge, Louisiana, and I know damn well the answer is in furniture!" He lurched in his seat as the plane touched down.

"You know something?" Sig said, still staring at Akley, "you remind me of someone but I can't quite . . ."

"Doubt it. Really doubt it. I seldom get out."

"Maybe we've met before. Or you have a brother . . ." Sig's brow developed three pleats across it.

"No. No brothers. I stay home a lot, and I'm very sure we've never met before. Very sure. Never knew anyone in the frozen food business. Don't *like* frozen foods, never heard of these here clubs. You're mistaken."

"Well, maybe. But you sure do look familiar."

"Hmph. Well, what were you doing in Hawaii? You never said." A. K. smiled broadly again, as if a switch had been thrown inside his face.

"Hmm? Oh. There'll be a big AKA Club convention over Labor Day weekend. I was helping our Hawaii chapter set up receptions for the Far East delegates. Lots of AKA Club members in Japan, China, the Philippines, Java, Borneo — places like that. Lots of people interested in *The* Blue Light."

"That so?" Akley slapped his hands on his knees and said something that sounded like "By gosh!"

"Lots of people," Sig repeated.

"We buy most of our wood from the Philippines. Wonderful place. Well, here we are. Been a pleasure. A real pleasure." A. K. shook Sig's hand and walked off into the crowd exiting the plane, Sig's *Fortune* under his arm.

"He sure does look familiar," Sig mumbled, watching A. K. disappear into the flow of people.

"Squirts," A. K. said to himself.

"What'd you say, Mr. Akley?" Ed Sox asked. He stood at A. K.'s elbow in the baggage claim area.

"I said, 'Squirts.' Frozen foods indeed. Anyone knows the answer lies in cheap furniture, eh, Mr. Argyle?"

"Sox."

"Yes, yes, right, Mr. Sox."

"Absolutely right, Mr. Akley."

"You still *believe* in Akley Republican Furniture, don't you, Ed?" A. K. asked as they rolled down the Bayshore Freeway toward the new Dunbarton Bridge and the road to Milpitas.

"Absolutely, Mr. Akley," Ed answered as they rolled off the bridge and onto the Nimitz Freeway. Ed turned radio station KAKA-FM down a bit to say, "Akley Republican Furniture is in every home in America now. It just came off the computer today, this morning."

"That's fine, Ed. Just fine," said A. K. as they swerved off the Nimitz into Milpitas. "But we want Akley Republican Furniture in every home in the *world!*"

"Yes, sir."

Akley Republican Furniture covered seven acres of choice garbage landfill under one roof. Seven acres of coffee tables, American Heritage fourposters, AkleyLoungers, couches, easy chairs, sofas, consoles, end tables, lamps — standing and table, sofa-convertibles, day beds, shelf-and-cabinet combinations, desks, dinettes, bar stools, dressing tables, chaises longues, love seats and settees.

"Magnificent, isn't it?" the president of Akley Republican Furniture asked his West Coast manager.

"Yes, sir," said Ed.

"That's a lot of furniture," said Akley.

"Yes, sir," said Ed, glancing down the tall aisles of stacked furniture, alive with the sounds of forklifts and warehouse personnel keeping the flow of furniture moving.

"Well, Ed," Akley said, looking at him for the first time since deplaning. "You appear quite fit, I must say. You and the little woman enjoy that bonus I sent you when you joined us?"

"You send us that bonus every year, Mr. Akley. Betsy Sue and I surely do appreciate it. We surely do." Ed glowed.

"I do believe you've lost a bit of weight, Ed. Since I first interviewed you at my little place in Hawaii, at Ka Lae. Yes, indeed. A bit of weight."

"Yes, sir." Ed was wiry and tanned pink, his fingers lean and strong, his chin single and clean. He had recently treated himself to a fifty-dollar razor cut, and his ears were free of unsightly hair. "And you should see my wife Betsy Sue, sir. She looks like a million dollars, if I do say so myself."

"Things pretty good on the, uh, you know?" Akley winked at Ed.

"The what, sir?"

"The, uh, you know." He winked again and jabbed Ed with his elbow.

"I don't quite get you, sir." Ed was puzzled.

"You know," said Akley repeated, winking and elbow-jabbing. "Like the brochure for the Crystal Grape. Like that. How'd you like it, eh? Wall-to-wall pussy, eh? That's the kind of stuff you like, eh?" He winked again.

"Ahhh," breathed Ed, grinning. "Yes, sir. Wall-to-wall. Amazing place. But things are pretty good with old Betsy Sue, if you know what I mean. Pretty good. Sir."

"I see, I see. Lots of fucking," said Akley softly.

"What's that?" Ed asked. A forklift had roared past them cradling a nine-foot couch in its arms.

Akley leaned toward Ed. "I said *fucking!*" he shouted just as the forklift's engine was shut off. Ed winced.

"Yes, sir," he said, trying to get into the spirit of it. "Like a mink. Fantastic."

"The Crystal Grape does that for you, Ed. And the little woman. They've got a secret."

"That's what Keb, uh, Mr. Armbruster, says."

"Just like Akley Republican Furniture, eh, Ed?" Akley winked again. "Just like Akley Republican Furniture."

"Yes, sir. That's what my wife Betsy Sue says. She says the Crystal Grape has made her horny as hell, and that must be part of the secret. And she says that Akley Republican Furniture must have a secret, too, even though it's cheap."

"Inexpensive, Ed. Inexpensive."

"Yes, sir. Inexpensive."

"So your little woman Betsy Sue says that, does she?"

"Yes, sir."

"Well, well, well. To quote an old Si Ronga proverb, Ed, 'A relative by marriage is an elephant's hip.' You just remember that, Ed."

"Yes, sir," said Ed with a strange expression. "An elephant's hip."

24 / Statistics Broth

"IT IS IN THE NATURE OF statistics to be both extremely precise and entirely meaningless." Above Dr. Ague's shaven head, backlit from the floor-to-ceiling window, floated a shining nimbus of sea green light in such high contrast to his face that Dick Peters was dazzled. He could discern only the glare from the doctor's thick glasses.

"For example," Dr. Ague continued with a nod that caused his glasses to blink off and on again, "the divorce rate in the United States last year was precisely one hundred percent of the homocide rate for the first time since the beginnings of statistical computation. That is, there were exactly as many divorces as murders. An astounding fact that the department and the FBI are helpless to explain. Further investigation and correlation revealed that the curves of those two social factors were exactly matched by the incidence of sexual impotence among middle-class whites. The birth rate dropped off in a perfect sine wave form. People simply stopped screwing. Very odd." Dr. Ague nodded again.

"But what does that mean, Doctor?" Dick Peters asked, glancing down at the red light on his pocket recorder to confirm it was still taping.

"Well." Dr. Ague leaned back in his huge leather chair and locked his fingers in front of his stomach. "Nothing."

"Nothing?" Peters looked up.

"That's correct. Meaningless. Completely meaningless. Why would anyone want to bother with studying correlations such as those, you might ask? Well, of course there's an answer to that question. Research funds, for one thing. Projects like that always attract grants. And someone ought to do them, for another. You never know, maybe those statistics *are* meaningful."

"I'm not certain I follow you, Dr. Ague. Are you saying we should stop keeping statistics?"

"Good heavens no! Listen: the ax has become the second favorite murder weapon in this country, a country where there is a murder every 17.394805 seconds, or 3.4493055 murders every minute. Imagine that, the ax! Foreheads creased to the nose! Limbs hacked off!"

"Gruesome, Doctor," Dick Peters muttered. "Please!"

"But what does that statistic mean? I ask you. Perhaps it means *more personal contact!* Perhaps it implies nothing at all." Dr. Ague's head bobbed, his glasses blinking a Morse code message Dick could not decipher.

"The big question is, are the ax murderers and the divorced people the same? That's the big question."

"And?"

"And the answer is, not always. Sometimes. In fact, 32.9678 percent of the time. Or take rape."

"All right."

"Actual rape has fallen off dramatically in the last five years." Blink, blink, blink, his glasses reflected the desk light.

"That's a good thing."

"No indeed. Terrible. *Attempted* rape has soared. Grandmothers, dogs in heat, fire hydrants — no one and nothing is safe anymore. My own sainted mother . . . Well, that's another story. The point is, the rapists *can't seem to follow through!* Voilà!" Dr. Ague's hands spread in an all-inclusive gesture.

"Yes?"

"Less robbery. No need to steal anymore. But armed assault has risen; sheer spite. People are unhappy, no doubt about it. For example: yesterday, one day alone, almost fifteen thousand people disappeared. Vanished without a trace. Gone. Think of that."

"So?"

"So, nothing. Doesn't mean a thing. All over America folks are hacking each other to pieces, divorcing each other, insulting and assaulting each other, dropping in, dropping out. Gangs of middle-aged accountants armed with baseball bats roam the streets of Kansas City at night, clobbering rival gangs of bank tellers. The amount of soot that falls on the streets of New York in a single day is now over three inches. Fourteen percent of the country's arable land is covered with cement. Ten years ago the President of the United States disappeared, and not one clue to his whereabouts has been found. Five years ago the Indians of the American Southwest stopped making blankets and pottery and turquoise jewelry and started an enormous traffic in *Amanita muscaria*, a mushroom that induces strange mystical states when smoked. There are rumors that the Mafia tried to create its own source for the drug and was unsuccessful.

"What has happened, you see, is that violence has become completely *random*. That's why statistics are meaningless."

"How is the Aldrich K. Ague Biosynthetics Clinic involved in all this?" Peters asked. Every year he made the rounds of various research centers, measuring the scientific pulse, as it were. This was his first interview with Dr. Ague, however, and the first time he was completely at a loss in understanding his informant.

"Ah, well." Dr. Ague sighed. He whipped his chair around and gazed out the window, presenting his shining baldness to the reporter, which winked its own coded messages at him as the light glanced off the ridges and rills of the round skull.

"Well," Dr. Ague repeated, talking to the window. "I investigate hormone levels, for instance. Hormone levels related to apathy and boredom. Apathy and boredom breed aggression, you know. And the hormone levels have been falling. Falling." He leaned forward and scraped something off the windowpane in front of him; he almost dropped out of the reporter's sight. Peters half rose from his chair and peered over the desk at Dr. Ague's back, and Dr. Ague sat up at that moment and said, "Look out there!" He leaned to one side and pointed to a huge man walking across the manicured lawn. "That man out there," he continued, "is the hope of the future. That man is William Lamplighter!"

A long pause fell between them as Peters waited for an explanation. "Who?" he asked at last.

"William Lamplighter." Dr. Ague swung his chair back around and started his glasses semaphoring, blink-blink, blink-blink. Peters saw a buxom girl in starched nurse's whites come running toward the huge man in seeming slow motion. She was holding the hem of her nurse's dress in both hands so her long legs, exposed, bounded up and down and scissored back and forth. She got to Lamplighter, who opened his arms to her, and hurled herself into them, knocking him backward off his feet. The two of them tumbled out of sight behind the rhododendron hedge. To Peters it looked as though she had her left hand in his pants before they disappeared

"He's a big man," the reporter said. "But he sure is ugly. All those scars. And who was that woman?"

"Woman? Oh, that must be Nurse Thinger. She's been quite taken with Bill the past couple of years. Quite taken with him." Dr. Ague rose and paced around his desk. "Let me show you something," he said.

Four yards of computer print-out unfurled into Peters' lap. "Those are hormone levels. Here are samples from a random population. The curve, you can see, is falling. *Here*, and *here*. And here are Lamplighter's levels. The androgen group here. Testosterone levels are enormous, abnormally high even. And why? Well, that's our secret at the clinic. You might wonder if Nurse Thinger has anything to do with it." Dr. Ague turned away from the charts and glanced out the window. Peters followed with his eyes and saw a furious cartwheel of clothing spewing from behind the rhododendrons. A brassiere followed the nurse's dress. A white shoe flew after it.

"Doctor, they're not . . . ?" Peters was standing up too now, craning to look out the window, staring through the slightly brownish air in the sedate hills above Menlo Park, California, across a respectable lawn at a hedge heavy with rhododendron blossoms. Another shoe flew over the hedge.

"Why, yes, I believe they are," the doctor smiled. "Well, to continue. Of course Nurse Thinger has something to do with it. It's her job."

"That's her *job*?" Peters said, pointing.

Dr. Ague looked out the window again. The broad ropy back of the underground film star was humping across a gap in the hedge. Under him, Nurse Thinger's thrashing arms and legs and the billowy tossing of her blond hair could be seen.

They watched Lamplighter's huge scarred buttocks bucking and plunging across the small opening in the hedge, knocking the nurse ahead with each plunge. Gradually the pair inched behind a new section of rhododendron and vanished again. The last to go were her curling toes clamped behind his ankles.

"What does she *see* in that guy?" Peters asked.

"You'd be surprised." Dr. Ague smiled again. "He has an implant, developed here at the clinic. The man is an anomaly, of course, a well-known underground movie actor who specializes in the erotic. We do all kinds of research here at the clinic."

"A while ago, you suggested that people were becoming less, uh, erotic."

"Indeed they are, on the whole. But there are pockets on the print-out. At times there is a resurgence, as it were. Sudden, inexplicable frenzies. The overall trend has been down, however. At least until recently."

"Aha. And what has happened recently?"

"Avery Augenblaue has returned, for one thing. The AKA Clubs and interest in *The* Blue Light. *Amanita muscaria*, now a highly illegal drug, outsells beer. William Lamplighter and Nurse Thinger and related phenomena. All signs of a change, perhaps. Here at the Biosynthetics Clinic we aim to do our share, work toward that change. We need it. Remember, a murder approximately every seventeen seconds."

Peters, looking out the window again, gasped when he caught a glimpse of Lamplighter's size. "My God!" he breathed.

"The implant," Dr. Ague said modestly.

"How can she . . . ? I mean, Lord!"

"Oh, Nurse Thinger has adjusted very well."

"So I see," Peters said, riveted to the window. He watched the couple move out of sight again. "What *is* the secret here? What is it that you do, precisely?"

"I wish I could tell you that, Mr. Peters. I really do. But research being what it is, it's best to keep things under wraps until all the data is in and analyzed. I'm sure you understand."

"Well, in general terms, could you summarize the clinic's goals, what you are trying to do? For the world, our readers."

"Certainly, Mr. Peters. In general terms, we're trying to put more love into the world."

"Oh."

25 / More Broth

BUCK SWEENEY'S FACE was red. "Yes, sir," he answered into the global black mouth of his telephone. "Yes, sir. I've assigned my best men, round the clock."

He hung up and reclined in his chair. He imagined himself in front of a room full of well-disciplined boys: neat rows of neat uniforms and close-cropped hair, faces at attention and alert. He imagined himself pacing back and forth in front of the room, slapping his thigh with a riding crop.

"You, Martinez!" he snapped, and dusky Martinez answered, "Yessir," with a salute. "Front!" "Yessir."

When Martinez had been punished sufficiently, Buck felt better. Some of the red had drained from his face. "That's the kind of world we need. If I had my way . . ." he muttered to himself, gazing up at the photograph of his father, General George Armstrong Sweeney. A swatch of black ribbon hung from the upper right-hand corner. General Sweeney had died recently under disturbing circumstances in a special "hotel" room in New Orleans. The disturbing circumstances included some disciplinary apparatus and strange welts on various parts of his body.

Buck picked up the phone. "Give me Team A." He drummed his fingers on the glass desktop while he waited. At last he heard a voice. "Who's this?"

"Harker, sir," twittered the receiver in his ear.

"Well, Harker, what the hell's going on? The Director's on my ass and you people haven't come up with anything yet!"

"We're at the house, sir," Harker said. "Just finished eating. Mrs. Augenblaue has ordered dinner and guests are arriving. No sign of Mr. Augenblaue."

"Well, find that son of a bitch, Harker. You're the three best men I've got. You've been familiar with this case from the beginning. You should have some idea by now where the hell he is, goddammit. We've got to locate him before something worse happens. Christ, if he shows up at that goddam convention tomorrow a leak'll spring in the social fabric so big the whole goddam country'll sink like a stale bagel, understand? Not to mention what will happen if he *doesn't* show up. Either way, we're in trouble. You should read the fucking statistics!" He slammed down the phone.

"Christ!" Buck turned on the radio. Then he hauled a pile of newspapers over and began scanning them stolidly. Outside his window an American flag hung limply from a pole in the sultry Washington air, air that had not noticeably cooled since the sun went down.

"Ooooo children of paradise," the radio crooned. "Ooooo

gooey Yin and throbbing Yang," it sang in a cracked but honest voice.

"God almighty, that song again. I can't stand it." Buck switched off the radio, then turned it back on.

"Ooooh, children of paradise, You are the everything and all!" the radio concluded the song.

"That was 'Children of Paradise,' as of course you all know," the WAKA disc jockey announced. "Theme song of all the AKA Clubs and number one smash hit on all the charts. Over four million singles sold. It's made its writer, Philbrick Weevol, an overnight rock sensation. And now for a word about personal security . . ."

Buck's face reddened again as he turned off the radio and went back to his newspapers. He read Dick Peters' interview with a Dr. Aldrich K. Ague in California. He read about the department's statistics and ground his teeth. "There are as many divorces as murders," he read, "an astounding fact that the department is helpless to explain." He paced furiously back and forth in front of the room full of young boys. He added some girls. *"Amanita muscaria,"* he read. That doesn't need any more publicity, he thought.

And he read about pockets or times when there seemed to be a resurgence of erotic activity.

Erotic activity, he mused, as he had Martinez bend over the edge of his desk. For a moment he couldn't decide whether Martinez had pants on or not. He raised his riding crop.

"Oh, hell," he groaned out loud and seized the phone. "Computation!" he ordered. The receiver beeped a few atonal notes in his ear.

"Computation," a voice responded.

"Article in the *Times* today," he shouted. "Interview with a Dr. Ague. Says, '. . . pockets or times of a resurgence of erotic activity.' Run a cross-correlation with Augenblaue, Avery K. And with President, disappearance of. Find out who the hell this Dr. Ague is. Find out where the hell this goddam song 'Children of Paradise' came from. Cross-index everything you can think of. I want to know what these pockets and times of erotic activity are. This interview with Dr. Ague says his clinic is trying to put more *love* into the world, for God's sake!"

He stabbed a button on his phone. "Get me Team A again.

Who is this? Harbin? What the hell happened to Harker? Listening? Is anything going on? No, I'll wait." He drummed the desk.

"Hello. Yes? Harker says Sparrow is worried? Sparrow, he's the frozen food guy, isn't he? What the hell is he worried *about*? He has no idea where Avery is? Nobody seems to know where Avery is. I received your report about this scientist, Merkin. I suspect he's hiding something. Did you bug him? He's *disappeared*? The U.S. Government has spent almost a million bucks training each one of you jerks and you can't even keep track of one lousy scientist! All right, all right. But I've got to ask you about erotic activity."

Buck's face began to glow an eerie red that seeped from his face down his neck to vanish under his collar as he listened to Harbin. Buck laid one massive hand, palm down, very gently on the desk and took a deep breath. "Whattaya mean, what?" he screamed. "Erotic activity. Is there any erotic activity there? Have you noticed any erotic activity around any of the people you have been investigating the past ten years? Yes, I'll wait."

"Where the hell have you been?" he shouted into the phone when Harbin at last returned to the line. "None of you has noticed any erotic activity, say, around the Augenblaue family, over the past ten years? What's the matter, why are you coughing? You'll blow your cover. Where the hell are you, anyway? Forsythia bushes? My God. All *right*." He hung up.

"Dad," he said, looking up at the photograph. "Things are getting worse. Be glad you're out of it."

The phone rang. "Yes."

"Computation. We have a run on those correlations you asked for."

"Well?"

"There could be a relationship between this Augenblaue and erotic activity. Or there could not be. For example, at the launch of the *A.K.A. Monastic* ten years ago an awful frenzy of sexual, uh, indulgence was precipitated. Four people killed outright. Three died later in the hospital. Seventeen critical injuries. And that's the time the President disappeared, although he had complete Secret Service protection. In fact, two of the injured belonged to Secret Service."

"You mean he was kidnapped?"

"No, sir. The injuries were of a, uh, *private* nature. The men were preoccupied; it seems they forgot about the President. For a time, anyway."

"Go on."

"Yes, sir. There might be a connection with Mr. Augenblaue's kids. They were in San Francisco a couple of years ago . . ."

"What?"

"Yes, sir. You weren't aware of that?"

"No. What the hell was Team A doing then? How could they miss something like that?"

"Well, it appears from the report we have that Mrs. Augenblaue didn't even know, so perhaps she couldn't have informed your agents."

"Christ, nobody talks to anybody these days. What has happened to *trust?*"

"Yes, sir."

"What did the kids do in San Francisco?"

"The younger one got a sex change. There were flurries of sexual activity above the statistical norm for that period in the area. Some of it centered around a small movie theater, the Accacia Kinetoscope Art Theater. There's a possible connection between the theater and this Dr. Ague you asked about.

"Here's another connection the computers came up with. Don't know whether it's significant or not. A furniture company in Hawaii."

"A furniture company?" Buck's eyes rolled toward the ceiling. Yes, Martinez definitely had his pants off, tight adolescent butt presented for punishment.

"Yes, sir. The divorce rate for people who have purchased furniture from this company, especially beds, has dropped dramatically. Over fifty-seven percent. The homocide rate has also dropped."

"This is beginning to look more and more like a conspiracy of national, no, *inter*national proportions. Is that all?"

"Uh, yes, sir."

Buck leaned back in his chair rubbing his eyes. Outside his double-paned window the sultry heat of the late August Washington air began to spread mildew on the American flag hanging there. Buck allowed Martinez to whimper a little when the whip struck his quivering sixteen-year-old flesh. The thick lips on Buck's beefy face thinned, showing the sharp edges of his widely spaced teeth. I'm the Deputy Director, and Martinez will toe the line. Martinez wiggled his ass. Keep still, Martinez, *thwack.* This hurts me more than it hurts you, *thwack!*

Buck was beginning to relax when the phone rang.

"What is it?" he asked.

"Computation again, sir. There is one other small thing you should be aware of."

"What's that?"

"Initials, sir."

"Initials?"

"Yes, sir. The same initials keep popping up, over and over."

"Coincidence."

"Yes, sir. Could be. That's what we figured too, at first."

"What initials?"

"A.K.A., sir. Over and over, A.K.A."

PART II/SEPTEMBER 1

A Chinese story tells of a doctor who fell ill and could not go on his rounds. A patient who had paid him large sums of money without getting any better grew very angry that the doctor was not coming around, so he sent a servant to curse the doctor. When the servant returned, the master asked. 'Well, did you curse him?'

'No, I did not,' the servant answered.

'And may I ask why not?'

'Because,' the servant answered, 'all the time I was trying to curse him he was being badly beaten and I couldn't get a word in!'

26 / A Bunch of Grapes

SIG SPARROW, GRAY-HAIRED AND tanned, dressed head to toe in his pea green velvet six-button jacket and flared brown trousers over brown Earth Shoes, glasses tinted a delicate amber, looked like a leaf on a twig beginning to curl in the first crisp frost of autumn. He stood before the stove preparing a frozen truffle omelet for defrosting. The sun streamed in through the kitchen window, dappling his brown and green outfit with gold. He hummed a catchy popular tune under his breath, "Oooh, children of paradise, hmmmmm, hmm-hm, dee daa de da . . ."

He peeled back the paper top and slid the aluminum package into the oven. Leaning against the counter, he crossed one Earth Shoe over the other and watched, smiling, as the crinkled lid slowly puffed up with dense, moist, aromatic omelet-stuff. Outside the window a leaf stirred gently in a vagrant breeze.

Dudee was out in the garage with Philadelphia snuffling wetly at her ankles as she stirred equal portions of cottage cheese, ground filet mignon, goose liver pâté, two raw eggs and a liquid containing twelve essential vitamins and minerals (nine, plus extra iron) into the dog's ceramic bowl. Although it was a crisp first of September, the garage door was open, so the same sunlight dappling her sweet Uncle Sig shone full upon her $95 Marshall Field denim jeans and satin v-neck blouse, under which her fresh melon-breasts circled as she stirred.

"Stop it, Philly," she said gently. "You're soaking my shoe." She placed the bowl in front of the dog and gave a delicious little shiver that sent her nipples tingling against the satin. Then she went inside to watch her dear Uncle Sig eat his omelet.

Virge Moses, down near the South Side, had his riot helmet on and was just inserting himself into his wife's roiling stew. Wanita, thrashing in a stupendous frenzy, caught a glimpse of her face reflected in the dark blue plastic of Virge's face protector and felt the metronome of lust ticking inside her groin notch up by a factor of ten. She licked the face protector with her long red tongue, hurtled her calves behind Virge's knees, and shoved him hard into her. The same sunlight that blessed Sig and Dudee up on the North Side was blessing Virge and Wanita on the South.

And *Forniculotermes brevis*, which had swarmed its nearly invisible swarm a couple of months ago, releasing into the bedroom air its minute quantities of PCPA, had now bored its way, led by a new queen, into the dresser, where hair-thin burrows threaded their way through the wood as the termites munched and munched.

Downstairs, Grandma and Grandpa Moses spooned Cream of Wheat into their toothless mouths. Grandfather Moses wheezed alarmingly between mouthfuls. "Disgusting!" Grandma Moses muttered to the chair in which her son Virgil was not sitting. The floor over their heads thumped, and a thin layer of plaster snow dusted the breakfast table.

Reba Hare idly scratched an old bite on her shoulder as she swished eggs and sliced carrots around in the frying pan. She and Bunny Darlitch had been to the Accacia Kinetoscope Art Theater the night before for the opening of Art's new film, *Blue Lite/Cosmic Connection*. It lasted three hours and invoked such a powerful sexual panic in the two of them that they had carried on — biting and screwing/gobbling/snarling — until two-thirty in the morning.

They got up early. She and Bunny had a plane to catch to Chicago for the AKA convention scheduled to begin that very evening, so she blearily stared at the eggs and carrots and scratched. In the other room, by the window where the sun was struggling through the fog outside to warm the scraggly row of marijuana sprouts on the sill, Bunny pecked at his typewriter.

Not only to review *Blue Lite/Cosmic Connection*, but to elaborate on the curious cultural phenomenon centered on the poem "Children of Paradise" he had covered several years before. Reba considered it a terrible poem then, but now she caught herself singing a verse under her breath. Damn, she thought, that's weird. And she thought about *The* Blue Light.

"Philbrick Weevol," Bunny typed, "one-time self-styled psychiatric dropout, painter, sculptor (there are still those among us who remember the smell of his *Virgin Sofa* as it rotted on the floor of the Occidental Gallery; one patron suffered a broken ankle when she slipped on a vagrant cherry) and poet, is something of a cultural anomaly. He has become, in the past six months, the patron troubadour of the AKA Clubs, singing, in his untrained but strangely compelling voice, the only poem he has ever written, the endless epic titled 'Children of Paradise,' which this reporter has learned through his research was published originally, in part, ten years ago in the August issue of *Arizona Highways* . . ."

When the eggs and carrots coalesced in the greasy pan, Reba called Bunny in to his breakfast of scrambled eggs with sliced carrots and seven-grain toast.

Stringy China was stuffing Philbrick into his tight black pants with the special padding in the codpiece. She had stitched sequins onto that part of the pants, sequins that would glow an enormous phallic outline when the ultraviolet lights went on. Phil grunted as she zipped him up.

"Well, asshole," seventeen-year-old China commented, "tonight's your big night, eh? Tonight you get to blow the minds of all the folks at the AKA convention. And then I get to blow you, eh?"

"Jesus, China, do you have to keep talking like that. You're only seventeen. What would your parents think?" Phil turned around, admiring himself in the floor-to-ceiling mirror of his dressing room.

"If my *father* knew I was having my little pussy reamed out by a creepy sixty-year-old asshole who's prolly older than he is, he'd prolly *shit!*"

"I'm only fifty-seven," Phil said, aggrieved. "And I can't believe the way you talk."

"OK, OK, cocksucker, let's go get something to eat. Real food. I mean. We've got a plane to catch."

Duane Hemp was humping Rhea, the cute attendant. He had been humping her regularly ever since he had read her "Children of Paradise" from his issue of *Arizona Highways*.

"Gosh almighty, Duane," she said, looking at her bright red fingernails over his shoulder as he pumped away at her. They were screwing in the dim green light of the empty early morning mudbath room. "Duane. Can't you even take your hat off? *I can hardly see my nails*." But they look real good in this light, she thought.

"Huh?" Duane grunted. He was perspiring freely. He always did when he had sex with Rhea. He perspired because he worked very hard at it, yet he couldn't tell whether she even noticed he was screwing her.

"I said, 'Can't you even take your hat off?' " She examined the nails on her right hand. The thumb was chipped.

"Oh," said Duane without breaking his rhythm; he was, he could tell, almost finished, and she always asked him that question. Duane never removed his hat. No need.

"Are you finished yet?" Rhea asked.

"Not yet."

"Well, keep me posted, will you, Duane? I'm getting hungry again, and we gotta get to the airport soon."

The temperature outside was climbing over a hundred, even this early, but it was very pleasant in the mudbath room.

Ed and Betsy Sue Sox gazed deeply into each other's eyes in the breakfast room of their $200,000 tract home in Milpitas, California, where the sun was also shining brightly. The low, coastal, early morning fog had dissipated, taking with it much of the rich walnut brown industrial and automotive residue in the air.

Before them on the table (through which the tiny jaws of countless thousands of *forniculotermes brevis* munched their thready channels) lay the remains of eggs fried sunny side up, chicken-fried steak and home-fried potatoes.

"Remember that time on the AkleyLounger back home in Tulsa?" Ed asked Betsy Sue with a broad salacious grin.

She smiled back and slid her dainty foot up the inside of his thigh under the breakfast table. Their new AkleyLounger, with its electronic improvements, sat, tested and sedate, in the living room.

"Uh, I guess we'd better get going," Ed said, "before something happens." Betsy Sue's toes wiggled on his sausage and Ed's grin widened.

Connie Hubble sneezed and yawned at the same time under the forsythia bushes near the Augenblaue mansion.

"Christ!" he muttered, and popped another Dexedrine into his mouth. All night the three of them had been crouching there waiting for some sign of Avery. Already it was getting hot. Harker slapped at his neck as he listened carefully at his earphones.

"Has the girl appeared yet?" he asked Harbin, who was at the scope, now tuned to daylight mode.

"Not yet," he murmured. "But I think she's headed toward the door. Hard to tell. This damn thing really isn't working very well. Gimme another Dex, will you?" He rubbed his chin.

Hubble, who was drinking coffee from a thermos, poured a cup and handed it, along with the pill, over to Harbin, who gulped both down.

"Here she comes!" At the bottom of the hill Ally Kate, as ripe and gorgeous an eighteen-year-old as any goat-god of universal groins could ever have dreamed, walked slowly up the driveway toward the forsythia hedge the three scratchy, tired agents were crouching in. Halfway up the hill she stopped, took a deep breath, gazed at the sky for a long moment, and turned back toward the house.

"The boss says to take her," Harbin muttered. The three agents ran in an odd, hobbling, bent-double run down the twenty yards of driveway, grabbed Ally and carried her, screaming, kicking and squirming, back to the hedge, where they hastily gathered up their equipment and dragged her and it to the anonymous sedan parked nearby.

The sun blazed on the slowly warming asphalt of the driveway. Inside the house, Kay sipped at her thirteenth cup of coffee and wondered what the hell would happen when the world discovered that Avery Krupp Augenblaue was missing.

27 / Rose-Colored Glasses

THE ARGO PALACE HOTEL WAS Chicago's newest and proudest adornment, a tall, round shaft 115 stories high, topped by a geodesic dome of tinted, polarized plastic. This dome covered the hall where the tenth annual AKA convention would take place. It was upriver from the Marina Towers, its twin, round predecessors, and overlooked the Loop, the Chicago River, and to the east Lake Michigan, now placid and serene in the early September sun, a blue sheet unwrinkled by thrashing bodies.

Ambrose Merkin stood in the empty hall looking down at the river winding past the building, 115 stories below. He tugged at his muttonchops and sucked a lemon lozenge. A suburban train crawling toward the hotel reminded him of a photomicrographic film of erythrocytes moving in line through a capillary. The train vanished beneath the hotel. The landscape was flushed slightly pink by the tint of the plastic dome.

A sound behind him caused Dr. Merkin to whirl around. Two men labored up the last steps to the hall, lugging between them a large crate with AUDIOVISUAL EQUIPMENT stenciled on the side.

"Where does this go?" asked the shorter of the two, whose name was Marty Huggins.

"Down there on the podium," Merkin answered, pointing across the room. He turned back to the window, lips pursed around his lozenge. Far to the south, Merkin thought he could spot the Kankakee facility of Augenblaue AeroSpace, closed for the Labor Day weekend, but he was not, at the moment, ruminating on AeroSpace.

He was thinking about Avery's appearance later in the day. He tugged at his muttonchops and smiled.

Marty Huggins and his companion used crowbars to peel away the sides of the wooden crate, revealing a standard speaker's lectern with built-in microphone and speakers, reading light and water dispenser. It coasted on silent casters, so the two men easily centered it on the podium, where the morning rose-tinted sunlight shone on the AKA insignias on the backs of their uniforms.

"It looks like an ordinary speaker's lectern," Marty whispered into his throat mike. "But it's a hell of a lot heavier than it should be."

"Give me more data," the tiny microphone implanted just under the skin over his mastoid process instructed.

"About four feet high," Marty whispered.

"What did you say," his companion asked him, straightening from his task of collecting the debris from the crate.

"Oh, nothing," Marty answered, "nothing." He pretended to notice crate scraps across the podium. "Simulated teak veneer, plastic for sure. Water dispenser, mike, reading light and so forth. Just like the real thing. Whatever they're doing here, the weight must be concealed in the bottom half, though I'll be damned if I can figure out where; there's nothing down there but a shelf and empty space. False bottom? Machinery in the sides? I doubt it, but the only thing I can tell for sure is that it weighs too much."

"Say, are you talking to yourself?" Marty's companion asked. "It sounds like you've been whispering over there."

"Oh. Was I doing that again?" Marty flashed a neon smile buzzing with innocence.

"Jeez," said the other man. "I always get stuck with the weirdoes!"

Across the hall, Dr. Merkin leaned against the waist-high wall skirting the perimeter of the room, gazing at the two men working on the podium. Idly, he watched Marty Huggins' lips move.

The vast hall under the dome gradually filled with people setting up chairs, adjusting lights, testing the sound system. They spread a blue velvet cloth over a table on the podium. Florists arranged exotic bunches of orchids and other tropical blooms around the room. Every country in the world that supported an active AKA Club was represented by a flower. Over all the activity, the dome arched gracefully and poured its pink benediction on the crowd.

At last Merkin nodded and trotted downstairs to the floor below, where the express elevator stood open. It dropped him the 115 stories to ground level in twenty-five seconds. He ducked into the manager's office and made a phone call.

The Countess was stroking her breast when the phone rang.

She wore a gold AKA Club pin, a twenty-four karat gold ring with the AKA intaglio on it set with small but flawless diamonds and tiny gold AKA earrings. She had grown considerably stouter since she dated the Able-bodied Seaman, but her appetite for the sleek pleasures of power and wealth had not diminished.

"Is Bob there?"

"He's asleep," she said. "Ambrose! Is that you?"

"It's me."

"Well, my goodness, I haven't seen you since the welcome home party. How are you? My goodness."

"I'm fine, Countess. Just fine. Do you suppose that you could wake Bob up? It's rather important." Bob was her current husband, the former Governor and current Secretary of the Army.

"Oh, of course, Ambrose. Of course. How's Avery? We were a bit concerned when he didn't show up at the party, you know. I hope everything's all right. I mean, it's strange that we haven't heard anything about him since he returned from *out there*. And there are rumors. He *will* be at the convention, won't he? After all . . ."

"Please, Countess. I'm sure we will all see Avery at the convention. Now would you please wake Bob up?"

"Oh. Why, yes. Well, see you later."

Ambrose reflected on the elegantly framed reproduction of Hiroshige's "Autumn Moon at Ishiyama" on the office wall while he waited for the Secretary of the Army. *The* Blue Light?

"What is it?" asked the Secretary of the Army when he got to the phone.

"You stupid son of a bitch! What the hell are you doing asleep? This is the big day and you were supposed to be over here at the Argo Palace by now!"

"Oh," said the Secretary of the Army, stifling a yawn as vast as his paunch. "Sorry. I'm just so sleepy these days. The Countess had us out to another party last night." He patted his tummy above his unbuttoned pajamas.

"Just get over here!" Ambrose slammed down the receiver.

It rang instantly. "Uncle Ambrose," Angel's fine androgynous tenor said. "Ally's gone and I'm worried. And angry."

"What do you mean, gone?"

"She went out this morning to walk around the house and she never came back."

"Oh, son of a bitch, what the hell are those jerks up to now?" Ambrose mumbled, looking at his watch.

"What's that, Uncle Ambrose?"

"Nothing. Listen, you just hang in there a while. I'll call back as soon as I can."

"Uncle Ambrose, I'm getting *pissed off*. First Dad disappears and neither Ally or I get anywhere finding him. Now Ally's gone. I'm getting pissed."

"I understand, Angel. Just stay with it. I'll see what I can do." He hung up and called the Secretary of the Army again.

"Bob. You were supposed to keep the federal government, and particularly the Department, in line, weren't you? Do you know those jerks have kidnapped Ally Kate Augenblaue?"

"Wha-at?"

"Listen, Bob. You're supposed to be maintaining control, yet things seem to be moving a bit too fast. Angel is very angry, and I can't say I blame . . . Anyway there's a rat stinking here, you understand? If you can't hold up your end, we'll find someone else. Avery is going to be cranky, you understand, very cranky."

"What are you talking about, Ambrose? Avery's disappeared, probably dead. At least, that's the rumor floating around the Pentagon. So how's he gonna be cranky, huh?"

"That's not your concern, Bob. I'm certain Avery will turn up. Tonight there will be almost fifteen thousand people in Chicago, all expecting to see Avery and learn about *The* Blue Light and hear the Answer. Fifteen thousand people from all over the world. We can't tolerate these jerks from the Department being underfoot all the time. So at least figure out what the hell is going on, will you? They aren't following the schedule."

"What schedule? Ambrose, you never gave them a schedule. You never even gave *me* a schedule. What schedule are you talking about?" Bob's voice was querulous.

"Christ almighty!" Ambrose muttered and hung up.

Two seconds later the phone rang. "Merkin."

"Ambrose, goddammit, I'm worried." Kay's voice resembled her hair, stiff and livid.

"What about?" Ambrose was cautious.

Somewhere in Kay's throat a steel stylus was drawn across a vast plain of slate, a hideous screech measured in grams of caffeine — thirteen cups of coffee. "The convention."

"Oh, don't you bother about *that*," he reassured her, realizing she wasn't leveling with him. Avery may have been murdered, but he certainly wasn't dead. Kay was off balance, of course. "By the way," he asked quickly, "how's August?"

"August?" The stylus skipped forward across the slate. "August?" Louder. "August has vitiligo. He looks like hell."

"August has what?" Dr. Merkin smiled.

"Vitiligo. A skin disease. Progressive depigmentation of the skin. Ghastly white spots with red rims. It's embarrassing to have him around."

I'll bet it is, Merkin mused. I'll just bet. "How long has he had this, uh, vitiligo?"

"A couple of months. It's horrible. He's covered with white spots. He looks like some kind of mushroom, for God's sake. Oh, why am I discussing this? I'm anxious about the convention. And I think there are people spying on me. What should I do?"

"Just take it easy," answered Avery's top scientific adviser.

"I think that son of a bitch knows something," Kay shouted at August after she hung up the phone.

28 / Cream of Wheat

"Virge, you're the greatest," said Wanita. He smiled his cherub smile behind the plastic faceguard.

"OK, babe," he said through the buzz of hormones in his head. He pulled himself from between her thighs with a soft *shlup* like the center of an éclair. He unsnapped his helmet, flipped it onto the floor, and beamed his baby smile at her, while with sounds too quiet for the human ear *forniculotermes brevis* munched on through the wooden frames of the dresser and bed.

"Today's the big day, Virge," Wanita reminded him, giving her sopping groin a little toss and slosh. "Labor Day."

"Yep," Virge answered, standing nude and wilting at the window. "And it's a lovely day. Not supposed to be so hot as yesterday, nor so muggy." Virge watched a young boy, couldn't be older than nine, crack the driver's window of a four-year-old

Chevrolet and swiftly and expertly remove the radio and tape deck.

"You'll be seeing him, home from *out there*." Wanita felt delicious, spread-eagled on the wrinkled satin sheets under the fringed canopy of the fourposter.

The Chevrolet's owner stumbled down the front stoop of his house waving a shotgun. Virge heard a faint yell. The boy, arms loaded with radio and tape deck, sped up the street. A dull roar from the shotgun sent radio, tape deck and boy sprawling across the sidewalk.

"I certainly hope I'll get a glimpse of him, babe," Virge said from the window.

"What do you mean?" Wanita demanded. "He'll be at the convention. We saw him return. The pictures were on TV."

Virge's neighbor stood over the body. "Goddammit," Virge could hear the man swearing. "Fucking radio's ruined. Shit."

"Yes, babe. But there have been rumors, at headquarters," Virge said, pursing his lips. Fifteen minutes, he thought. It'll take fifteen minutes for the squad car to get here.

"What kind of rumors, Virge?" Wanita was sitting up now, her pink toes grazing the floor.

"Maybe Avery has disappeared. Maybe he won't show up. Nothing definite, just rumors." Virge was surprised to see the black and white patrol car roll up alongside the body just then. The man with the shotgun was staring disgustedly at the smashed radio in his hands.

"Disappeared?" Wanita asked. "What do you mean, disappeared? He can't have disappeared. We'd have known about it. The whole world's watching him."

"Broke my fucking radio," Virge heard the man say to the policeman. The officer said something and got back in his car. Calling the morgue, Virge thought. Get that body off the street.

"It's been kept real quiet," Virge answered her. "There are several million members of the AKA Clubs. There might be a panic or something. So the word has come down to keep the whole thing under wraps. Don't breathe a word, even to Grandfather Moses." The squad car drove away, leaving the neighbor gazing mournfully at his broken radio.

"But who could keep something like that a secret?" Wanita

wanted to know. She was a member of the AKA Club; she had an enormous faith in Avery and *The* Blue Light and the Answer he was bringing back from *out there*.

"Help! Oh, God, help!" wafted up to the bedroom window from the street below. Virge squinted and saw an elderly woman being robbed in the doorway of her house.

"The word seems to come from the very top," Virge answered.

"You mean . . . ?"

"That's right," Virge finished her sentence, "the President." He gazed sadly out the window. He'd been looking forward to seeing Avery and finding out firsthand about *The* Blue Light; he, too, was a member of the AKA Club. The old woman was still crying for help, but her voice was noticeably weaker. Across the street, the neighbor continued to stare at his radio.

On the first floor, Grandma Moses suddenly shrieked in a voice that penetrated through the floor under Virge's feet like an icepick through tender flesh.

"What was that?" asked Wanita in alarm. "Oh, Grandma Moses. I bet she said, 'Disgusting!' "

"Oh, Christ," moaned Virge near the window, hairy arms hanging at his naked sides. "I'll see what's the matter," he offered but didn't mean it.

"No, dear," said Wanita, sliding into her pink satin robe with a bunny-fur collar, "I'll go."

"OK," sighed Virge.

Wanita found Grandma Moses at the breakfast table, clacking her teeth and waving her spoon in front of her face. Little Jimmy sat in front of a bowl of Cream of Wheat. He had one finger in his nose and his mouth hung open. It was full of cereal.

"Disgusting! You disgusting little boy!" she screamed at Jimmy. "You're a nasty, disgusting boy!" She turned to Wanita. "He's disgusting! You ought to punish him!"

"Kak kak kak, hhhhrrr, guck!" coughed Grandfather Moses across the table. He seemed to be laughing.

"Oh, for God's sake, Jimmy, you stop that. You know it upsets Grandma Moses."

Jimmy looked disappointed, but he closed his mouth and swallowed.

"Kak kak kak, huh huh hnnph!" said Grandfather Moses.

"And you better get on your breathing machine before you croak, Grandfather!" Wanita was annoyed.

"Knk, knk knk," said Grandfather Moses in strange, short, snorting noises. Very solemnly he stuck his finger in his nose. "Knk knk knk!"

"Disgusting!" Grandma Moses got up from the table and stomped into the living room.

Grandfather Moses turned a deeper purple and raced for his room. Wanita waited to hear the wheeze of his breathing machine before she went back upstairs.

"Just Grandma Moses. Little Jimmy was teasing her." She took off her robe and gave a delicious stretch.

"Hmph," said Virge. The old woman had collapsed in front of her door. The robber picked up her purse and walked off down the street, passing the man with the shotgun. The two men said good-morning to each other. The robber whistled as he rummaged through the purse.

"Virge, you must tell me about Avery. You've just *got* to." Wanita sat down on the bed.

"Oh . . ." Virge began but was interrupted by a tremendous explosion on the corner of his block. Orange flames and black smoke billowed from the Italian delicatessen. Two men raced up the street. "Verdi's place is on fire," he said.

"Christ!" said Wanita. "What a neighborhood."

"Ten minutes. At least ten minutes for the fire department."

"Well?" Wanita asked.

"Well, what?"

"You going to tell me about Avery?"

"Oh," said Virge. When he turned away from the window Wanita noticed the gauzy curtains tinged pink by the fire. Virge crossed his arms and leaned against the bedpost. It gave way under his weight, and the bed collapsed with a terrible screeching sound. His heavy body hit the mattress, crashing the two of them to the floor in a tangle of arms and legs. The termites released an intensely concentrated dose of p-chlorophenylalanine into the closed bedroom.

With the first breath the surprised couple drew, massive quantities of the PCPA poured through their lung tissue into their blood, where chemical switches switched, hormones raced, and the most intense imaginable lust coursed through their bodies, propelling them into a mindless rut of such ferocity that an hour later their exhausted bodies continued to twitch spasmodically.

Inside the dresser, *forniculotermes brevis* chewed happily on.

When he finally regained consciousness, Virge realized that he was already two hours late for his duty at the Argo Palace Hotel.

29 / A Glass of Milk

ANGEL CHECKED AROUND the driveway and the forsythia hedge, where he found the remains of three hero sandwiches and a jumble of foot- and kneeprints in the soft ground. He also found a small cluster of mushrooms, the three depressions left by the tripod and forty-five cents in change. Whoever left all this crumpled paper and bits of tomato had snatched Ally. Angel stared down at the bits of tomato. Ants were boiling over them, and they seemed to disappear before his eyes.

Ally Kate had disabled Joseph Harbin with an accidental kick, and he was now hobbling across the room toward her, his knees pressed tightly together, carrying a glass of warm milk.

"You don't really expect me to drink that?" she asked. He set the glass on the table beside her and glared at her.

"Now, Miss Augenblaue," Jonathon Harker began in a patient voice. "You do understand that we are from the government, don't you? The federal government? And that we are trying to find your daddy?"

"So?" Ally stretched her feet out in front of her and curled her toes. Her arms were strapped to the arms of a chair in what she assumed was a hotel room.

"We suspect you might know something about his where-abouts." Harker sat in a straight-backed chair opposite her. He watched as Harbin limped back to the door. "For Christ's sake, Joseph! — Quit walking like that!"

"She damaged me," said Harbin in a mournful tone, his pasty face glazed with sweat.

"Miss Augenblaue," Connie Hubble addressed her from behind. "You are in serious trouble. It's very likely that you are concealing evidence."

"You can't hold me like this!" she protested.

"Of course we can. National security. We can do anything we think necessary to perform our job properly. We could kill you if need be."

"That's not true! It's against the law!" Ally felt a shiver course down her spine.

"We are above the law," said the voice behind her.

"Let's not be hasty. After all, Miss Augenblaue is our guest, and I'm sure there is no need to threaten her, is there, Miss Augenblaue? I'm sure you want to cooperate with us." As he spoke, Jonathon Harker stared at Ally's neck, thought about her mother — orange hair and red fingernails — and experienced an odd sinking sensation in his stomach. Maybe later, maybe later, after she tells us where her father is. She's very young.

Ally felt very alone all of a sudden. Where was her Angel, in whose arms she had rocked to sleep so many nights since their daddy disappeared? He would search for her, but he was only sixteen. Though a very wise sixteen. He'd get help from Uncle Sig or Dr. Merkin. She tried to concentrate on the hotel room, on how long it had taken them to get there, how many turns they had made — things she had seen in the movies. But it all kept sliding into fear.

Near the forsythia, Angel felt fear as the ants carried off the last of the tomato. Then he began to cry soft, silent tears, feeling deep down inside a gathering rage padding back and forth, and as the rage paced and growled low in his throat he forgot to cry, and the tears dried.

"Oh, it's you, Miss Angela." He wheeled around at August's cadaverous voice. August still didn't know Angel had changed sex.

"Hello, August. Yes, it's me. August, Ally's vanished, someone's kidnapped her, we've got to call the police or somebody. Who would do such an awful thing?" He ran out of breath.

"Probably she went for a walk?" August's voice was shrouded in cobwebs.

*

"Take a walk," Harker snapped at Harbin, who stood in the doorway clutching his groin.

"Christ," Harbin said weakly, "I can hardly stand up. She might have broken something."

"Then go lie down. Just don't stand there doubled over like that. It's bad for morale." Ally had been persuaded to drink the milk and was nodding sleepily in her chair. "Jesus," Harker said to Hubble, "sometimes he acts like a kid!"

"Yeah," said Connie Hubble, his hand resting on the nape of Ally's neck. He was reluctant to remove it. She had a soft neck, and her billowing chestnut hair tickled the back of his hand. He was the only one of the three of them not to have had a relationship with Ally's mother. He guessed the daughter, though, might be similarly inclined. "Tell me again about your relationship with Mrs. Augenblaue," he said, stroking the fragile neckbones under his hand.

"Christ!" said Harker, rolling his eyes toward the ceiling, eyes so pale that even when only the whites showed, as now, there was little discernible difference in color. "I was in her house ten years ago as a member of the fire department rescue squad. You remember. The butler pinned to the bed. I've never seen such a mess. Someone had fallen through the skylight. Anyway, there was something very strange about the woman. She kept coming at me!" His tapioca face looked inward for a moment. "Finally I got away."

"Yeah," said Connie. His fingers dipped beneath the back of Ally's dress. "She fucked the brains out of ole Joe a while back. He told me she led him into the solarium, closed the door, and practically raped him."

"Oh, come on," Harker said, his irritation showing. "Let's question her. We haven't got much time."

"If you wish, I will call the police," August said to Angel, his monotonous voice displaying no conviction whatsoever.

"Oh, damn, August, we haven't got time for the police. I've already called Dr. Merkin, but surely there's something else we can do to find Ally, something *immediate*. Maybe the same people got her that got Daddy. What do you think? August? August, are you all right?" The butler was sitting in the driveway pulling at his tightly knotted tie.

"Air!" he gasped. "Need air. Hhhhhhhgk." He sounded like a pump gone dry.

"What's going on around here?" Angel asked as he tugged with August at the constricting tie. This close Angel could smell the damp-earth odor the butler always broadcast and was vividly reminded of the small clump of mushrooms under the forsythia hedge.

When August was breathing more easily, though his face was still shining wet, Angel, concerned, asked if he would live. August nodded, swallowed, and answered yes.

"August," Angel asked, remembering Philbrick Weevol's theory and momentarily distracted by August's smell, "do you like mushrooms?"

"Angel . . ." Ally Kate was saying in a slurry voice. "Angel, come . . ." She dozed again.

"Christ almighty," Harker said for the tenth time. He slapped her gently a couple of times.

"Who's Angel?" Connie asked, sliding his hands back and forth over the soft flesh over her collarbones.

"Must mean Angela, her kid sister," said Harker. He slapped her again. "Unless she's turned religious. Wake up, Alicia."

"Hunh?" Ally said. Her luminous brown eyes opened and looked blearily at her questioner. She didn't seem to notice the hands working on her shoulders.

"Alicia, who is Angel?" Harker leaned forward anxiously. There was not much time, he hadn't slept in two days, and he could feel the Dexedrine buzz faltering in his system.

"Angel? Mmmm. Brother. My brother," she said sleepily. "Wanna sleep."

Me too, thought Harker. "You don't have a brother, Alicia. You have a sister. Where is your father?" She had fallen asleep.

Hubble buried his nose into her thick chestnut hair, taking long shuddering inhalations. His hands slid past the light dusting of freckles on her chest and worked feverishly at the buttons of her dress.

"For God's sake, Connie, *stop that!*" Harker ordered sharply. The sudden shout awakened Ally, who whipped her head up to focus on Harker, striking Hubble viciously in the nose with the top of her head. Blood gushed from his broken nose as he screamed and, throwing both hands up to his ruined face, fell over backward.

August climbed unsteadily to his feet with Angel's help. "I think I'll be all right, Miss Angela," he said in a voice so close and airless it seemed to yawn before him like a freshly opened grave.

They had started down the driveway when abruptly they both stopped in amazement as a dwarf, dressed from head to toe in a rabbit costume, bounded in a hopping lope down the hill in front of them and around the house.

30 / Rabbit Stew

VIRGE MOSES was more than two hours late to his post at the Argo Palace. By the time he got dressed and down to the street, his car had been vandalized, all four tires were flat, the trunk had been pried open, and the spare was missing. He had to wait for another car from headquarters to fetch him. It was delayed by the crowds gathered to watch Verdi's delicatessen burn down while Mr. Verdi banged his head on the curb in front of his store.

The second the car pulled up at the Argo Palace, Virge ran inside, trying to buckle on his gun belt and carrying his helmet. He dropped the helmet twice, further delaying himself, so when he arrived at his post at the express elevator, where he was to check everyone's pass, he just missed seeing the dwarf in a rabbit costume hopping into the elevator.

"I certainly hope no one's gotten by this elevator," he muttered to himself. He adjusted the NO ADMITTANCE sign. "Christ, I'm really late."

"What'd you say?" Dudee Sparrow stood beside him waiting for the express elevator. Philadelphia cowered and drooled at the end of his leash.

"Nothing. Nothing," Virge mumbled. "Uh, are you waiting for the express?" He gave her a suspicious glance.

"Yes, I am. Be quiet, Philly," she said, glaring at her whining, repulsive dog.

"May I see your pass then, please? No one is allowed up to the top floor without a pass."

"Of course," said Dudee, rummaging in her purse. "Where is the damn thing, I wonder?" She glanced up and asked, "Isn't my AKA pin enough? Never mind, here it is."

"Thank you, ma'am. You can go on up."

"It's Ms."

"Yes. Ms."

"But I don't understand why I have to show my pass. What about the dwarf that just went up? You weren't here to look at *his* pass."

"Dwarf?" Virge felt a cold wind pass over his face.

"That's right. The dwarf."

"What dwarf? What'd he look like?"

"In a rabbit suit," said Dudee firmly. "Very odd."

"Oh, my God," groaned Virge, grabbing his walkie-talkie from his belt and calling for help.

"A dwarf?" Ambrose asked into the telephone. He drummed his fingers on his box of lemon lozenges.

"Yes, Dr. Merkin. A dwarf. We thought you ought to know." August's sepulchral voice seemed to contaminate the earpiece of the phone with mildew, and Ambrose held it slightly away from his ear.

"In a rabbit suit, you say?" Merkin was standing behind his desk in the manager's office on the ground floor of the hotel. He felt with his tongue for the lemon lozenge lodged behind his left molars and tugged thoughtfully at his muttonchops.

"Yes, sir. Hopping on the lawn."

"Hopping? Oh, boy. All right, August, I'll check into it."

He hung up and punched another number. "Avery? Do you know anything about a dwarf? In a rabbit suit?" He listened for a moment. "Hopping on your lawn. That's right. OK."

He dialed another number. "Bob? You find out anything about what the Department's up to yet? Well, what the hell have you been doing all this time?"

"Gee, I'm sorry, Ambrose, but I can't seem to get hold of Buck Sweeney. He's left Washington. But I'm pretty sure he's the one behind the snatch of the girl. They're beating the bushes for

Avery, and according to my sources, they're getting desperate. Something about their computer and statistics." Bob sounded troubled; his political career was at stake, and if it should be made public that he was connected with all this AKA stuff, he'd be fired from his job as Secretary of the Army and thrown out in the street.

At least I'll still have the Countess, he consoled himself, but somehow it wasn't a very comforting thought.

"Bob, do you know anything about a dwarf?" Ambrose flicked the lozenge from behind his molars and sucked on it vigorously.

"Dwarf?"

"Yeah. A dwarf in a rabbit suit hopping around Avery's lawn this morning. About two hours ago."

"Oh, come on, Ambrose. What would I know about a dwarf in a rabbit suit? Who told you about it, anyway?"

"August."

"For God's sake, Ambrose. That creep is probably hallucinating. He's got some kind of weird skin disease, you know. Maybe it's attacked his brain."

"OK, Bob. Keep trying to get hold of Buck. We'd better rescue Avery's daughter before tonight, when the convention starts, or heads will roll." He slammed down the phone and chomped down on the lozenge, which shattered in his mouth. He spit out the pieces and left the office, walking swiftly to the elevator, where he found ten police officers checking their weapons.

"What's going on here?" he demanded.

"Who are you?" Virge asked.

"Dr. Merkin. I'm running this convention. Who are you?"

"Officer Moses." Virge shoved the last slug into place and clicked the weapon shut, holding it loosely in front of him. "I didn't recognize you, Dr. Merkin, sorry. We're about to go after the dwarf."

Dr. Merkin's tongue probed at a loose filling. Have to stop sucking these lozenges, he was thinking, when the word "dwarf" penetrated. "Dwarf? Oh, God . . ."

"Yes, sir. In a . . ."

"Rabbit suit," Ambrose cut in. "I heard. And where is he?"

"Uh, he sneaked past the guards, Dr. Merkin. And onto the elevator." That cold wind howled across Virge's face. He tried to smile, to pretend it wasn't his fault, that he wasn't the guard the dwarf had gotten past, but his little cupid mouth spread into a sad cherub pout.

"Who's supposed to be guarding this elevator?" Ambrose allowed some dark clouds to gather on the horizon of his voice.

"Uh, I am," Virge answered, his sweet eyes nearly filling with tears. He wagged his gun briefly. "I was, uh, detained. My car was vandalized and there was a fire . . ."

"I don't give a damn about that! If you don't find that *dwarf* your head is going to be on the chopping block. He can't get far, for God's sake. The express elevator stops only at the floor just below the dome. He must be up there somewhere!"

The elevator door opened, and Virge hoped the dwarf would be inside. But the elevator was empty. Virge, the other nine officers and Dr. Merkin all piled into the car, and Virge stabbed at the buttons.

The car sank swiftly to the basement and the door opened. The twelve of them rushed from the car, eleven of them waving their pistols in the air. They ran ten or twelve paces before they realized they were not on the top floor.

"Jesus," Virge grumbled. They rushed back into the elevator, Ambrose the last in, and when he turned around to face forward, a smile flickered across his face.

"What was that all about?" Marty Huggins asked the man next to him. They were uncrating more sound equipment.

"You got me. Looked like a bunch of cops."

"That's what it looked like to me, too," Marty said. "Hey, I gotta go to the bathroom. Be right back." He headed off to the janitor's toilet. Once out of sight he whispered, "Listen. There's something going on around here. Bunch of cops just ran out of the elevator and then back in. Waving guns. Seems like some kind of manhunt."

"OK, Mr. Sweeney," he answered. "I'll get right on it." He sauntered back to the half-opened crates. "Let's haul some of this stuff upstairs," he said. "We can finish uncrating this other stuff later."

"Suit yourself," the other man said. "You're the boss." They rang for the elevator.

"You mean this elevator goes to the basement?" Virge was asking. "Oh, my God. Why didn't they tell me that when I was briefed for this job? There could be millions of people in the convention hall by now!"

The express rose to the top. Ambrose had just asked Virge in a surprisingly calm voice if anyone had been guarding the basement. Twenty-five seconds later the elevator opened on the top floor, and once again the twelve rushed out into the corridor.

They stopped in absolute horror when they saw a bunny suit lying crumpled at the foot of the helical stair that wound around the inner wall of the hotel to the convention floor. Ambrose picked it up and dangled it in the air. It would fit a stocky man forty-two inches tall perfectly. But there was no stocky forty-two-inch-tall man in sight.

"All right, men. Spread out. We've got to find that dwarf!" Virge shouted, and the eleven policemen scattered, opening doors and poking into corners. Five of them sprinted up the stairs, still waving their guns. Behind Ambrose the elevator doors sighed shut, and the car dropped back to the basement to pick up Marty Huggins and his companion, who arrived fifty-five seconds later with a pair of public address speakers and a microphone.

"Hey! What's going on?" Marty asked with a languid wave of his hand at the busy policemen. Ambrose, tugging gently at his muttonchops and probing his filling with his tongue, shrugged.

"Looking for a dwarf," he said, squinting at the ceiling.

"Oh," said Marty. He touched his throat. "Looking for a dwarf," he whispered.

"A dwarf?" his earphone twittered. "Whose dwarf?"

Buck Sweeney, racing in his Lear jet to Chicago, was very puzzled. "A dwarf," he said to himself. "We didn't send in any dwarf."

31 / A Pot of Jam

CHICAGO WAS A POT OF JAM this day. The air above was filled with bees, circling in for the sweet news of *The* Blue Light and the strong round tower of the Argo Palace Hotel. As jets wound down from holding pattern to approach, their places were taken instantly by other jets, and all were buzzing with members of AKA International fingering their little gold lapel pins and whispering to one another. From plane to gate to taxi to hotel, a high, faint whine of excitement kept them all keyed to one common frequency: *The* Blue Light, and over and over, Avery, Avery, Avery.

Betsy Sue Sox was no exception, a small, slender, smooth woman of forty-two, former Reformed Baptist and farmer's daughter, wife to Edouard, beside her dressed in blue, looking out the window at the gradually browning air over Chicago and the sluggish yellow river that sucked and bubbled at the foot of the Argo Palace tower as the plane banked back westward for the approach to O'Hare — no exception at all. She felt in her trim self from knee to throat a fine wire, drawn tight, resonate with the high blue fiddle-pitch of AKA.

Eddie all in blue was still large and tough. She let her head sink against the headrest and closed her eyes. As the plane touched down a fleeting image of Duane Hemp at the Crystal Grape floated across her inner lids. Duane in his Stetson hat, tanned and muscles jumping, and she reached over and held her Eddie's arm.

"Do you feel it, Eddie?" she whispered.

"Feel what, honeypot?" Ed whispered back, giving her dainty hand a squeeze, and thought, I probably do, whatever.

"The excitement, Eddie. I don't know, anticipation, something." Maybe it's just me, she thought.

"That's it for sure, honeypot. I'm nervous, a bit. On accounta the speech tomorrow."

"You're gonna be fine tomorrow, Eddie. You know the furniture business like nobody else, except maybe Mr. Akley, and he had the confidence in you to ask *you* to give the speech tomorrow, so don't you worry none at all. You're gonna do just fine. I know it." She patted his arm and felt its hardness.

"Can't say I really understand why they want a session on furniture, honeypot. This is the first AKA convention we've been to, so I suppose I wouldn't understand. I'm gonna do it, but I don't really know why. What does furniture have to do with *The* Blue Light?"

But Ed smiled his new wide California smile, white and tan, when he asked the question, because Betsy Sue really wanted him to give the speech, and Mr. Akley, whom Ed had never, ever understood, wanted him to, so by God he would.

In the limousine from the airport they sat behind William Lamplighter, who was wearing his bulky overcoat. Nurse Thinger radiated her love for him through her fingers in his overcoat pocket as well as through her eyes. She slid her hand down through the opening inside the coat pocket until it rested on the slumbering dragon in his pants.

"We're to take notes, you know," she said. "Dr. Ague was most insistent. We're to take notes. He thinks *The* Blue Light may have something to do with his research at the clinic."

"I didn't know that," Bill rumbled, "but it makes sense. Art wanted me to come for the same reason. Thought eroticism might be related, like what happened at the launch. I think he's got a crew here filming the convention too." His dragon turned in its slumber as Nurse Thinger's fingers ran up and down its back.

It wasn't until the limousine pulled up in front of the Argo Palace Hotel and the agitated press corps popped flashbulbs and video cameras in their faces that they all realized that among the other passengers in the car were the famous Philbrick Weevol and his girl.

"Philbrick! Philbrick! Philbrick!" chanted a huge crowd of eleven-year-old girls held back by a staggering line of uniformed policemen with linked hands and plastic bubble heads. "Philbrick! Philbrick! Philbrick!"

"Philbrick Weevol's here!" squeaked Betsy Sue to Ed. "He was on the plane with us and we didn't recognize him. Gosh, Eddie!"

"Philbrick! Philbrick! Philbrick!" chanted the crowd, and Betsy Sue, peering out the window as the car slid to a stop, noticed that they had all painted their faces blue.

Even Nurse Thinger looked up. "That's the man who sings 'Children of Paradise,' isn't he? We used to see him at the Third Eye. Remember, Bill? He's coming to the convention!"

"Wonderful," said Bill. "With him here, Art's movie is going to be bigger than *Woodstock*."

"Philbrick! Philbrick! Philbrick!" chanted the thousands of prepubescent girls, and even the police holding them back tried to crane their heads around to get a glimpse. Philbrick Weevol was *big*, and they knew it. This was something to tell their kids about.

A uniformed Argo Palace doorman opened the limousine door, and Phil and China sprinted through the cleared lane to the hotel while the crowd screamed and shoved against the weakening line of helmeted police. The rhythmic chant continued during the screaming. Betsy Sue and Ed, dazed by the shouting and chanting, the sea of blue faces and the frenzy, climbed out and stared around them. Lamplighter and Nurse Thinger emerged smiling and unrecognized. They made it inside the hotel just as the line of police collapsed and was trampled under the crush of wildly screaming groupies.

"Philbrick! Philbrick! Philbrick!" The roar continued from the street, though muted by the heavy door that closed behind the delegates.

The lobby was more peaceful, despite the energetic bustle, as delegates from every nation milled around the registration desk. They picked up their programs from a large table in the center of the lobby and pinned on their nametags, with AKA, in gold, at the top.

"What's going on there, Eddie?" Betsy Sue asked, pointing. A cop with a worried expression raced from one end of the lobby to the other. A moment later two more sprinted after him. They disappeared through a revolving door.

Then they returned, followed by a man in a business suit carrying what appeared to be a rabbit costume, and vanished through an arch that bore the sign ELEVATORS. A man in muttonchop whiskers emerged through the arch glancing back over his shoulder and shaking his head. Two policemen escorted Weevol and his girl to the elevators and whisked them away as the front doors crashed open and a small, frenzied knot of blue-faced girls hurtled through.

"There he is!" someone shouted, and the chanting began again, "Philbrick! Philbrick! Philbrick!" Reinforcements of riot police poured through the swinging door and finally managed to push the girls back outside.

The man carrying the bunny suit reappeared and handed it to the man in muttonchops, who shook his head again as the man raced back toward the elevators.

"What's that?" Nurse Thinger, who'd been observing the racing back and forth, asked the man in muttonchops.

"This? Oh, it's a rabbit suit," he answered. He walked over to a door marked PRIVATE and disappeared inside.

"They're searching for a dwarf," someone said.

"This place is going nuts," someone else said.

"I'm told the dwarf was wearing a rabbit suit."

"You know who that was? That was Dr. Ambrose Merkin. The guy who invented the orgone drive that propelled Avery into intergalactic space."

"I thought he looked familiar."

"Oh, Eddie. Isn't it exciting!" said Betsy Sue.

"Sure is, honeypot. Listen."

Over the noises of milling delegates and scurrying police, faintly, as if from very far away, from intergalactic space itself, the strains of the AKA Club theme could be heard over the hotel's music system:

> Shiva dancing in Buddha's navel
> The dance of Cosmic Coitus . . .

32 / Angel Food Cake

A DOZEN SMALL BORDER WARS were being fought inside Kay Augenblaue's stunned and compact body that first of September morning. She sat in the glinting dazzle of the kitchen, pouring down those final drops of her fourteenth cup of French roast with hot milk, and her outraged neck and shoulder nerves marched discordantly into combat with the muscles there, raising a terrible din.

Coffee acid hit her stomach and hurled the combined weight of fourteen cups against her stomach wall; a hot tendril of distress crawled up and down, infiltrating the already panicked regions of her lower abdomen. Vast armies of fear, hatred, vengeance, revulsion and lust swept through her, fought bitterly, retreated and advanced, dug in, collapsed, reformed, made wedges and phalanxes and pincer movements in such strange and chaotic actions that one foot was fibrillating and the other seemed to have fallen asleep.

In her crimson mouth lay the bitter taste of hatred for Avery, who had wished on her so long ago the distorted lust she had for the butler. Things had never been the same since that column of blue light had dissipated into the crowd on that day ten years before when her husband left for the silence and velvet darkness of intergalactic space. In those ten years her hatred grew and fed upon itself, a dry but slithery snake forever swallowing its own tail, because the one thing she had always hated more than anything else in the world was sex, and Avery had catapulted her onto the rigid organ of their unctuous underground butler, who was equally helpless to stop it.

The cook, a ghostly woman starched in white, crept fearfully around the kitchen, careful not to bang pots together or slam the cupboard doors. She cleared a circle around her mistress, a sacred space five yards in radius into which she would not enter, so charged was it with the ions of hate and fear.

Kay slammed down her dainty cup so hard she cracked the saucer. "Damn!" she groaned under her breath. Across the cinerama of her imagination walked the youthful, handsome Avery, a smile crinkling the corners of his ice blue eyes: a mockery. She replayed that night of his return: August's sloshing in the steam in his wetsuit, knife in hand and hatchet, and gun, herself close behind him whispering urgently in his ear.

The screams: terrifying and satisfying at once.

And the catatonic moment when Avery was gone.

"Ma'am," August said at her elbow suddenly, and Kay realized she had been crushing her coffee cup into its broken saucer like an unwanted cigarette.

She turned to him with a soft hiss. "What is it?"

"We'd best be going. Mr. Sparrow has called twice. And Dr. Merkin just called back. He wants us both to come down to the hotel. He says we can't do anything about your daughter here, and he may have some information for you."

"My daughter? Oh, God, I forgot about her. Which one was it again?"

"Alicia Katherine, ma'am. She was kidnapped, apparently. Remember?"

"Yes." Kay stood up and hopped numbly on her sleeping foot. "Let's go."

"Mom," said Angel through lips thinned with rage as Kay and August marched in step across the parquet to the front door.

"Yes?" Angel was at the doors to the solarium.

"Somebody better locate Ally." Kay felt more menace in that sentence than she deemed possible for a frail sixteen-year-old girl; the armies of hatred temporarily retreated and the armies of fear advanced. What the hell is going on? Kay wondered, and the small orange hairs at the back of her neck rose.

She thinned her own lips. "Of course, Angela. We're leaving for the hotel now. Dr. Merkin and Uncle Sig are working on it. We'll find out what has happened, so don't you worry about it."

There was a long pause as the two of them faced each other across the polished parquet, and August stared down at his shining shoes, his eerie face glowing with an unhealthy pallor through his spots.

"And someone better find Dad," said Angel at last, coming toward them. "Let's go."

"You're not coming with us?" Kay asked, though she had meant it to be a command. The three walked out to the car and drove downtown in utter silence.

It was almost noon. The Chicago air was gradually shellacking the city with layer after layer of dirty brown, and through the bottom layer the large white Augenblaue Rolls-Royce Silver Cloud flowed like a leucocyte on its way to an infection. August sat stiffly at the wheel, hat brim down, dark glasses over his eyes, collar up, hands gloved. But nothing could conceal the moldy smell of cellars and fear that exhumed itself from his clothes and overpowered the car's climate control. He stared straight ahead at the road, resonating, in part to the violent tides of hatred, fear and rage that crackled inside Kay and in part to the clouded memories of the steambath that rose unbidden in fragments. As he drove, the road seemed to rise and fall under the car, reptilian and alive, and the early September trees, some of them beginning to clothe themselves in vibrant fall colors, writhed obscenely in the dirty air. It took all his concentration to keep the car on the road.

Kay sat in the back and simmered in her agonizing stew of caffeine, rage and fear.

Angel, too, felt fear, a fear that gusted in waves from his livid mom, but he had to acknowledge that it was fear *of* Kay that he felt, staring out the window at the passing cityscape and early autumn leaves and tarnished buildings. And fear of Ally's absence, and fear that Avery was gone forever, in some strange way destroyed by the thin-lipped bloody dagger that was his mother.

But at Angel's core was a powerful, righteous certainty that the truth would assert itself, that the world was waiting for Avery and would welcome him if it could, and that when the truth appeared Angel would act, no matter what. At last the Argo Palace loomed before them.

When August saw it, the rubber road started to burble under the car. He twisted the steering wheel, trying to control the feeling of changing altitude, though in reality the street was perfectly level. The hotel wavered in front of him as well, and the doors, as they pulled up, yawned dark and wide and then snapped shut with a sound of teeth. August squeezed his eyes closed and opened them again, and the hotel smiled at him with a knowing leer. A window winked in invitation, and August gripped the ivory wheel tightly in his gloved hands. What is happening? he thought, and through his groin a terrible *tsunami* of powerful lust roared in a mindless rush and as swiftly passed, leaving peculiar wreckage on his beach. He stopped the car with one tire on the curb and sat perfectly still, clutching the steering wheel.

Kay waited. In the silence, the ticking of the digital clock in the dash was loud.

"August?" He didn't answer.

"August! Turn off the engine. We're here."

In the back seat Angel smiled a mirthless smile, watching his mother furrow her brow, a brow slightly dewed with sweat in spite of the climate control.

At length August, with a mechanical movement, reached down and switched off the engine.

"August. We'd like to get out of the car. Please open the door." Kay was in command once more.

Angel opened his own door and breezed into the hotel without a backward glance. Kay continued to sit in the car, waiting for August, her butler and lover, to open the door for her. This was one power struggle Kay was determined not to lose.

August stared straight ahead for a time, watching the hood of the car slither toward him. Strange, he thought. Very strange. His fear had disappeared. Finally he tore his eyes away and stepped out into the radiant air. For several seconds he caressed the side of the car, whose velvety flanks rose and fell under the gloved palm in quiet breathing.

"There, there, boy," he murmured, gently stroking the door. "There, there." Then he opened the door for Kay and watched as she bounded gracefully from her seat, one slender leg before the other, in a long slow-motion ballet leap to the ground. Her hair, he noted, formed a rosy halo of flame around her face of wrath, and deep inside August experienced the first stirrings of something very much like awe. She's an avenging angel, it dawned on him. Terrible love, he thought, two thousand years of Balkan Christianity descending on him.

"Christ, August," she hissed. "I want you to snoop around. We've got to find out if anyone knows anything about Avery. *Someone* removed his body, dammit, and it wasn't us."

August's silvered sunglasses glared impassively at her, reflecting her anxious expression. She curled her crimson lips and stained her teeth with lipstick.

She couldn't see the rapture on his face as he stood in the noon heat gazing at her. "Let's get going," she said.

He followed her, in step, into the hotel.

33 / In the Oven

BUCK SWEENEY'S LEAR JET banked over the lake and entered the noon pollution at nine hundred feet on its approach to Meigs Field. The sun was by now working its alchemical magic on the brown stuff, turning it slowly to poison. Two hundred and seventy-three people would die of causes directly related to the polluted air that strangely windless day.

Buck chewed on his fingernails, his florid head filled with ranks of well-disciplined and naked seventeen-year-old girls delivering snappy salutes. He had stopped off for a couple of hours very early that morning at a special place in Washington to administer some very satisfying spankings. But the satisfaction had evaporated. Two members of Team A had been disabled by their prisoner, a small slip of a *girl*, for Christ's sake! And now he had a missing dwarf to worry about as well. Whose dwarf?

"The sister is here, in the hotel," Marty Huggins tinny voice twittered in Buck's ear. "Mrs. Augenblaue and the butler are here, too — the one she's been, uh, you know . . ." Marty's voice trailed away.

"I know," said Buck. "Get on with it." The jet's tires squeaked twice on the runway and the engines reversed.

"No sign of the dwarf. If there is a dwarf; I'm beginning to have my doubts."

"You're not paid to have doubts. You're paid to report."

"Yes, sir. This place is in turmoil, anyway. The police have been examining the rabbit costume. That, at least, exists."

"I'll be there in twenty minutes." Buck slammed his receiver back into its cradle and the projector in his head shut down. The girls disappeared. A waiting patrol car sped him to the hotel with rotating beacon and sirens wailing.

"It has come to my attention," Dr. Merkin said to Buck when they met in the manager's office, "that your department has, uh, detained Avery's daughter Alicia Katherine. Avery will be very upset about that, I assure you. I suggest that she be, uh, released as soon as possible. Sooner, in fact. Avery may already be on to you." Ambrose tugged hard at his muttonchops and winced.

"This is the first I've heard of it," Buck lied, but he was visibly disturbed. Not only were his agents being disabled left and right, but word had somehow leaked that the department was responsible. He'd have to plug the hole in his security.

The hole in his security was puffing across the lobby at that moment in the shape of the Secretary of the Army, who mopped futilely at the soggy back of his neck as he jogged toward the elevators. Things were slightly amiss, he huffed. Who the hell was this dwarf everyone was so excited about?

He ran into Officer Moses at the elevators.

"Any sign of this dwarf?" He mopped at his neck with a damp handkerchief, one of the three dozen monogrammed the Countess had bought him for Christmas. He had given her the diamond broach.

"No, sir. He's simply disappeared. The boys are checking the ventilation system right now, but I doubt they'll find him." Virge still felt that Arctic breeze across his face, though it had picked up some and was blowing through his abdomen as well. The dwarf was his responsibility. "He seems to have vanished into thin air."

"That's not possible," said the Secretary of the Army, swinging around to jog to Ambrose's office. He entered just as Ambrose was confronting Buck Sweeney.

"My source is very good," Ambrose was saying. "We are aware that you ordered Alicia's detention. She knows nothing about her father's whereabouts, so you might as well let her go. You are annoying some very important people, Buck. Some very important people."

"*I* happen to be a very important person, *Doctor* Merkin." Buck assumed his professional voice. "I have the backing of the Director himself. There is no one more important than the Director. Anywhere. I follow his orders. *Everyone* does. His word is the Law, *Doctor* Merkin. The *Law*. To deny that is to be a fool!" That'll show him, Buck thought.

Ambrose sucked on his lozenge, tugged at his muttonchops, and glanced at the Secretary of the Army standing in the doorway dabbing at his forehead with his monogrammed handkerchief.

"Buck." Ambrose spoke at last in a quiet voice. "Do you remember what happened, ten years ago, to the President?"

"Huh? Why, he disappeared." Buck was confused.

"That's right," Ambrose continued. "He disappeared. And your Department searched for him, didn't it?"

"Yes," Buck answered, and somewhere deep in his hindbrain his father selected a birch rod.

"You haven't found him yet, have you?" Ambrose asked, and in Buck's animal synapses the birch fell and fell on his trembling backside.

"No. But we will, Dr. Merkin, we will. The Department never fails. The Director has decreed it, but you must understand that this matter has a rather low priority right now. At the moment the Director is very anxious to find Avery Augenblaue. Do you have any idea where Avery Augenblaue is, *Doctor* Merkin?" Buck shifted back to the offensive, stiffened in his resolve by the beating he had just received.

"Of course not," Ambrose lied in turn. "No one does. But he *is* somewhere, of that you may be sure, Mr. Sweeney. Of that you may be sure. And I think you should keep in mind that former President, *Mister* Sweeney."

"Do you really think he's somewhere, Dr. Merkin?" Angel's tight small voice curled around the bulk of the Secretary of the Army standing in the doorway. "Do you *really* think so?"

"Come in, Angela," Ambrose said. "Of course he is. Now don't you worry. He'll show up. I'm sure of it."

"This is the younger daughter, isn't it?" Sweeney asked, lining up in his head Angela's file photo with the androgynous youth in front of him.

"Yes," said Ambrose. "Angela, this is Buck Sweeney, of the Department of . . ."

"I'm familiar with Mr. Sweeney, Dr. Merkin. He's almost as famous as the Director. How do you do? Are you trying to find my father, Mr. Sweeney?" Angel gravely shook Buck's hand, his smooth face handsome and sober as he looked him in the eye. "Someone has kidnapped my sister Alicia, Mr. Sweeney. Three men who eat sandwiches with tomato in them. Three men who have been spying on our house, men with a telescope, or at least something on a tripod. Men who lost forty-five cents in change under our forsythia hedge. Here it is. She was grabbed this morning about nine. Are you on it, Mr. Sweeney?" Innocence rose from Angel's words like steam from a bowl of chicken soup.

Buck had a smile on his face. It was a strange sort of smile, a smile that seemed to start very far inside his face as Angel began talking, and the smile-stuff behind it evaporated as she continued, leaving a set expression resembling a decal carefully applied to the front of his face. Behind the smile was a growing bewilderment. As he smiled and smiled at the solemn and determined face of this sixteen-year-old, Buck's mind worked rapidly: this teen-age girl is really a *boy* and no dummy at all. Buck eyed his watch.

"Twelve-thirty," he muttered, still smiling.

"Well, are you?" Angel insisted. He knows something, Angel realized, he *knows*.

"Uh, what? Oh, no, no, nothing. We'll look into it. I mean, Dr. Merkin here just told me about it, that is. Damn. And who are you?" He turned swiftly to the Secretary of the Army.

"Who, me? I'm Bob . . ."

"Oh, hello, Bob. What're you doing here?" Back on the offensive. Keep things moving. Keep the opposition off balance. That's the ticket.

"Me?" said the Secretary of the Army. "Oh, uh, well, hmm." Bob cleared his throat. "God, it's awfully hot in this hotel, isn't it, Ambrose?"

"No," said Ambrose. "It's a constant seventy-one degrees." No help there.

"Well?" Buck asked, leaning on Bob a little.

Ambrose smiled. A real smile. This was kinda fun.

"Well," said Bob, straightening. "I'm here for the convention, of course. Ambrose asked me to help him out a bit, do a little investigating on my own, as it were."

"Jesus!" Buck said. "Investigating?"

"It seems there's a mysterious dwarf loose on the convention floor that the police can't find. In a rabbit suit." Bob mopped his sweating face.

"Right," said Buck briskly. "Well, better get busy. There's a lot to do. I'll check with you later, Ambrose."

"Remember," said Ambrose, halting Buck at the door, "the President."

"Aaah," said Buck and continued out the door, slapping his thigh with the imaginary riding crop.

"Dr. Merkin, there's something very weird going on around here!" Angel was close to tears, but they were tears of rage.

"Don't fret, Angel. We'll find your daddy and sister."

He called me Angel, Angel thought. Was it a slip? Something is definitely going on.

34 / Cold Cuts

"SOMETHING'S UP," squabby Bunny Darlitch, soft and dimpled, murmured into Reba Hare's sweet right ear. The ear was faintly blue, a cyanotic shell half buried in the littered beach of her hair.

"Evidently," she whispered back, gazing through the coffee

shop window into the lobby of the Argo Palace, where uniformed policemen paced, hands twitching nervously near the butts of their pistols. A half-dozen hard-eyed cops in nondescript suits, narrow ties and short hair lounged around the lobby trying very hard to pass as guests.

"It can't just be the convention," he whispered. "I've never seen so many cops in one place before outside of a policeman's ball. They all look worried, too." He fished out his *Boric Acid Weekly* press card. "I'm nosing around."

It was 4:30 in the afternoon on the first of September. Tomorrow was Labor Day, and tonight the AKA convention began. The dirty brown air outside the air-conditioned hotel had already claimed the first thirty-seven of its victims. The temperature had topped ninety at 3:14 P.M., then dropped to eighty-seven. The stagnant high pressure area over eastern Iowa, Wisconsin and northern Illinois showed no signs of moving. Lake Michigan seethed with violet bubbles, soapsuds, hydrocarbons and acids.

Angel Augenblaue seethed as well while he pretended to read the latest issue of *Lake Michigan Boater* at the magazine stand. He'd uncovered no clues to Ally's whereabouts and had no concrete help from Dr. Merkin, despite his promise. Angel had combed the hall for Sig Sparrow in vain, though he had spotted Dudee on the convention floor stroking her slavering dog, Philadelphia. She had no information.

Angel was gazing blankly at an article about a new, jet-powered racing boat with a 795 horsepower engine, capable of speeds in excess of 237 mph, when two men in white carried a stretcher through the lobby toward the elevators. He had a hunch and followed them.

Bunny Darlitch also followed them, his journalistic intuition buzzing for attention. So Angel and Bunny watched the numbers on the elevator climb to 96, then they both took the next car and reached together to punch 96.

"Sorry," Bunny muttered.

"Quite all right," Angel said, and they stood in silence as the local car lifted them to the ninety-sixth floor. They stepped out together and saw the two men with the stretcher scurry around the corner to the right.

"You watching those guys?" Angel asked.

"Hm? Oh, yeah. I'm a reporter. There's something very funny going on around here."

"You're damn right!" Angel responded with considerable energy.

"Name's Bunny," he said, "Bunny Darlitch. Of the *Boric Acid Weekly*."

"Call me Angel. I used to read the *Boric Acid Weekly* in San Francisco. Right?"

"Right. Come on, they're turning left up there."

The door to Suite 9614 was open when Angel and Bunny strolled by. Inside, the stretcher lay on the floor. They stopped to listen.

"This is the second time we've been up here today. Just what goes on in this room, anyway?" The voice was squeaky and petulant, obviously one of the medics.

"Never mind," said a voice so soft and bland and filled with tapioca curds that it could suffocate, a voice that was nonetheless white with strain. "Just get him to a hospital."

"That voice sounds very familiar," Angel whispered.

"Not to me," Bunny answered. "But then, I'm from San Francisco."

"Jesus!" said the first voice. "What the hell happened to him? I've never seen anything like that in all my years chasing accidents. Looks like a dog got him."

"You wouldn't believe it if I told you," said the second voice, its pudding surface glazed with sweat.

The first voice said, "You don't look so good yourself. Come to think of it, you didn't look so good when we picked up that other guy. The one with the smashed nose. What's happened to you?"

"Never mind, will you? Just get this man to a hospital."

"Oh, don't worry about *him*. He'll be all right. Just now he don't care about nothing. He's out cold. Like a light. But we gotta know what happened to him. Otherwise, how we gonna treat him?"

"Oh, he tripped," said the tapioca voice.

"And tore his pants like that? Come on. And look at his hand; it's in shreds. He didn't do that tripping."

"He had some help. He got bit."

"Ánimal or human?"

"Huh?"

"Animal or human? Who bit him? Or what?"

"Never mind, just get him . . ."

"Come on, buddy, we gotta know. You say he tripped, huh? Just like the other guy, the one with the shattered nose. He had a little help, too, huh? Sa-ay. There's something suspicious about all this. Oh, I see. Well, OK, Mr. Harbin. Government. OK, whatever you say. Come on, Max, let's load him on the stretcher. These guys are from the government. Official."

Max grunted.

"That must be the second medic," Bunny whispered.

"Yeah." Angel couldn't decide whether to peek into the room as a curious passer-by or hide around the corner until the medics left. There was something familiar about the name Harbin as well as the voice. "We'd better not get caught here," Angel whispered. "These men are from the government. We could get into trouble."

"Tell you what," Bunny whispered. "You sneak around the corner and listen. I'll stay here. I've got a press pass, so I have a right to ask questions."

"OK."

"Ahem." Bunny cleared his throat loudly as the two medics loaded the unconscious Jonathon Harker onto the stretcher. "Excuse me, I'd like to ask a few questions."

"Wha?"

"Bunny Darlitch, *Boric Acid Weekly*. I have a couple of questions . . ."

"*OUT!*" Joseph Harbin screamed. "Out! Scram! Christ, everything goes wrong."

Surprised, Bunny retreated a few steps as the medics lifted the stretcher. Harker's hand was a bloody mess. It *did* look like an old slipper a dog had attacked. He was intrigued. How could this happen in a hotel room?

Harbin's voice was extremely menacing, however.

Just then there was a loud groan from the direction of the bedroom. Angel's tiny body hurtled into the room. "Ally!" he shouted, tripping against the man holding the front of the stretcher. The medic fell, and the unconscious Harker rolled off the stretcher onto the floor, taking the sheet with him.

Before a stunned Harbin could stop him, Angel raced into the bedroom. Bunny flashed the agent a big smile and sauntered in after Angel.

Joseph Harbin stooped in despair to help the medic reload the stretcher. Harbin had been awake for forty-eight hours and was speeding on a red haze of Dexedrine and coffee, on top of which the intense pain in his lower abdomen had not abated. Ally's kick had been extraordinarily accurate, and she was wearing hiking boots. The haze filled the room, and the corridors outside, and rolled up and down his tapioca torso.

Slowly, almost majestically, Joseph Harbin's knees turned inward and his large law enforcement body tilted forward and dropped, face down, on the floor beside the stretcher.

"Oh, boy," said Max. "We'd better call for another ambulance."

"Ally," Angel was saying in the bedroom. "Boy, am I glad to see you!"

Angel untied his sister's bonds. Her head lolled as though unhinged, but she managed a smile of such radiance and joy that Bunny's cynical critic's heart dissolved into something very much like unfettered pleasure.

Bunny said, "*You* look familiar to me. Is it possible that I used to see you both at the Third Eye in San Francisco?"

"We spent some time there. With Philbrick Weevol and his girlfriend, China."

"China!" Bunny exclaimed. "Of course. I remember. Who are you two?"

"Well," Angel said, "this is Ally, my sister. Ally Augenblaue."

"You mean you're *Avery's* kids?" The word "thunderstruck" was invented for Bunny's response just then. "Oh, my God!"

"Yes," said Angel modestly. Ally rubbed the back of her neck.

"Wow, Ally," Angel asked. "What did you do to that man?"

Ally smiled a Mona Lisa smile.

And inside all the Akley Republican Furniture in the room, and in all the other rooms in the Argo Palace Hotel, *forniculotermes brevis*, sensing a drastic change in the weather, began happily to munch to the outside to swarm.

35 / Spinach Soufflé

"Ho ho ho. Hello, there, are you a little boy or a little girl?"

"What?" Angel had put Ally to bed in Bunny and Reba's room (number 8246, double with bath, no windows) and was walking along the muted rose-colored corridor of the eighty-second floor toward the elevators when he heard the voice from an open doorway.

"I said," the voice repeated, " 'Are you a little boy or a little girl?' "

"I'm not a little anything, and what's it to you? Where are you, anyway?" Angel stared into the empty room.

"Ho ho ho. I see. Yes. Not a little anything. Very good. Ve-ery good! Ho ho ho."

"Who are you?" Angel was getting annoyed.

"Ta da-aa!" A stocky dwarf leaped from behind the door and spread his arms as though he had just completed a spectacular vaudeville turn and expected applause.

Instead of applauding, Angel jumped back with a shrill cry. "Aaach!" he said. A little shock, a little fear, a little anger, all stirred together and baked in Angel's abdominal oven. A loaf rose in his throat.

"Never fear," said the dwarf. "I'm a dwarf!"

He had, Angel noticed, big blue eyes that glittered and shifted with the light from malevolence to sadness and back.

"I can see that," Angel muttered, not sure whether to be polite or not under these peculiar circumstances. This dwarf was disconcerting.

"Of course you can," said the dwarf and quickly jumped into the air and vanished, but not before Angel noticed his green suede shoes of a creamed spinach soufflé color.

"Hey!" Angel shouted.

"Ho ho ho," came the resinous voice, a piny-pitched, sap-filled, rich-timbred voice, and the dwarf somersaulted off the top of the door to land on his feet staring straight at Angel with his big sad eyes.

Instantly his face changed, writhed in a peculiar way; he stuck out his tongue and his eyes glazed over. "Goddammit, suck fuck shit shut up, oh fuck *shut up!*" he shouted.

The state passed as swiftly as it had arrived and the dwarf blushed deeply, a crimson god of embarrassment.

"Oh, I am terrible sorry," he apologized. "I really can't help that." He drooped in the doorway.

"What do you mean?" Angel asked. "You can't help it? Really?"

"Can't help it at all," said the dwarf. "It's a kind of fit. Just comes over me, suddenly, like that. A myocloniclike disorder called Gilles de la Tourette Syndrome, ho ho ho. Sudden outbursts of obscenity. Nothing personal, I assure you. Very embarrassing." The dwarf smiled a dazzling smile and did a back flip, landing on his feet and still smiling at Angel.

The smile snapped off like a light. "Are you a little boy or a little girl?" he asked again, eyes now glinting with malice.

"I'm a boy."

"But you were a girl, weren't you?" The third degree.

"Was. Yes." Angel frowned. "Who wants to know?"

"Ho ho ho. Wouldn't you like to know," the dwarf answered before vanishing again.

Angel waited, but the dwarf did not reappear. Angel took a step or two into the room and looked around. It was empty, an ordinary room. In the bathroom, he guessed, but the bathroom was empty too, a white ceramic dazzle with an empty shower-tub. Nor was the dwarf under the sink or behind the door or in the toilet. Gone.

Angel peeked under the bed. That's the weirdest thing I've ever seen, he mused.

"I didn't really disappear, you know," said the dwarf from across the hall as Angel leaned in the doorway scanning the hall.

"Ah!" Angel jumped, and the dwarf, grinning broadly, hopped up and down on his green feet.

"Hey! Come on. Who are you?" Angel ambled into the slumbering rose hall.

"Shhhh!" The dwarf's finger flew to his lips. He beckoned to Angel and whispered into his ear. "I'm the Degenerate White Dwarf," he announced, straightening up, very pleased with himself.

"Huh?"

The dwarf frowned. "I'm the Degenerate White Dwarf," he repeated in his normal pitchy voice. "You know," wink-wink.

"I'm afraid I don't," Angel said.

"The Degenerate White Dwarf. I'm a *star!*" He did another back flip.

"A star?"

"That's right. An inner-galactic star, a white dwarf, a compact and delicious condensation of normal folk. I'm very bright."

"Have you been on TV?"

"Ho ho ho, no, silly, not that kind of star. Oh, goodness, no. A heavenly star. I'm a friend of your father's. That kind of star. But there's someone coming down the hall, ho ho. He says hello, he does. Hello!"

The dwarf vanished again.

"Hey! Who says hello?" But the dwarf had gone; the door was closed and locked, there was no one home.

"Is that your room?" a voice behind Angel asked as Angel tugged at the doorknob.

"Uh, no," Angel said, spinning around. "I was talking to someone right here, and suddenly he was gone."

"Sure," said Virge Moses. "Say, you're not Angela Augenblaue, are you? Mr. Sparrow has been looking for her."

"Uncle Sig? I've been looking for *him*. Where is he?"

A new weather front formed in Angel's chest: someone had said hello; had it been Avery himself? If so, where had he been all this time, and why? A warm mass slid underneath the cold and caused turmoil.

"Up in the dome. Come on, I'll escort you." Officer Moses led Angel to the elevators, and together they rose swiftly through the central column of the Argo Palace to the top, got out, and climbed the helical stair to the rosy-lighted convention hall. It was 5:15 in the afternoon. The temperature outside had dropped to eighty-five, and 113 more people had succumbed to the air, which in this heat had undergone a photochemical process producing a particularly virulent poison. Aid was on the way, however, in the shape of a Canadian low pressure area filled with Arctic air, which at that very moment was crossing the Canadian border into northern Minnesota and North Dakota.

The low was full of water, and throughout the hotel the termites in the furniture reacted to it.

Ninety-three million miles away, enormous dark spots were forming on the sun, ready to add their strange magnetic confusions to the weather. Ho ho ho.

"Uncle Sig." Angel waved to him when Virge pointed out the king of frozen foods on the convention floor. The air up there was overwhelmed with the odors of the exotic blossoms that were heaped and banked around the huge room. Fifteen thousand chairs had been arranged in a semicircle facing the western end of the room and the podium.

"Hello, Angela. Listen, we think we have some information about your sister's whereabouts. Ambrose just called up. Seems three government men were taken to the hospital late this afternoon. One of them was a bit delirious, a fellow named Hubble. He interviewed Ambrose yesterday, so we recognized him. At any rate, this Hubble rambled on about some kind of kidnapping. Poor fellow had a badly smashed nose."

"Hey, Uncle Sig, Ally is all right, we found her. I'm not familiar with this Hubble, but three men from the government snatched Ally this morning. They had her here in this hotel the whole time. They questioned her about Dad, like where he was and all that, but of course she has no idea. They drugged her and everything. Who are they?"

"Whoa, whoa, slow down. They are merely doing their job. There's a growing panic about Avery, whether something happened to him. They've been watching your house. Now don't worry. Where is Alicia, by the way?"

"She's resting in a room. Some people I met, Bunny and Reba, he's a reporter. But Uncle Sig, they can't simply kidnap somebody like that, can they?"

"Uh, well, I suppose they can, if they do. But it seems that Ally disabled all three of them. That could be assault."

"It was accidental, except the one she kicked, and he was messing with her. And the one whose hand she bit a little, but she was drugged."

"Bit a little! She chewed it to shreds, according to Ambrose." Uncle Sig seemed distracted. "Wait a minute," he said in a strange voice. "That lectern over there has moved. I'd swear an hour ago it was closer to center stage. You don't suppose that dwarf . . . No, he couldn't hide in there. Hmmm. Oh, what is it, Angela?" Angel was tugging at his sleeve.

"That reminds me, Uncle Sig. What's a Degenerate White Dwarf?"

"Huh? Oh, I'm not certain. It's some kind of star, as I recall." He stared at the peripatetic lectern.

"A star? Like in the sky?"

"Yes, yes. That's right. A collapsed star. The matter in it is called degenerate, nothing to do with morals. You really should ask Dr. Merkin about that, though. I'm in frozen foods."

"OK. Thanks, Uncle Sig."

Angel ambled away, humming the theme of "Children of Paradise" under his breath in time with the music system of the Argo Palace Hotel.

36 / Fumet de Champignons

AMBROSE MERKIN PASSED Angel on his way up to the geodesic convention dome and greeted her, Hello, hello, tugging at his muttonchops as he climbed the helical stair. Angel nodded and smiled for the first time since that morning when Ally had been hustled away by three soft men from the department of something or other.

"Angel certainly appears cheerful this afternoon," Ambrose mentioned to Sig, who was gazing across the floor at Dudee Sparrow arranging a bouquet of heady orchids beside the podium. "Say, has that lectern moved since I was up here last? We had it set up the way it was supposed to be."

"That occurred to me too. It's moved all right."

"Did the police search inside that lectern for the dwarf, I wonder?" Dr. Merkin murmured.

"One thing's for sure, he's not in there now. I just checked. Ah, there's Kay." Sig lifted his hand in greeting and noticed that August, hat brim snapped down, dark glasses and gloves, snuffled along behind her like Dudee's bulldog, Philadelphia, on the trail of a skunk.

"What about the dwarf?" Kay asked in her strident voice. "Is it the same one August saw hopping down our lawn this morning or not?"

"We're on the lookout," Sig answered. He noted the two new grooves etched into her forehead between the eyes. They gave her face a peculiar meanness.

"Are you tired, Kay?" he asked. "Why don't you go down to your suite and get some rest before the convention begins. It won't start for almost three hours."

"I don't need any rest," she said tiredly, and flakes of rust settled, a rotten snow of red-brown bitterness, in her abdomen. She experienced an overwhelming hopelessness and observed, in her inner landscape, wide treacherous flats, brown and desolate, stretching to the horizon of homocide, where she and August had slaughtered Avery in the bath and he had disappeared, leaving the marble tub clean and mocking. The problem, she assumed, was that she and August hadn't planned what they would do when Avery was dead, after they had killed him forever. To complicate matters, Avery had refused to stay dead, and now Kay was very confused.

We killed him, she thought, and I wish we hadn't, and someone is on to us. She glanced at Sig and Ambrose's faces and saw only mild concern.

"Perhaps you're right," she said. "I do feel a bit tired. It's been a trying day."

"By the way," said Sig with a reassuring smile. "Your daughter is safe. She's here at the hotel."

Kay frowned. "My daughter?" Her voice slid across an endless expanse of glacial ice.

"Alicia Katherine. She was abducted this morning."

"Oh. Yes, yes. Of course. Well, Angela should be pleased, I suppose. Come on, August."

August swung around in unison with her and step for step marched along behind her. At the top of the stair she paused and leaned against the waist-high sill to gaze through the rosy glass at the city.

The top of the brown layers of air had settled at the 108th

floor, so she looked down on the smog. Downriver a mile or so she saw the tops of the two Marina Towers, the Sears Tower, the Prudential Building and the John Hancock Center, but the smog blocked her view of the city streets and the river. The spires of the skyscrapers seemed to float on a dead brown sea. The view, she decided, resembled the inside of her mind.

August was quivering on the knife edge of pure sensation. He was hallucinating like crazy, imagining that he was connected by an unbreakable but invisible wire from his navel to somewhere in the furrow of Kay's tightly clenching buttocks. When she turned to descend the stair, he turned automatically and step for step followed her down, and into the elevator, and down again to the 108th floor, where her suite awaited them. Glancing out the window once more, she was level with the very top of the impenetrable brown layer of hydrocarbons lapping at the exact center line of the window. A clear boundary of some kind, she thought, but what kind she wasn't sure.

"August," she said in a bitter tone, "hold me."

So August, spotted and serene, gloved and hatted and dark so his spots hardly showed, held her, and Kay, used to his odors of fungus and damp, clung to him as tightly as the smog hugged their window. And far, far to the west, the long, slanting rays of the sun began to throw the curious warps of *its* spots down the wires of light into the earth's Van Allen belt to jazz the western air with tiny balls of blue-gray light, all dancing the dance of orgones.

Kay, with a despairing sigh, felt through the coffee acid of fear and hate the rising tides of estrogen and lust, and her nails, which had so long ago furrowed August's back in eight neat rows under the skylight, unsheathed and began reluctantly to tear at his coat and pants and shirt. August smiled a silly seraphic smile, a smile so foolish and serene, so utterly awful, that Kay, as the powdered rust blurred her vision, whimpered before succumbing to the infinite winds from her groin: "Oh, August, God, how I hate it all!"

Her words tore and flew away, shredded forever in a satisfying violence.

August bobbed balloonlike at the end of his rigid string, feeling new connections wind him closer and closer to her pale

freckled flesh that at the same time released him into a strato-
sphere of calm. And in the sun's corona the storms of protons
raged and photons flew and the seething mass of gases flared
with a strangely soothing fury.

They thrashed, two speared fish, on the Akley bed; tossed on
crisp white sheets, floundered through different mists toward
one another, and were shaken by the finest of fine frenzies. August plunged into her, and she issued one terrible scream containing everything of her turmoil, her fear, her hate, her rage,
and, God forbid, her love, her ravenous love that devoured its
way through August's amnesia and hallucinogenic poisons to the
raw center where he lived, and his body sang.

Thirty floors below them Duane Hemp flexed his tattooed bicep
before the mirror in his bathroom; it bucked and kicked under
his tanned skin, his tattoo thrashing violently. Then he pulled
back the corners of his lips and examined his teeth, gleaming
perfect and white in the simulated sunlight of the bathroom
lamps. He cocked his head to the right, he cocked it to the left,
and his molars glistened like Christmas Eve.

He straightened his hat, admired his pristine T-shirt, which
matched his teeth, stepped into a clean pair of Jockey shorts, and
flexed once more before the mirror. Then he strode into the
bedroom.

Rhea lay on the bed examining her nails. "Duane," she asked,
"don't you ever take off your hat?" She buffed the right index
nail.

Duane stood at the foot of the bed, T-shirt, Jockey shorts and
Stetson hat all flawlessly white, flexing his rippling muscles for
her.

She didn't notice.

He went to the bedside table and opened the drawer. Inside,
carefully wrapped in white linen, was their supply of *Amanita
muscaria*, the reddish mushroom spotted with white, sheer
poison and transportation to another land indeed. He unwrapped the linen package.

"Oh, is it time for us to do a little of that?" Rhea asked. She,
too, was dressed in white, her simple floor-length gown draped
across her languidly reclining form on the pale blue bedspread.

Duane grunted and selected two shriveled pieces. "The convention starts in a couple of hours," he said. "We might as well get ready for it now."

"And then have dinner," Rhea said. "I always get hungry."

"Right!" said Duane, tamping the shriveled scraps into his pipe.

Four floors above Duane and Rhea, Bunny Darlitch finished typing up his notes. Ally was awake and sipping hot tea, and Angel was smiling and humming under his breath.

"It's all going to come together," he said. "Oh, yes, it's all going to come together."

"How do you know?" Ally asked between sips.

"The dwarf." Angel smiled broadly. "The dwarf told me Avery said hello. And you're OK."

Ally beamed, her eyes filling with liquid love.

"Well," said Bunny, pushing back his chair and rising, "Reba and I are going to smoke a tiny bit of *Amanita*. How about you kids?"

"Not for me." Angel shook his head.

"Nor me," Ally chimed in. "I'll wait a bit."

In many hotel rooms, *Amanita muscaria* was being solemnly smoked or sniffed or eaten or ground fine.

37 / Fillet of Sole

WILLIAM LAMPLIGHTER DIDN'T KNOW IT as he stood at the window of his room on the ninety-ninth floor of the Argo Palace Hotel and let the westering rays of the troubled sun fall full length on his naked body, but in Philbrick Weevol's taxonomy of personalities he was a dicotyledonous angiosperm, a gnarled California live oak, an evergreen with shade tree properties; and what he was shading just now was the bounty of Nurse Thinger's abundant cereal self, also angiosperm, fresh as new bread, ancient as hunger. She was lying on the double bed with the blurred silhouette of Bill's ropy shadow falling across her groin. Her face and torso and legs toasted in the red-gold evening sun as it fell through the top layers of the amber air.

"Do you know," Bill said in the grating rumble that was very dear to Nurse Thinger after these years of impossible love with this former porn star whose face could express such transports of ecstasy. "Aldrich — Dr. Ague — once told me that Wilhelm Reich said that sexuality and the living process were identical, and at the core of it all was what Reich called the *enigma of love*. What do you think of that?" He turned away from the window to Nurse Thinger, and as he turned, the *instrument* of his enigma turned with him.

"I think he was right," she said. "Because I am filled with love, but I don't fully understand it."

William Lamplighter, blasé veteran of a hundred explicit flicks, survivor of a wide array of electromagnetic and atomic radiations and Dr. Ague's implant, felt deep in his oaken heart the carefree rising of sap through xylem and identified it there as love; he was looking down at his beloved's wheaten form lying on the sheets, and he was thinking too of how very dear *her* dicotyledonous angiosperm person was to him, though he did not think it in those botanical terms. He felt, gazing at her, her generosity for including his homely welted face and form in the circle of her arms and heart.

I'm becoming a romantic sort of fool, he thought as he sat on the edge of the bed and ran the furrowed bark of his hand down the smooth and silken-tasseled length of Nurse Thinger, up over the round (*generous*, he thought again) hills of her breasts, the great plain of her belly and its gentle rolling swell, the golden peninsula of her leg. He cupped her foot in his rough hand and gently squeezed it.

"We'd better get ready," he rumbled at last, overcoming the syrupy silence that had glued them in place for what had seemed an endless time, and he waited a long, long time for her to answer.

"Yes," she finally said, sighing a soft breeze.

They took the elevator down to the Mycenaean Room on the third floor of the hotel for a dinner of wine and sole filleted and drowned in golden butter sauce.

They left behind them in the room the long rays of the sun

falling across the bed. It was a sun that rotated in twenty-seven days, and as it rotated now it brought around its eastern limb the turbulent umbra of a new and truly gigantic sunspot cycle. And although Lamplighter knew about Reich's enigma of love, he did not know — and how could he? — that sunspots fostered the formation of blue and energetic orgones in all kinds of matter organic and inorganic.

Nor did he know (there was no need, really) that orgones were plentiful in cooked food. And in sea sand, sea water, and most especially in sole filleted and drowned in butter sauce. If he had known, he would have been very pleased.

The hour for the kickoff of the tenth annual AKA convention approached as the sun lowered itself toward a horizon that held on its northern front a wild change in the weather. Bill sat and ate and gazed and at length in a starchy voice asked his lovely Nurse Thinger to marry him, and of course she most graciously consented.

At the next table, Ed Sox chewed his way through an enormous portion of *tournedos Rossini* with *haricots verts*, and a side order of French fries.

"Betsy Sue, honeypot," he said, munching a mouthful of steak and potatoes. He took a gulp from his foaming glass of beer and looked up, for Betsy Sue had not replied.

"Honeypot," he said, a question in his tone. She was staring over his shoulder at the three injured men walking single file behind the headwaiter to a rear table. She gave a start and returned to nibbling her *jambon braisé morvandelle*, which the menu informed her was ham braised in a wine, cream and mushroom sauce. Ham she recognized.

The first man in the injured party had a dazed look and his arm hung in an elaborate sling, his hand encased in a white cloud of bandage to the fingertips. The second man hobbled, knees pressed together, his back and stomach held rigidly. The outlines of a very painful truss over the midsection of his body were visible. The third man had two black eyes emptied of all meaning and an enormous bandage was taped across his nose; he drooled a little, too, though not enough to embarrass his companions. The three looked as though the farmer's wife had just cut off their tails with a carving knife.

Buck Sweeney drummed his fingers on the white tablecloth,

exasperated, impatient, annoyed and harassed. His brain was full of clams steaming open in a simmering broth of ire and fear, a chowder of despair. "What the hell have you been up to?" he hissed as soon as the trio was seated and the waiter had placed menus before them and left.

"Uh," Jonathon Harker said, his brain fizzing with concussion, Dexedrine and fatigue. "We ran into a little trouble."

Constantine Hubble smiled vacantly under his white bandage and drooled; there was no one home there at all, but he could, Harker had discovered, follow simple commands.

"Yes," Sweeney said, his voice quiet only because he was being strangled by two immensely powerful, invisible hands. "I can see that."

"The girl," Harbin whispered. It sounded as if his truss had drawn his larynx down the drain of his throat, leaving only the ghost of his voice behind.

"What happened to you?" Sweeney snapped. "And what about the girl? You were supposed to get information, not injuries."

"She kicked me. She whipped all three of us. She's a menace." Harbin's voice whispered through the dry stones of the Mojave Desert; it wavered in the still air above the stones, a thin wail on the horizon of grief.

"I'm aware that she kicked you, Harbin. Christ!" Sweeney oozed sarcasm like pus, but before he could continue a weird wind wafted past the diners in the Mycenaean Room and all heads turned toward the door, where three waiters, smiling unctuously, practically prostrated themselves before the spangled figure of Philbrick Weevol in his heroic black and silver rock-star idol's outfit. Beside him, hugging his arm, was pale quillwort China, her mouth twisted in a swampy smile.

A few women pressed next to the author of "Children of Paradise," large, lonely women desiring to touch the magic person who later that night would perform his one powerful song for the fifteen thousand AKA Club members attending the convention. They wanted only a little of the *mana* gathered around Philbrick's famous smile, but behind them, inevitably, the word was going out, like a rising tide, and a crowd was gathering, clouds on the hotel horizon.

"Oh, Christ!" Buck repeated, loud enough for Lamplighter to hear through his romantic haze.

38 / Au Jus

BUCK MUSED, "That son of a bitch looks familiar." He was glaring across the Mycenaean Room at the rapidly dissolving knot of people surrounding Philbrick Weevol. Blue uniformed leucocytes had raced to the source of the infection, and only their quick work had prevented a full-scale riot. "Dammit, he looks familiar."

"His picture was in *Rolling Stone* a couple of weeks ago," Harker said through his codeine fog.

"What the hell's *Rolling Stone*?" Buck's words felt to Harker like somebody stepping on his injured hand.

Through the laryngeal corridors of the vast hotel the Degenerate White Dwarf's ghostly laughter raced, but the halls were empty as eight o'clock approached, and no one heard those phantom ho ho hos as they sped past locked doors at seven hundred mph hardly louder than the whisper of the air conditioning. Somewhere the Dwarf was holding one hand over his mouth and the other to his tummy and shaking with wheezes and gasps of ho ho ho. Why was he laughing so? Ho ho ho!

Weevol and China secluded themselves at a corner table out of sight of most of the diners. Soon good manners caused the crowd of hungry conventioneers to leave the couple alone and focus on their own plates of roast beef *au jus* (the Homeric cut for men, the Sappho cut for the ladies), or steak Diana (goddess of the hunt), or chicken Agamemnon, or fillet of sole or any of the other succulent dishes ordered from the enormous menu with the fluted Ionic columns down the sides and the Corinthian capitals supporting the words Mycenaean Room.

Betsy Sue Sox pushed her plate of *jambon braisé morvandelle* to one side and smoothed out her program for the AKA convention.

"Read it to me, again," said Ed, shoveling chunks of *tournedos Rossini* into his mouth without a pause in his rhythm.

"All right, Eddie. At eight o'clock an opening address will be delivered by Mr. Sigismund Sparrow, president of AKA International and chairman of the board of Sparrow Frozen Foods. He will speak on" — Betsy Sue bent closer to read from the program — "the origin and history of the AKA Clubs."

"I suppose that could be interesting," Ed said doubtfully through a mouthful of *haricots verts*. He was giving his talk at the express orders of A. K. himself. The note in his pocket directed him to do so. "How long will that address last?"

"At eight forty-five a Dr. Ambrose Merkin will give a speech on intergalactic space, which Avery explored, and on the orgone engine."

"Whatever that is," Ed mumbled, forking a gardenful of salad and pushing it in behind the *haricots verts*.

"Oh, Eddie, that's what powered Avery's spaceship."

"Ha," said Ed, "but what's 'n orgone?" He sopped up Rossini sauce with another slab of *tournedo*.

"I'm not positive, but I think it's related to *The* Blue Light everyone is buzzing about."

"I'm not up on it," said Eddie after he had swallowed his mouthful of food. "I'm a Reformed Baptist, myself. Or at least I was." He flashed Betsy Sue a dazzling smile, and Betsy Sue, tan and smooth and delicious, dazzled back.

Ho ho ho echoed through the brachial branches of the breathing hotel, and in a room somewhere the Degenerate White Dwarf was doing back flips with his twinkling green shoes describing perfect circles in the air, over and over again, around the room with ho-ho ho-ho ho-ho, through miles of rosy corridors swelling and contracting and gloomy boiler rooms where the hotel beat with the hot heart of its heat, and ducts and tubes breathed the whispers of that mirthful laughter ho-ho-ho, ho-ho-ho, ho-ho-ho!

"How long is this Dr. Merkin's lecture?" Ed asked. He heaved a great sigh, loosened his belt, and leaned back in his chair.

"Only half an hour, until nine-fifteen. Then there is a twenty-two-minute break, until dark. I wonder why until dark? During that time, according to the program, refreshments will be served. I hope they aren't too fattening."

"The refreshments?"

"Yes. We've just eaten a rather large meal."

Ed nodded, and Betsy Sue went on. "At nine-thirty-seven Mr. Avery Krupp Augenblaue will address the convention on the subject of *The* Blue Light."

"Is that so?" asked Ed with a hint of stage fright in his voice.

"Yeah, I guess that's what everyone is waiting for, to hear about this stuff, this *The* Blue Light, whatever it is." Neither Ed nor Betsy Sue was very involved in the AKA Clubs, and they were a bit unclear about their purpose.

"I wonder why they gotta wait for dark. Does he prefer to talk after dark?" He and Betsy Sue were not the only ones puzzling over that, for around the dining room people were now unfolding programs and questioning this strange gap.

Ed and Betsy Sue fell silent, and conversation drifted toward them in fragments from the neighboring tables.

"Gee, Eddie, do you suppose there's a chance Avery isn't going to show up?"

"No chance," Ed answered.

The Degenerate White Dwarf ho-hoed his way through the hotel trachea, green feet all a-twinkle as he skipped and somersaulted and flipped and vanished and reappeared, as he held his belly like a bowl full of jelly and laughed, ho ho ho, with his delicate sensitive fingers held over his tittering mouth and he rocked and shook and quivered and quaked with irrepressible giggles and laughs. He did another back flip and said to himself with a giggle and a shake, Oh yes, and I'm a STAR, I am, ho ho ho.

"What's after Avery's appearance?" Ed asked his savory wife, the farmer's daughter. She gave him a cheerful smile and bent over the program.

"After Avery speaks, the evening will end with Philbrick Weevol performing the theme song for the AKA Clubs, 'Children of Paradise.' "

"What's that?" Ed knew his furniture, he did, but music was not in his ken.

"Oh, Eddie, my goodness. It's all over the radio. 'O children of paradise/Two teen angels in the San Francisco/Hills who walk together/In the Cosmic Dharmas of love/In the chill and warm weather/Falling from above/Where Che and Buddha dwell . . . !"

"Oh, yeah, yeah," said Ed, "it does sound familiar." And in his inner ears the melody wafted, filling all the gloomy empty stretches in the Milpitas furniture warehouse, where busy forklifts hummed down the aisles bearing couches and chairs and beds to the waiting trucks. The warehouse radio was continually blaring that very song.

"I can't really say I understand that song, though," he added. "For instance, who are Che and Buddha? And all the cosmic darning stuff — never heard of it." But I'm an expert on furniture, he thought.

"It's a *song*. You're not supposed to think about the words. Anyway, Philbrick Weevol is the biggest sensation in pop music in twenty years!"

Betsy Sue sat back and folded her arms in a so-there attitude. She had read it all in that paper on the plane, *Rolling Stone*. As it happened, the article had been written by Bunny Darlitch, who at that very moment was enjoying a religious experience in the hotel room shower with phthisic Reba Hare. He soaped her very slickly under her thin arms and gave no sign of, even if he heard, the ghostly *ho ho ho* that tiptoed with the speed of sound past their door. Reba soaped Bunny under his plump arms and lovingly kissed each of his purple bite marks. They lathered each other's crotch and slippery bottoms and laughed, *ho ho ho*.

And in the still-empty but fully decorated geodesic rose-colored convention dome at the very top of the powerful pillar of the hotel, the Degenerate White Dwarf was laughing and laughing until his face transformed instantly and he said, "Dammitshit, suck fuckshut up shit SHUT UP!" and stuck out his tongue, then stopped as suddenly as he had started, blushed a clashing crimson, and then began very softly, once more, to laugh, Ho ho ho.

Buck Sweeney sat in steamy discipline and stared at Philbrick Weevol at his corner table eating chicken paprikás and dabbing at his mouth with a snowy napkin. "Dammit," Buck mumbled, "that guy really looks familiar."

He glanced over at Constantine Hubble. The enormous white bandage that covered his nose was pressed firmly to the edge of the dining room table. The one terribly blackened eye that Buck could see was closed, and a small silver thread of saliva connected Hubble's mouth to his right thigh just above the knee. His breath rasped softly through his sagging mouth.

"Christ!" Buck Sweeney exclaimed for the third emphatic time that meal.

39 / Apple Tart

"CHRIST!" Kay moaned in her febrile afternoon sleep as she tossed her gory ferruginous hair fretfully against the cool hotel pillow, while beside her, stiff and straight, August breathed the dank exhumations of his own body and stared at the ceiling, a small and innocent smile twitching his thin liver-lips.

"Christ!" she moaned again, and she threw her left arm outward so her forearm fell heavily across August's nose. He didn't move, merely blinked once as the bridge of his nose began to empurple with damaged blood vessels. August bruised easily in his new condition. But he didn't care.

The blow woke Kay, and she bolted straight up, staring wildly into the dresser mirror opposite the foot of the bed. Her pale, startled face stared back under its stiff, disordered crown of orange hair.

"What was that?" she asked. There was no response from August, who still stared at the ceiling with wide, wondering eyes.

Kay rubbed her eyes and glanced over at his daydreaming face. "Oh," she said, and watched for several minutes, bemused, as the bruise alongside and over his nose gathered in virulence. Then she shook her head to clear it, swung her legs over the side of the bed, and walked over to the drawn curtains. Suite 108B was on the west side of the building, so when she pushed aside the heavy drape, the nearly horizontal rays of the sun speared her in the eyes. She squinted and noticed beneath the sun a gathering layer of dark cloud, and then observed with a small furry part of her mind that the very top of that ocean of tired brown air was even now being gently whipped into inch-high ripples that lapped against the windowpane and receded or shredded off to either side. But nowhere in her head did she connect this with a change of weather, for to Kay the swiftly moving ripple patterns were abstract and annoying correlates to her own despair. Nor would she have cared had she known that at that very moment the two hundred and twenty-sixth person of the day was succumbing to the poisoned air: he was an eighty-seven-year-old retired bookie from Oak Park who would receive no obituary in the *Tribune*.

"August," she said firmly, turning away from the window and letting the curtain fall. Her round buttocks clenched tightly and relaxed. "August! Wake up!"

But August was not asleep. August was far away, his dim fungous eyes on distant rollicking horizons blazing in colors not yet invented. He breathed quietly, and his pale, hairless and spotted chest rose and fell evenly, ripely, mutely and damply, the susurration of frenzied dark life well below the humus of his consciousness.

Outside the hotel, the sun lowered its long arms and slipped itself into a buzzing nest of clouds.

"August, dammit, you've got to wake up. You've *got* to. Something awful is going to happen! I can feel it!"

A ripple ran up the length of August's stiff body, a ripple that reflected the ripples now running regularly along the brown top of the hydrocarbon layer inverted over Chicago. When the ripple reached the crown of his head and slid quietly into the thin layer of damp black hair that lankly covered his balding scalp, his eyes achingly rotated toward Kay and locked on to her worried face. He smiled broadly, an expression that could not be described as sunny but was at least far warmer than the look it had replaced.

"Yes, Kay?" he said very softly in a voice that felt like soft, rich, decaying leaves underfoot.

"Thank God," she said and returned to the bed. "Are you all right? That's a nasty bruise."

"Bruise?"

"On your nose. I guess I must have hit you in my sleep. God, the dreams. Oh, August, what made us do it? We never should have done it." She bit at her crimsoned lips and outlined every sharp tooth in red.

"Done what?" August asked in that same soft voice.

"We never should have killed Avery. We never should have."

The ripple that had crawled up August's body now reappeared at the top of his head and crawled back down, pimpling his spotted flesh, section by section, from damp scalp to cracked feet, but his smile did not change at all.

"Did we do that, Kay?" The soft voice again.

"Oh, God!" Kay started pacing the room. "What time is it?" she asked finally.

August lifted his arm mechanically and looked at his digital watch. "Seven-thirty."

"We'd better get ready. The program says Avery is addressing the convention tonight. Do you know that, August? Something awful is going to happen."

She stood in front of the dresser mirror and gazed at her naked body, its pale freckled skin with the newly visible networks of blue veins along her sides and the length of the undersides of her arms. She raised one hand and patted absently at her stiff orange hair. With another shake of her head she set to work, opening her small make-up case and removing the bottles, compacts and containers, the brushes and applicators and combs. Carefully, she arranged them on the dresser.

Then she roused August and led him into the bathroom, where she showered and scrubbed away as much of his dankness as possible and doused him with cologne (a concoction called Sauvage). She braced him against the wall and dressed him in a clean shirt and suit, combed his lank hair across his balding skull, and left him standing there to prepare herself.

Cream on her face, rest, wipe it off; cream again, rest, wipe it off. Gentle pancake make-up, to heighten the supple skin tones. Then the eyes: first the shadow, a very pale green to match their color and blend with her hair. A line across the lids, top and bottom, and lashes curled out and darkened. Eyebrows, plucked and shaded. The cheeks, subtly rouged to bring out a healthy color and distract from the tired lines under her eyes. The nose sculpted and highlighted with lights and darks. Lips smoothed and crimsoned again, a white cloth cleaning the lipstick from her teeth. She rubbed her lips together and smiled at herself. It was a hideous smile, but it would have to do.

Next, her hair, combed a hundred times, brushed this way and that way, curled carefully and sprayed in place to curve under and behind the ears. To which the sapphire earrings are locked in and held tight. With the hand mirror she checked all the angles — front, sides and back — and tilted her head to the left, and to the right, and watched her hair fall just right with the tilt. All right. The head was done.

She powdered and sprayed and deodorized the rest, and began to clothe it all, garments to hold in and garments to hold up, and garments to conceal other garments. Legs sprayed clean, smooth and sheer. And over it all she spread silk the color of clear water while August stood against the wall and gazed at her, the innocent smile again twitching the corners of his lips.

She stood before the mirror and turned slowly around, watching the glass. Everything was in place, the culmination of three thousand years of cosmetic science. Peering over her shoulder at the mirror, she clenched her buttocks once.

If August had been watching carefully (which of course he wasn't), he might have noticed the tiny globes of blue light flicking away from the very tips of Kay's violent orange hair. She was, he had to admit in the dim interior of his mind, quite beautiful in her way.

"What time is it?" she asked, interrupting his reverie.

He wound his arm upward on its pulley and glared at the face of his watch once more. "Almost eight."

"Let's go," she told him, and taking his arm, she led him from the room. They joined the flow of people streaming to the elevators that ran through the central shaft of the building in one vast duct and rode to the top, where they all would climb that final helical staircase to the rose-colored glass geodesic dome at the tip, where fifteen thousand chairs waited in a semicircle.

She released August's arm in case someone they knew should see, for Kay liked to pretend that no one was aware of her involvement with the butler. He snuffled dutifully along behind her, eyes fixed on those clenching fists inside her dress. Kay flowed in watered silk like water herself, and August damply sloshed along.

The round shaft of the building had come alive with movement as crowds of people emerged from their rooms to join the flowings through the veins and arteries of twelve miles of corridor. The elevators were in ceaseless motion, rising swiftly, filled with people, all of whom wore small gold AKA pins on lapel or dress, to return as swiftly down, emptied, to rise and stop and rise again. The crowds were all carried upward to the opening moments of the AKA convention, the one where Avery would bring to the world the message of *The* Blue Light after ten long years (though only a month to him) in intergalactic space, and somewhere in that vast maze of halls the Degenerate White Dwarf was going *ho ho ho* quietly to himself.

Electronic Interlude

Who has ever stopped to think of the divinity of
Lamont Cranston?

– Le Roi Jones

40 / Raisins

"TELL ME about Avery."

"All right. Avery Krupp Augenblaue, born September 2, 19 —"

"No, no, no. Not that. I know all that. Tell me about Avery."

"Height, six feet. Hair, black; eyes, blue; weight —"

"Not that, either."

"What then?"

"What's he like? What kind of person is he?"

"He was a distant relation of the German Krupps. His father was a brilliant but somewhat erratic scientist who immigrated to America after World War Two. He was an engineer, did rocket research on the V-Two in Germany, at Peenemunde, worked with Von Braun in the States. Started his own aerospace company, enormously successful. Avery took it over."

"Anything else."

"Mother was a film star. Norwegian originally. Internationally admired beauty. She retired from acting when she married Avery's father and became his assistant."

"His assistant?"

"Yes. But not in his aerospace work. He moved into another field."

"He did?"

"Yes. He became a follower of Wilhelm Reich."

"Who?"

"A psychoanalyst who discovered the orgone. Life energy. Small blue balls of sexual power."

"Such as Avery used to power his intergalactic voyage?"

"Correct. There was only one problem."

"What was that?"

"The orgone doesn't exist."

"What?"

"In 1954 the United States Government declared the orgone to be nonexistent. Reich was sent to prison for selling what he called 'orgone accumulators,' boxes to collect and focus orgones; and for doing research generally on the orgone. Of course, in the process he messed around with radioactive materials and contaminated the building he was working in. Reich died the day before he was to be released from prison."

"What happened to Avery's father?"

"He continued his research. He died when Avery was twenty-four years old, and Avery became president of the company. Now he is one of the richest men in the world, if not *the* richest. In the sixties, when everyone was diversifying, Avery diversified. Cosmetics. Plastics and petroleum products. Biomedical research. Transportation, an outgrowth of his original aerospace plants. Communications — film, television, radio, satellites and so forth. Furniture."

"Furniture?"

"That's affirmative. Avery has a hand in almost everything by now. He owns hotels, airlines, health facilities, movie theaters, real estate, sugar plantations, computer companies . . ."

"Stop. Give me some examples."

"He owns the Argo Palace Hotel in Chicago."

"What?"

"Argo Palace Hotel. Tallest structure in the city, convention center, on the river. Has a pink dome on top. Named after the city in Greece, reputed to be the oldest city in that country. Home of Agamemnon, whom his wife Klytemnestra and her uncle-lover Aigisthos murdered upon his return from the Trojan War. The hotel could also be named after Argus Panoptes, the all-seeing, who in myth had a hundred eyes all over his body. Or it could be named after Odysseus' watchdog, who, recognizing his master when Odysseus returned home after twenty years, wagged his tail and died. The word means 'plain.' Appropriate for Chicago at the edge of the Great Plains. It might also have been named after both the builder of Jason's fifty-oared boat and the boat itself, the *Argo*."

"What does this have to do with Avery?"

"Everything. He has a classical mind."

"How do you mean?"

"When he was nine years old he built a machine that ate his mother's favorite carpet, in the dining room. I believe it was a Persian."

"Yes?"

"The machine ate the carpet and converted it into, uh, into . . ."

"Into what?"

"Well, into *droppings* would be the correct word, I think."

"Droppings?"

"Affirmative. He had made an electric goat."

"That's a classical mind?"

"Yes."

"And?"

"His mother was annoyed, so he made her a new carpet."

"Let me guess. Out of the, uh, droppings?"

"Affirmative."

"Then?"

"Later, when he was thirty-seven, he married a Kay Mynad, a strange but very ambitious woman. She bore him two children, girls. Nearly three years ago the younger one, then fourteen, became a boy, on his/her own initiative. The Augenblaues are very strong-willed."

"I begin to get the picture."

"Avery and his assistant, Dr. Ambrose Merkin, developed the orgone engine. Avery is supposed to have recently returned from ten years at translight speeds in intergalactic space, somewhere between here and the Andromeda Galaxy."

"That classical mind?"

"Yes."

"What do you mean, 'supposed?'"

"Insufficient data."

"Explain."

"There were no witnesses to his journey since he was alone, and he disappeared the day he landed. He has not been seen since, though there has been speculation that he met with foul play."

"What kind of foul play?"

"Murder?"

"Who speculates this?"

"Your assistant, Fairfax 'Buck' Sweeney, among others."

"You are suggesting, if I am not mistaken, two things. One, Avery has not actually traveled for ten years in intergalactic space . . ."

"The concept is ridiculous. We do not possess the technology for such a trip. And it is theoretically impossible in the framework of the Theory of Relativity."

"So is the orgone, is it not?"

"The orgone doesn't exist. In 1954 —"

"All right. And two, Avery has been murdered. By whom?"

"Kay Mynad Augenblaue."

"His wife? What motive?"

"Revenge. Remember, this is pure speculation."

"Revenge for what?"

"That is the question. Insufficient data, again. There is some talk, less probable this time, that she has been, uh, involved with the butler, a man named August, surname unknown."

"Why is that less probable?"

"The butler is repulsive."

"I see. Then why revenge?"

"Answer unknown."

"Is there any direct evidence that Avery has been on this planet for the past ten years?"

"Such evidence is unavailable."

"That answer is equivocal."

"Yes. Some information is coded."

"What is the code?"

"Insufficient data."

"Is there any direct evidence that Avery *has* been in space for the past ten years?"

"Yes. He appears not to have aged. This is commensurate with the theoretical effects of the Lorentz-Fitzgerald equations and the contraction of time at near-light speeds. He would only be about a month older."

"So he probably was away?"

"Insufficient data."

"This is getting us nowhere. I am learning nothing new about this man except that he once constructed an electric goat."

"It indicates the presence of a sense of humor, I believe."

"Not to me."

"As you wish. There are other things, stranger things, about him, but they are only rumors. No hard data at all."

"Such as?"

"He's been cloned."

"Cloned? What do you mean?"

"He has had replicas of himself grown from his own genotypes. Tissue samples. The rumor is that it didn't work out."

"Jesus! You mean it's possible that there are several of him around?"

"Only rumors. And it wasn't supposed to have worked. Clones have not proved viable."

"Still, that could explain the recurrence of the initials. Everywhere we look, A.K.A. They could all be clones."

"Maybe. But if they were, they've all disappeared."

"What's happening now?"

"The tenth annual AKA convention is beginning at the Argo Palace Hotel in Chicago. Avery is supposed to address the meeting after dark tonight. Something will become clear then."

"Good lord. I see. All right, terminate program."

"Program terminated. Good night, Mr. Director."

Part III/Convention

But silken nets and traps of adamant shall
   Oothoon spread,
And catch for thee girls of mild silver, or of
   furious gold;
I'll lie beside thee on a bank & view their
   wanton play
In lovely copulation bliss on bliss with
   Theotormon:
Red as the rosy morning, lustful as the first born
   beam,
Oothoon shall view his dear delight, nor e'er with
   jealous cloud
Come in the heaven of generous love; nor selfish
   blightings bring.

– William Blake, *Visions of the Daughters of Albion*

41 / Sweet and Sour

SIG SPARROW WAS exhausted. He leaned against the waist-high sill of the convention hall dome and sighed as fifteen-thousand people flowed up the spiral stair into the huge semicircle of chairs. AKA marshals directed them to their seats, where earphones were provided to give the various foreign representatives simultaneous translations in their own languages: Japanese, Burmese, Swahili, Urdu, Bantu, Basque, Mandarin and Cantonese and Fukienese, Turkish and Greek and Serbo-Croatian, Norwegian, Baluchi, Rumanian, Bihari, Romany and Singhalese, Yiddish, Manx and Wendish, Sogdian, Kurdish and Persian and all major European languages.

Sig adjusted his glasses, polarized now to counteract the long, slanting beams of the setting sun that skipped off the foaming caps of the pollution ocean. The dark clouds, he had noted, were visibly closer, and the weather report gave a 73 percent chance of heavy precipitation, up from 67 percent an hour earlier. The light falling across the shuffling lines of people was, of course, tinted a splendid rose.

Sig had freely admitted, not only to himself, but also only half an hour before to Dudee — Dudee who knelt at his feet stroking her repulsive doggie and murmuring about velvet ropes into a vaguely defined area somewhere between his belt and his knee, an area that Sig felt charged with a familiar kind of energy that could not at the moment be discharged because he must discharge other, more pressing, duties — Sig admitted that he had

had a *tough day*. The kidnapping, police, the Dwarf (which had acquired a capital letter in his mind).

It was with remarkable precision that the delegates found their seats, but one confused Burmese, who had been given the wrong lapel button, a Flemish one, was directed to the wrong area and had to be reseated in his section when the people around him noticed that he didn't look Flemish. Vermeer, for one, had never painted anyone like him. There were surprisingly few such episodes.

Sig sighed again and mulled over his speech, which he'd rehearsed last night after a dinner of *Sauté de boeuf à la Parisienne* with his darling Dudee while gently chained to the special rings set into their bedroom wall. Dudee's perfumed breath moved over his quivering naked body in an intensive and ultimately successful effort to distract him. He had, however, under these trying circumstances, made it through the entire forty-minute speech two and one third times before breaking down into strangled screams. When Dudee released him, he fell on her with terrible vigor.

Dudee was now seated, sated and replete, in the front row, her slavering beast sleepily mumbling and twitching in her warm lap, its red tongue lying on her firm, tanned thigh, now discretely covered with a form-fitting, earth orange, double-knit jersey dress. Absently she stroked the dog's misshapen head while she waited for her Uncle Sig to address the convention.

At last eight o'clock arrived, the delegates were seated; Kay and August had been settled in the front row, two seats away from Dudee. Angel and Ally, also in the front row, waited expectantly. Buck Sweeney was in the back of the hall mentally whipping in a frenzy while his three damaged agents drifted about the hall, looking vaguely for suspects, though the crime was by now unclear to all of them, so long had they been awake, so painful were their injuries, and so zapped were their soggy brains with stimulants, antidepressants, tranquilizers, antibiotics, painkillers, amphetamines and coffee. Duane Hemp and Rhea were in the back, Duane with his hat on, Rhea buffing her nails. Bunny and Reba sat in the press section, Bunny with his ballpoint pen poised over his steno pad.

Downstairs, in a dressing room, China dusted the sequined

outline of Philbrick Weevol's rock-star codpiece with a small feather duster and mumbled lurid sexual invitations. Phil gazed at the ceiling, shifting from foot to foot under China's obscene tickle. He had a long wait, sequestered here from his murderously engorged fans, but he'd been provided with a large color television on which he could watch the earlier events of the evening. At the moment the set was focused on the cheerful, confident face of Dick Peters, who was telling the world about some minor aspect of the AKA phenomenon, a pregame warm-up as it were, presided over by the also smiling, but somehow more *serious* face of the avuncular Walter, grayer and wiser than it was ten years before when he covered Avery's launch.

"Ream, ream, ream," China was saying. And, "Tongue!" And, "Stroke. Suck. Blow." Phil barely heard her, but he glanced down briefly at the top of her stringy head of blondish hair and smiled slightly. Her head moved in little circles as she attentively dusted and muttered. Then he turned back to the television.

Dick Peters faded away to be replaced by a depressed-looking woman with HOUSEWIFE printed on her drab dress. It was dinnertime, and her husband, a businessman carrying a briefcase bulging with important papers, arrived home. He was hungry, but no dinner had been prepared. A nasty argument began, and the husband dropped his briefcase to take a swipe at his wife. She fell backward and slid across the freshly waxed kitchen floor. The word HOUSEWIFE was printed all over her jumpsuit. Her head hit the base of the refrigerator, the door of which opened, and a small cartoon man popped his head around it and whispered into the woman's ear. She had HOUSEWIFE emblazoned on her uniform. Her face, despite a large purpling bruise on her cheek, visibly brightened. She stumbled and steered her irate husband, who kicked his briefcase angrily on the way, into the dining room and sat him down at the head of the table, which was recently polished. In the kitchen she opened the freezer and took out a carton of Sparrow Frozen Foods, a complete Chinese dinner: won ton soup, chicken and black mushrooms, spring rolls, Mongolian lamb, shrimp in lobster sauce, sweet-and-sour pork. She popped the plastic sack into the boiling water. She could boil water. The word HOUSEWIFE flashed on and off on her dull gray smock. Suddenly, in a blinding flash and a puff of stage smoke, her dull gray uniform was replaced by an elegant, low-cut evening gown. The Sparrow Frozen Foods Gourmet Chinese Dinner was ready. As she carried it into the dining room to serve to her husband, now soothed, the word SUCCESS blinked on and off on her back, alternating with the word GOURMET.

She was replaced by the sagacious Walter, who announced the opening of the AKA convention at the Argo Palace Hotel in Chicago, Illinois, brought to you live!

Phil noticed that Sig was tired, leaning there against the lectern. Sig removed his glasses and rubbed the bridge of his nose. The rosy plastiglass of the dome polarized itself at the touch of a button to dim the setting sun behind the podium. A spotlight (several people twisted in their seats to locate its source but couldn't) pinned Sig in its formal circle. He folded his glasses and put them in his inside coat pocket. As he straightened, a hush fell over the fifteen thousand delegates. The throat-clearing, foot-shuffling, ear-whispering, nose-sniffing, seat-adjusting and program-folding all died away, leaving a vast Precambrian silence in the hall.

Into which Sig Sparrow began to speak.

He welcomed all the delegates and briefly listed some of the places from which they came, the six continents and sixty-three nations. He promised they would all soon learn the truth about *The* Blue Light and what it had been like *out there*. He reminded them of the time ten years before when the entire world watched via satellite that historic launch of the *A.K.A. Monastic* into intergalactic space. He referred, in a quiet tone, to the results of that launch, the people whose lives had been transformed merely by being present, the column of blue light that may or may not be *The* Blue Light. That it was a coherent beam of light, something like a laser through the collecting and focusing action of the orgone drive, as developed by Augenblaue AeroSpace and Dr. Ambrose Merkin, who would be speaking to them next on the nature of intergalactic space and the orgone engine itself.

Sig outlined the history of the AKA Clubs, how they had started in California soon after the launch when a rootless and unhappy population had seen in that, uh, flamboyant launch cause for hope in a world where, statistics told them, criminal violence and divorce and misery were, in spite of the welfare state, guaranteed annual wage, free medical insurance, political freedom and free speech, on the increase. Were, in fact, epidemic.

These first brave people in California had found in Avery's daring voyage a hope for the future, a hope that was not open-ended and vague, but a finite, clear-cut, reasonable hope for the future, when Avery would return from touching the Face of God (as some expressed it) to tell the world about *The* Blue Light, and about the Answer.

Many scoffed at this idea. (There was some whispering and movement in the audience at this, a slight shuffling of collective feet.) But the idea grew until, now, tonight, the Answer would be given. (More shuffling, a vagrant breeze of excitement and anticipation.)

There had been rumors, Sig acknowledged, that Avery had disappeared, that he would not show up here tonight. Rumors of foul play. (Shuffling again.) These rumors are false. Entirely false, started by those who oppose the AKA Clubs and what they represented.

And he wished, as he said it, that he believed it himself. Oh, he wished that. He was very tired because he didn't really believe himself that those rumors were false.

42 / Banana Split

THE COUNTESS, pouter-pigeon plump and proud, stroking her feathery bosom in the front row, was not aware while Sig recounted the rumors about Avery, and while her tall, good-natured husband, Bob, the Secretary of the Army, daydreamed beside her, that Constantine Hubble, bandaged and black-eyed, a former navy man, was staring at her from the side of the auditorium. There was something intent, tip of the tongue, dazed and yearning about that gaze.

Absolutely motionless, he stared at the Countess, his ears deaf to the ringing voice proclaiming the glorious growth of the AKA Clubs and their culmination in this very evening in only an hour or so. The Countess, oblivious to Connie's attention, smiled at Sig. And once shifted uncomfortably as somewhere in her brainstem a small red flag was haltingly hauled up the yardarm and began to snap in the vagrant currents of her basal ganglia. She was the only one of fifteen thousand to shift in her chair at that moment, so raptly involved was the crowd in the ringing phrases of Sig's concluding remarks. No one even shushed her, and she herself hardly noticed; but her discomfort grew.

Among all those fifteen thousand, in spite of the most stringent security precautions, there were no less than forty-three potential assassins, armed with a variety of lethal weapons from poisoned spitballs to frozen rubber knives. Many of these were agents of governments who had attended the launch, ten years before, and found the experience not only unforgettable but pregnant with vital secrets.

Not all the assassins were assigned to Avery. In fact, only one was. Among the rest, there was an Albanian agent with instructions to eliminate the head of the Chinese delegation in the Albanian national interest. There were two Turks whose targets were Greek, and three Greeks whose targets were Turkish. The Israelis and the Arabs, the Irish and the English and the Basque had sent agents to the convention, but to a man they were absorbed in Sig's speech, political and cultural disputes temporarily forgotten.

"And now," Sig was saying, "it gives me pleasure to introduce the chief architect of the orgone drive, that very drive that sent Avery Krupp Augenblaue on his ten-year voyage into the unknown, Dr. Ambrose Merkin, of Augenblaue AeroSpace. Dr. Merkin."

Dramatically Sig swung his right hand out. The spotlight widened, and into it stepped Ambrose, his muttonchops glowing around his wide smile. He paused just inside the circle of light and gave a slight bow to acknowledge the ocean of applause for Sig's wonderful speech and welcoming him to the lectern.

A woman in the thirty-second row fainted from the excitement when Ambrose appeared. Her condition went unnoticed for the next sixty-seven minutes.

Sig edged to his left, out of the light, and vanished from view as Dr. Merkin, smiling, approached the lectern. He rested his foot on the ledge that bordered his side of the lectern and narrowly missed crushing the third and fourth fingers of the left hand of the Degenerate White Dwarf, who was curled contentedly in that small space, thoroughly enjoying himself. As Ambrose addressed the crowd, the dwarf amused himself by tying and untying the scientist's shoelaces together. It was, he ho-ho-hoed to himself, like playing "She loves me, she loves me not" with a daisy. Would Merkin's laces be tied together when he finished his speech? Ho ho ho.

Ambrose, in his mellow sensual voice, wove for the world the fabulous tale of the conquest of the orgone, from its first faltering and unhappy origins in Reich's research to the final triumph of the engine that gathered and focused them to launch Avery's spaceship.

"Tomorrow," Dr. Merkin announced, "Augenblaue Aero-Space will release to the world, for any and all countries and individuals who want it, the secret of the orgone engine. We have not and will not file for a patent on the process, save to assure that no *one* person or organization will control it, that it will be available to all.

"The relatively simple directions for the engine's construction will be published in every language represented here tomorrow morning at eight o'clock, local time. The formula will appear in a special issue of *Reader's Digest* tomorrow, the second of September, Labor Day, in all these languages. Avery Augenblaue, who recently purchased *Reader's Digest* expressly in order to publish this information, will then return the magazine to its former owners. The purchase was conducted under such secrecy that the owners themselves, until this second, were unaware of the buyer's identity.

"Augenblaue AeroSpace has been, for the past ten years, exposed to considerable pressure to release this information prematurely. The pressure has come, not only from our own government, but from no less than twenty-three national governments and six private groups or corporations, all of whom lobbied for exclusive rights to the orgone engine.

"Naturally, it is Avery's wish that no one power be allowed such exclusive domain over what will, I assure you, prove to be the most revolutionary technological breakthrough in the history of this planet — and, perhaps, all other planets as well.

"Among the benefits of the orgone engine is *unlimited free power* in the hands of anyone who builds one, and they can be built very cheaply out of readily available materials. Unlimited free power because the orgone and its energy are everywhere: in soil and sun, in sea water and dead leaves, in food and air. Unlimited free power, and free power means freedom undreamed of before."

Unseen in his cubby in the lectern, the Degenerate White Dwarf nimbly untied a square knot, his mouth forming a silent *Ho ho ho*.

"Avery, whom you all are awaiting, I know, has empowered me to make this announcement here this evening. Mr. Sparrow has mentioned rumors of foul play, and it is true that Avery has been detained. That is, he has not been present at the hotel. But he will address this audience at the scheduled time."

Kay paled under her elaborate cosmetics, and August's brain — as did that of many others who had smoked, sniffed, or eaten dried bits of *Amanita muscaria* before the convention — hummed in a diapason of bright actinic light. August began, very slightly, to glow.

Kay's vision wavered. How could Avery address the convention if he were dead? And if he weren't? She couldn't contemplate that. But in her sacral region a stiffening resolve straightened her spine, and she seemed unmoved by the swirls of guilt and rage roaring in her body. She glanced over at August and immediately realized there would be no further help from him, for his pupils were larger than his irises, making his eyes resemble the deepest black of intergalactic space, a velvety black that seemed for one oddly disconcerting minute to *glow* with unfathomable darkness.

Ambrose went on to describe the conditions in intergalactic space. He spoke, in simple terms, of the Lorentz-Fitzgerald equations, which explained the time discrepancy. He described Avery's return to Kankakee that blustery unseasonable day in late June, when he stepped, dashingly dressed, from his bagel-shaped ship and saluted.

In the back of the room Fairfax "Buck" Sweeney, Deputy Director, was grinding his teeth, and in the theater of his mind his arm swung a birch rod in a blurred whir at the naked buttocks of row upon row of naughty adolescents. It had been Buck's mission to discover that secret, and now almost no time was left to forestall its release to the world, the world! for God's sake — the orgone engine, an engine that should belong exclusively to the United States of America. Jesus, Avery was going to destroy us all! and Buck had only one healthy agent left.

He whispered into his walkie-talkie to Marty Huggins, seated on a crate in the basement of the Argo Palace eating a banana. He instructed Marty to get his goddam ass in gear and find out where the hell Avery was hiding in the hotel, and for Christ's sake catch the sunuvabitch by force if necessary and prevent him from appearing at the convention, but most of all keep him from publishing those secrets so vital to national security in, oh Christ, *Reader's Digest*, of all places! Use whatever tactics necessary.

Marty swung his feet off the crate. They touched the floor just as Dr. Merkin wrapped up his concluding remarks. Thunderous applause rolled through the hall.

Thirty-three minutes remained until dark and Avery's address.

43 / Mushroom *Duxelles*

AND HO HO HO, Ambrose Merkin lost the daisy test, She loves you knot. His shoelaces were tied together, so as he stepped away from the lectern after the applause had died down, this solid, dignified scientist, from Argyle socks to muttonchops, toppled like a ponderosa pine before Paul Bunyan's ax.

Most of the delegates did not see it happen, however, since they had been sitting on their clubby dedicated behinds for an hour and fifteen minutes, were eager to stand and stretch, and were in the process of vacating the hall. So they were surprised indeed when a crackling and enormous HO HO HO coursed through the vast dome. The crowd turned back toward the podium to see the Degenerate White Dwarf squatting on top of the lectern, microphone in hand, hugely shaking with deep, rich, moist and humid wonderful laughter, like a bowl full of jelly, shaking and ho-ho-ho-ing.

Then he performed a back flip off the lectern, scuttled to the wall, pivoted rapidly, and threw something at the floor that exploded with a loud bang, releasing an enormous cloud of *green* smoke (the color of his shoes). When the smoke dissipated, sucked into the air-conditioning ducts near the floor, the dwarf had disappeared.

Buck Sweeney grabbed Virgil Moses, standing at the back of the room completely dazed. "Grab that sunuvabitch!" Virge reacted as if he'd been stuck with a cattle prod. He leaped forward and sprinted toward the podium, but he was too late.

"Find that sunuvabitch!" Buck hissed into Joseph Harbin's ear, and Harbin, painfully trussed, trotted off in his curious gait to the front of the dome.

"Find that sunuvabitch!" Sweeney ordered Jonathon Harker. Harker lifted his damaged hand in a gesture of compliance and jogged after Joe Harbin's retreating back.

"Find the sunuvabitch!" Buck yelled at Connie Hubble, near the front row, staring at the Countess. He did not hear his boss's command over the buzzing of the crowd curious about the dwarf. So as the Countess made her way up the aisle and toward the refreshment tables at the back of the dome, trailed by her smiling husband, Bob, and while Joe and Jonathon tottered their separate ways in search of the dwarf, Connie Hubble wandered blankly after her, stupefying his boss.

"What the hell . . ." Buck muttered under his breath.

Connie trailed two paces behind her, and when she picked up some mushroom *duxelles* in pastry cups he stood his ground, and she turned directly into his staring face.

"Excuse me," she mumbled, and started to step around him in the crush of AKA delegates striving for refreshment. Then she peered at him, at the bulb of bandage covering the bridge of his nose, at his greenish purple eyes, at his finely chiseled mouth. "You look familiar. Do I know you?"

Connie did not answer.

"Bob," she said, drawing her husband's attention away from piling *duxelles* onto a paper plate imprinted with a gold AKA. "Doesn't this man look familiar?"

"He does look a bit *familiar*," Bob answered, meaning *fresh*.

"Do you suppose he realizes we're talking about him?" she asked.

"It doesn't seem so," said Bob.

"Wait a minute," she said, circling Hubble as if he were a piece of antique furniture. "Oh, my God, Bob! This is . . ." She held Hubble's chin firmly and ran her hand down what she could of his profile: mouth, chin, neck and chest. "The Able-bodied Seaman! Quick, Bob! His eyes! We've got to get away from him!"

She grabbed her still-smiling husband's arm and dragged him after her, but Connie Hubble, stiff-legged and vacant, followed inexorably behind, emitting small mewing sounds deep in his throat. His eyes, previously as blank as two pages of foolscap fresh from the paper factory, now were printed with a reddish text of strange yearning. *Clomp clomp*, he chased after the openly fleeing Countess, *clomp clomp*, to haunt her very dreams.

The small crowd that had gathered around Ambrose Merkin after his fall and the dwarf's ho ho ho began to gravitate toward the refreshment tables when it was clear that nothing was injured but his scientific dignity.

"Tied my shoelaces together," Dr. Merkin told Joseph Harbin, who, in spite of his truss, was still the only agent on the floor with what passed for a clear mind.

"Shoelaces together?" he answered haltingly. His response, filtering through his Dexedrine and caffeine haze, sounded like, "Shoo places tool leather?" The switches had crossed somewhere between his ears and his left hemisphere language center.

"Yes. He tied my shoelaces together." Ambrose brushed off his knees, not terribly annoyed.

"You must be furious," said Jonathon Harker, waving his injured hand. The gesture was too extravagant, however, and his hand connected solidly with the lectern. "Aaaah!" he screamed, bending double over the offended hand. While stooped over he noticed a piece of paper on the floor: "The end is at hand." When he read the word "hand" a terrible throbbing shot up his arm. The message was signed: "The Degenerate White Dwarf."

"What is it?" Angel's sweet voice asked at Harker's ear, and Harker, wincing in pain and fatigue, nodded at the floor and staggered away, cradling his bandaged hand in front of him.

Angel picked up the paper. "Look, Ally," he said. "A message from the Degenerate White Dwarf."

It was a business card. Angel turned it over after reading the handwritten message. On the reverse side in twelve-point Times Roman type, was printed: HO HO HO.

"That's him, all right, Ally. Ho ho ho. Just like Santa Claus. What do you suppose it means?"

"Must mean we're gonna know soon. About Dad. And everything. You know, the end is at hand." Ally smiled at her beloved brother and took his arm.

"I've been ordered to capture that dwarf," Virge Moses informed Ambrose. "Did you see which way he went?"

"I really couldn't say," Dr. Merkin answered with a flicker of a smile, a smile that was a shy elf at a cobblers' brunch.

Virge was stymied, and he stood bemused for a time watching the two Augenblaue children amble around the hall arm in arm and smile at the card Angel carried. Then his walkie-talkie beeped and Marty Huggins' voice twittered thinly in his ear.

"Who's this?" Huggins asked.

"Officer Moses," Virge murmured back.

"Huggins here," Marty said.

"Huggins?"

"Huggins."

"Oh. Did you see a dwarf?" Virge asked more for something to say than from any hope that the dwarf had recently been in Marty Huggins' vicinity.

"Nope. Have you seen Mr. Augenblaue?"

"No, but he's due here in about fifteen minutes. Should I ask him to get in touch with you?" Virge heard static in his earphone. "What's that?" More static. He shook it, but Huggins had evidently signed off. "Oh, well," he said to himself, and oddly, a vision of the fourposter bed wafted through his mind like a languid minnow in a bowl of mock turtle soup.

Down in the basement Huggins was fuming. Fifteen minutes! Sweeney would have his ass if he didn't locate Avery. He rode the elevator to the top. I can grab him here, he figured, before he goes onstage. Marty leaned against the foot of the staircase opposite the elevators. While his mind occupied itself with baseball, his eyes — keen, alert, brown — darted swiftly around the hall. He's gonna come up in the elevator, he thought, and then he mused about who was going to win the World Series.

Then the image of Sweeney having his ass spiraled out of the turgid depths of his unconscious, followed by a red tendril of fear hauling behind it all that remained of Marty Huggins' future.

While Marty felt despair and hope contend for their own World Series in his abdomen, fifteen thousand people on the floor above his head munched on mushroom *duxelles:* mushrooms minced fine and sautéed with shallots, Madeira, bouillon and tarragon.

But someone, and it was never discovered who, had introduced small but significant quantities of *Amanita muscaria* into the *duxelles*, and far far away, in the American Southwest, the Indians were counting their cash and going ho ho ho.

The chemical formula $C_{17}H_{23}NO_3$ zipped to fifteen thousand brains, where it intersected precisely with the arrival of their beloved Avery Krupp Augenblaue.

And ninety-three million miles away, the sun, a giant furnace of peppy blue orgones, was gathering itself to hurl a truly wondrous quantity of those little devils right into the heart of the storm that was even then preparing to throw itself on the Argo Palace Hotel.

And, elsewhere, the dwarf was saying, "Ho ho ho. The North Pole was never like this!"

44 / The Blue Light

THE STORM TIPTOED LIGHTLY across western Illinois and shook its mane of curly gray and very wet locks over the Argo Palace Hotel, splattering that monument to heavenly aspiration with gentle drops. Those gentle drops fell also into the brown soup swirling around the 108th floor. Water and hydrocarbons mixed, fused, and fell together to the crumbling streets below in a toxic, acid brew that would have been fatal if drunk. (Fortunately, no one was drinking the rain.) All over Chicago umbrellas unfurled like shiny black ferns to shed the poison rains. Umbrellas never lasted long in Chicago.

The sun set, sending a posy, a bouquet, a final floral tribute of blue orgonotic forget-me-nots into the dank depths of the storm, adding their mayhem to the festivities. And darkness descended.

At a printing facility in Elmira, New York, 137 agents of the department, on the express orders of the Deputy Director, who had *his* orders from the Director himself (who sat in a room underground in Washington, D.C., scanning a bank of television screens and sucking vigorously on a cigar given to him personally by Fidel Castro as a token of appreciation), smashed the sacred doors of *Reader's Digest* and charged into the building with drawn guns.

Fairfax "Buck" Sweeney followed the entire caper via his implanted radio receiver.

The raid was extraordinarily successful, Buck learned while watching AKA delegates wander around the pink-lit dome, chatting about the dwarf and Avery's appearance and slowly elevating to more mystic realms. All four hundred employees of the *Reader's Digest* printing plant were arrested and 1,675,000 copies of the special issue were seized.

Only one injury ensued from the operation. An agent's weapon accidentally discharged, severing him from his left little toe, which was shattered to paste.

Buck had no way of knowing, of course, about the other seventy-five million copies of the *Reader's Digest* speeding at that very moment through the dusk in Akley Republican Furniture vans to warehouses all over the country or already stored in Akley warehouses in Milpitas, Baton Rouge and Squash, Idaho.

He would find out in the morning, and the discovery would prove most uncomfortable for him. But by then the special issue would be in the streets.

So up in the cosy dome Buck paced and the rosy light grew. Buck munched a *duxelles* pastry cup and nodded as he heard about the stacks of *Reader's Digest* impounded by his agents. He munched another *duxelles* as he heard that the printing plant and its inventory had been burned to the ground, the most expedient way of disposing of the dangerous literature.

Buck did not notice the man standing next to him.

The man standing next to him did not, for that matter, notice Buck, either. He was an Albanian named Puta Lum, and his job at this convention was to assassinate the head of the Chinese delegation. Puta was unclear as to *why* he was to assassinate the head of the Chinese delegation, but he had in his pocket a new kind of weapon, a plastic machete that telescoped into an innocuous package disguised as a pack of filthy postcards. Puta had supervised the cover himself, and he smiled through his blackened tooth stumps as he fingered the package in his pocket. Wall-to-wall pussy, he thought, and he ate another *duxelles*. The addition of this small hors d'oeuvre to the *Amanita* already seething in his brain was all that was needed to give Puta Lum an intensely religious experience.

So when the lights suddenly faded and Avery appeared on the podium before the delegates could get to their chairs, Puta Lum saw visions of cataleptic rage in which his rigid body was seized by a powerful longing to rend and destroy, which, after all, was what he had been trained to do.

The spotlight in the huge room wavered and dimmed, leaving only a pool of warm light around the almost deified Avery K. Augenblaue, who sat on the podium in a comfortable armchair smiling warmly at the befuddled crowd of Akaians, who were either standing stunned or scrambling for their chairs dribbling half-eaten *duxelles* behind them.

In a strange kind of lock-step, Puta, stiff-legged, leaning slightly forward, marched around the periphery of the room toward the dais on which Avery sat beaming foolishly.

Avery sat quietly for five minutes while the delegates stumbled to their seats in the growing darkness, then gave him a standing ovation that seemed interminable. At last they were settled and reasonably quiet. There was a long silence in which only the faint sound of small raindrops drumming on the pink plastic dome could be heard. Puta Lum stood transfixed at the foot of the stage, and although the Chinese delegate bowed and smiled somewhere in his mental disorder, Puta couldn't quite keep him in focus.

Avery smiled a broader smile up there in the glow of light, rosy and warm. Then he opened his mouth to speak.

"Goddam suck fuck shut up shit fuck shut up *fuck!*" he said, and in the front row Kay felt very faint. Avery was alive!

"Oogie boogie," said Avery, and throughout the hall the delegates tapped their headsets, trying to make sense of the garbled translations the earphones were spitting out in all those languages.

"Screeek," Avery added, and then he made a terrifically loud throad-clearing sound and smiled again.

"Excuse me," he said. "Ahem. Ladies and gentlemen, let me welcome you personally to the tenth annual AKA convention. I realize you have all been anticipating my return from intergalactic space son of a bitch shit fuck shut up. And I want you to know how deeply I appreciate the confidence that you, and the people watching this event on television all over the world, have placed in me. I only hope that I won't disappoint you, goddammit."

Angel whispered to Ally, "I have a feeling I know who's behind all this." He glanced over at his mother, whose mouth had dropped open like an oven door, a look of overwhelming and blank terror in her eyes. Beside her August, now transported beyond all human dimension, gazed into a blue vibrating world of his own. He was smiling a beatific smile, and around his dank hair a faint blue nimbus was visible.

"So I won't delay," Avery continued "but will tell you right away about *The* Blue Light. *The* Blue Light about which you have all been eager to hear."

At that moment there was a tremendous crash of thunder just over the dome and a fierce lance of lightning penetrated the polarized plastic. A loud flurry of rain on the roof drowned out Avery's next sentence completely.

"And that's what *The* Blue Light is," he concluded.

Puma Lum was beside himself. His English was rudimentary at best, and he was not wearing his earphones, which would have translated for him, but he did catch the drift of Avery's remarks, and they somehow sounded *Chinese* to his cerebellum, drenched as it was in a massive overdose of psychotropic hyoscamine. He emitted a terrible cry, drew from his pocket his pack of dirty postcards, pressed the hidden button that transformed them into a plastic machete, and leaped onto the stage with the intention of decapitating the head of the Chinese delegation smugly lecturing about blue light.

With a hearty "Ho ho ho," the Degenerate White Dwarf tumbled from behind the chair, giggled as the Albanian agent took a powerful swing at Avery's neck and the blade sailed through, leaving behind no sign whatever of any damage, only a slight watery wavering of air disturbed by the blade's windy passage.

Puta Lum was carried in a complete circle from the inertia of his swing. Since the blade met no resistance, the Degenerate White Dwarf said, "Ho ho ho," and neatly tripped the agent as he finished his 360-degree spin. "Ho ho ho," as Puta Lum whirled off balance off the podium and dropped heavily to the floor, skidding seven feet into Kay's pointed toes. She didn't move, though her mouth, if possible, widened even more.

There was a shocked silence. Then Avery explained, "I am speaking to you through holographic projection, so I am not really here. Not really here."

Heads rotated in search of the source of this projection and faced forward again at the sound of a loud bang and puff of smoke. The dwarf vanished again.

"Well. To continue," Avery said, apparently oblivious to the strange and disturbing events that had taken place around him, including the dwarf's stagy vanishing act. "As I was saying, *The Blue Light* is really nothing. "

This announcement caused a long, long pause, a silence that crouched under the torrential sounds of rain sloughing away the brown air outside, shouldering it downward to the streets, where it ran sluggishly in gutters, and from there into the river, and down the river to the lake. As the fish were already dead, the pollution could do no further damage.

The rain brought with it an intense concentration of orgones, and the air of Chicago was turning slightly blue, though, because it was evening, no one could tell.

Nothing.

Nothing.

The word echoed through the minds of the fifteen thousand delegates, many of whom were floundering under double doses of *Amanita muscaria*, the sacred mushroom.

Nothing, nothing, nothing nothingnothingnothingnothing.

The Blue Light was *nothing!*

"And of course I didn't really travel into intergalactic space. All nonsense. There's nothing out there, you know. It's *empty*. Ho ho ho!" Avery smiled as he pulled the biggest rug from under the collective feet of the world.

"This is some kind of circus," Buck Sweeney screamed into the tiny microphone in his hand, and Bunny Darlitch stopped scribbling on his steno pad for the first time since Sig had gaveled the convention to order.

Ed and Betsy Sue Sox were confounded. Angel and Ally, though confused, were also delighted. The room burst into a cacophony of conversations when Buck's microphone somehow got patched into the hall's public address system, and the word "circus" echoed repeatedly in over 150 languages.

45 / Children of Paradise

PUTA LUM LAY ON his back, his crossed eyes gazing, unfocused at first, up Kay's watery silk dress, and as focus slowly gathered in the Albanian's narrow eyes, his religious experience swiftly increased in intensity. It became so intense, in fact, that when he was finally released from jail he returned to Albania and took his vows at that country's only remaining religious establishment, a convent, as it happened. He spent what was left of his life fingering beads and looking into distances no one else could see.

Neither he nor Kay heard the collective roar of conversation as it washed across the room to surge against the podium, retreat, and attack again. Avery basked in all his holographic reality, relaxed and smiling, legs crossed comfortably in his easy chair, while waves of undiluted emotion of mounting intensity scudded at his feet.

Those emotions varied. Ed and Betsy Sue Sox, for instance, were profoundly puzzled. Did this mean that Ed would not have to make his furniture speech tomorrow?

In the first row Angel grinned a wide skin-stretching, cramp-causing beamish grin. "Ally," he whispered into his sister's fountain of sweet-scented hair. "If he's here in that holograph, then he's here in the hotel. And we can tell him at last."

Ally threw her arms around his sixteen-year-old neck, hugged him closely, and nibbled on his shoulder. "Let's go look for him." They edged their way through the surf of dazzled conversation to the stairs. At the bottom Marty Huggins leaned against the banister waiting for Avery to arrive. He was preoccupied with sports and had not received the news.

"Leaving so early?" he asked the pair.

"Uh? Oh, yeah," Angel answered. "It's too noisy up there."

"What's happening?" Marty asked without real interest. His eyes darted around, two rodents on a hot plate, looking for Avery.

"Oh, nothing," said Angel.

"Oh, nothing," Ally agreed, and they went on to the elevators.

Marty would have had his ass busted flat if it were not for what happened later.

He lapsed into sports again, musing hard, while 120 floors below an irate father was making his way through the lobby to the express elevator. Ho ho ho.

Up in the dome Avery, wise and serene, smiled down on the crowd. He smiled on Duane Hemp and Rhea seated near the back. Rhea had, for the first time since Duane met her, rested her slender fingers and crimson nails on his thigh *of her own accord*. Under his Stetson the chemical messengers hummed.

"Take off your hat," Rhea whispered in his ear. "Duane. Take off your hat." Reverence was evident in her voice.

Slowly Duane reached up to touch the snappy brim of his Stetson.

The rain on the roof had settled down to a steady drumming, a soothing monotone that slowly insinuated itself into the conversational confusion, oil on troubled ocean, and an expectant silence began to grow.

Ambrose Merkin approached August, in his own intergalactic vacuum, and firmly suggested he take Kay downstairs to Suite 1001. August rose, took Kay's arm, and led her from the hall. Puta Lum, transported far beyond the need of looking up her dress, remained on the floor, ignored for the moment (Virge Moses would drag him away later), and stared into the vivid blue afterimage.

The silence grew behind Kay and August, and as they passed Marty Huggins alertly guarding the stair he asked them the same questions he'd asked Angel and Ally. But this time there was no response.

Boy, these people are nutty, he said to himself, and thought some more about the World Series.

Avery smiled on and on into the collective silence as fifteen thousand faces eyed his insubstantial form. "Never mind," he said at last, and sighed gently. "Never mind. You don't need *The* Blue Light, any of you. Other things are happening in the universe, wonderful things. These things are inside every one of you."

Avery smiled for a long time.

"Look here." He finally broke the silence and winked out like a burned-out bulb.

A group of marshals at the back began to walk up the aisles distributing from buckets what appeared to be topsoil, dirt, humus, and the rich smells of freshly turned earth filled the dome and mingled with the flower scents.

Duane's hand wavered near his hat. "Duane," Rhea whispered again, burning suddenly with unquenchable curiosity about another person for the first time in her life. "Duane! Take off your hat!" Again his hand lifted to the brim.

It was time for the finale, when Philbrick Weevol would give, live, the climactic performance of his artistic career, when he would sing "Children of Paradise" for the fifteen thousand in the hall and the millions glued to their TV sets.

Together, he and China climbed the stairs, passing Marty Huggins, who regarded the gray-haired man in the tight black uniform and gulped at the decoration on the front of Phil's trousers. Nutty, he said to himself, unaware that at that moment a thin blade of anger in the shape of an irate father was pushing the button for his floor in the express elevator.

Sig Sparrow escorted Philbrick Weevol and China to the podium, and the frenzied screaming of fans around the world could almost be heard on the moon. In New York City alone, twenty-three people expired of hysterical adoration.

Duane's hand had fallen in disbelief, so Rhea, staring at Philbrick, prompted him again. "Duane, your hat!"

Weevol's band arrived onstage: five pieces, two girls and three boys, all of whom seemed to be *naked*. The blonde slid behind the drums and tapped out a gentle intro, her perfect breasts (Reba Hare observed through her hyoscamine haze, and noticed too that Bunny beside her — his notepad forgotten on the floor — had also noticed) rippling with the rhythm she set.

Duane whipped his hat from his head, and Rhea exclaimed, "Amazing!" Duane's tight curly hair had grown and compacted into the shape of his Stetson hat. A brimless cowboy hat. The effect was very strange, but Rhea loved it.

The other girl in the band strapped on her saxophone. By God, Ed Sox murmured to himself, she *is* naked. By God, and he almost noticed Betsy Sue's little hand dancing on his knee.

Her hand was dancing because the electric flute player was a real blond, and *he* was naked, too. Betsy Sue had never been exposed to anything like this in public, except at the Crystal Grape, and somehow there it didn't count. Or did it? Betsy Sue wasn't certain, but a thrumming in her blood started her fingers dancing up and down her Eddie's thigh. The bass player was also undressed. And the electric dulcimer player was naked. Oh, my.

Philbrick Weevol wore clothes, though obscene ones, and at his side, crouching and hugging his calf, occasionally ripping her fingernails up the back of his thigh, China was clothed.

Phil got out his electric kazoo, and the crowd went wild. In Kuala Lumpur seventeen spontaneous orgasms were recorded.

The group started slow, tap-tap, tap-tap, tootle-toot. A slow rhythm, a new arrangement. The saxophone, muted, began to swell and fall, a luxurious stretching sound without melody as yet, the music of breasts and thighs, of reaching arms and curled toes, the whisper of breath on the neck, the cheek, the throat, of blood flooding spongy tissue and growing excitement.

What the hell is this? Buck Sweeney asked himself, and despite it all he began to imagine that those endless rows of naked bottoms invited him not to whip but to touch instead.

The flute began to warble, and the crowd could *see* that the music was exciting, the flute player's root twinging with the music, yes, sir. The bass, thump, thump, thump, almost subsonic, heartbeat below the soft drumming and smooth sax and warbling flute. The dulcimer, an ancient instrument, entered, picking out the melody, and in that mushroomed collective mind Philbrick's moronic words developed a corona of new and real meaning:

> *Shiva dancing in Buddha's navel*
> *The dance of Cosmic Coitus!*

Philbrick in his cracked, untrained, tone-deaf voice started to sing, and around the world, 57,413 couples reached their relatively low thresholds and fell upon one another in a rush of hunger and ecstasy they had never before experienced, and the orgones popped like flashbulbs.

The Argo Palace glistened in the rain, clean and tall.

46 / The Heart of the Artichoke

As Phil's cracked voice threaded though the humus-drenched air of the dome and the rain sluiced away the hydrocarbon corrosion on the hotel, leaving it pink and shiny, the two children of paradise themselves, who had been waiting inconspicuously one floor down by the elevators, trailed their mother and her fungoid butler to Suite 1001.

"Shhh," said Ally, pressing her finger against Angel's delicately pursed lips. In return, Angel whispered a kiss against the finger.

Kay walked as if all her major joints had been partially disconnected, so leg preceded pelvis, followed by thigh and head, then shoulders, and arms trailing out behind. The next step she took might alter the sequence — shoulders first, perhaps, then knees and elbows, breasts and thighs. Had she been undressed instead of fully clothed she would have resembled *Nude Descending a Staircase*, a cubist interpretation of motion. August shlumped along in front of her, leaving in his wake an easily detectable scent of crushed mushroom smells and hallucination.

He knocked at the door to 1001 on the one-hundredth floor, and the door swung open. August entered, and Kay assembled herself behind him.

"Oh, boy," said Angel, and the two kids huddled together

against the wall next to the door. The "oy" of "boy" echoed into Kay's penetrating scream, a scream that shot up and down the twelve-tone scale like an ambulance on the way and propelled Angel and Ally into the room.

To see:

Kay drooped against August's rigid form, but no help available from August, his hands lying as they were like two dead spores along his trouser seams, and opposite them Avery, seated and relaxed, in two easy chairs, two Avery's, one of them with a hatchet planted firmly in his forehead and a foolish grin on his face.

"Oh, my," said the other Avery, the one without the ax, smile departed as the buffalo from the plain of his face.

"August," he suggested, "please help Mrs. Augenblaue to a chair. I think she needs to sit."

August, whose mind was now a wolf running free through the moonlit mountains of the Transcarpathian Alps, breath frosty in the silver light, a howl and a yelp on his curled lip, moved his body to a distant rhythm indeed. But Kay collapsed in the chair, and he assembled her sections as best he could into an approximate order. She stared dazed at both Averys.

"Forgive my little joke, Kay," Avery said very tenderly. "This" — and he waved his hand at the motionless Avery grinning beneath the hatchet — "is a life-sized latex dummy. I'm afraid I substituted it in the bath a couple of months ago. I was hiding in the steam, singing."

Kay shook her head, and a loose heap of metal parts seemed to tinkle inside, though probably it was only her earrings making that curiously musical sound.

"Oh, Kay, I'm way ahead of you, you know, and I wanted to wake you up."

"You're alive." The words were two wafers pressed through the ancient mangle of her lips, two yeasty uncooked cookies ready for the baking sheet, ready to rise in the heat. But there was no heat, and the two words lay on the air between them like a pair of pallid oysters. She meant them to be a question, but she was beyond questions.

"Very much," said Avery, and his smile returned, and with it the heat came on again.

"Ho ho ho," came from the hitherto unnoticed dwarf in the chair behind the door. "Very much alive," said the dwarf, his voice making a two-note chord of Avery's.

"The Degenerate White Dwarf!" Angel exclaimed. "Look, Ally!"

"My pleasure, I'm sure," said the dwarf, nodding to Ally, who nodded politely back. He was squatting on the chair, his feet tucked under him, and he suddenly sprang into the air and executed a neat flip, landing on the floor before them. He bowed. "Nice to see you again, boy Angel," he greeted.

"Boy?" Kay asked. Things were moving awfully fast. No one noticed August's eyes fall shut as his mind raced on through the rich autumn nights where the trees formed dark outlines against a full moon.

"Yes, Kay. You didn't know, of course," Avery said. "Angel is our son, now."

"I had no idea."

"But Daddy, how did you find out I was a boy? That's what we wanted to tell you when you got back, but then you disappeared and everything and we got worried. And what's that dummy doing, with an ax in its head? And who is the Degenerate White Dwarf? And —"

"And where have you been?" Ally inserted in Angel's wordy rush.

"Easy. Easy," said Avery, patting the air gently in front of him. "One thing at a time. I don't need to be mysterious, at least not anymore. You remember who performed your operation, don't you, Angel?"

"I never met the doctor who did it. I was sound asleep."

"One member of the surgical team was a Dr. Ague, from the Ague Biosynthetics Clinic in Menlo Park."

"That's right, Angel. I remember his name," Ally said.

"Well, I am Dr. Ague," Avery said.

"Ho ho ho," said the dwarf, seated again, his green feet swinging a foot above the carpet.

"You did the operation?" Angel couldn't believe it.

"Well, I did have some help. A very good team," Avery said modestly. "But, yes, I did the work. I'd realized all along there was a mistake with you. You should have been a boy in the first place. But please understand that you have had a rare opportunity because you have experienced both sexes. Your understanding is great, and it is very important. If you hadn't chosen to change your sex I might have had to suggest it to you. But you *knew* and you chose. You are a new kind of person and will be very important to the world."

There was a long silence. Kay's head moved constantly back and forth, looking at Avery, then at Angel, then at Avery, then at Alicia Katherine, but avoiding the latex dummy with its goofy grin bisected by the shadow of the hatchet handle.

"OK," said Angel. "I like being a boy, and I like remembering what it was like being a girl, and I guess I do understand a few things, but just a few. And what about *him*?" He gestured toward the dwarf, who went *ho ho ho* with his rounded mouth but made no sound.

"Oh, he's me."

"Come on," said Ally.

"No, no. That's quite correct," said Avery. "He's me."

In August's head the night began to flash, the trees to sway, the moon to howl. Light dripped from the needles of wind, and popped and phosphoresced from his flying fur, running, *running!*

"Well," said Avery, "He used to be me, anyway. He's a clone, grown from some of my cells. He should have been another, younger me, but it didn't quite pan out. Still, he's my closest friend."

"Ho ho ho," said the dwarf. "Son of a bitch shit suckfuck!"

"Besides being a dwarf, he has Gilles de la Tourette Syndrome," Avery said.

"He already explained that," Angel said.

"You're alive," said Kay, and this time the cookies were rising. There was, in Kay's voice, a new tone, a fifth that chimed with Avery's tonic and the dwarf's third, a perfect major chord. There was something of wonder in her tone, a little less of fear, a hint of, not happiness exactly, but not misery either. Pleasure? Relief?

"I'm alive, Kay. And you are, too." Avery smiled at her, and this smile was new: it was hearth, and warm, and it held concern; but most of all, it was indescribably *tender*.

"Yes," said Kay and tentatively, shyly, uncertainly, a furtive twitch uncovered first one tooth, then another, until a smile appeared on her lips.

A real smile.

And her face, which until now had been (and no one had ever noticed that it had been such a permanent part of her face) an architecture of hard steel and flat planes, of small straight lines, of asymmetric tension, her face *relaxed*. Lines became curves, something inside that face broke, the rigid structure dissolved into dust, the scaffolding that had supported the unnatural shape of her face collapsed, and what remained was, well, beautiful. Even her hair, her stiff, orange hair, seemed to soften and frame that face. A face to love.

"I feel . . . strange," Kay murmured, her voice full of rich harmonic overtones.

"You've put up with a lot," said Avery, and his voice curled around her like the steamy warm odors of a healing broth. "But you see, you didn't kill anyone, everything is fine, now. You had a lot of hate, Kay. It was very unfair."

Kay, smiling, cried. Big silver-crystal tears rolled off her cheeks into her lap. And seated in the chair, her body subtly meshed, her joints knit and flexed, she sat up straight. And in her lap her hands relaxed, fingers gently curled, in a small gesture of acceptance.

"But if you didn't go into intergalactic space, why haven't you aged?"

"Oh, that," Avery smiled. "Ague Biosynthetics Clinic. One of my operations. A, uh, client of mine, a William Lamplighter, has something in his blood. We're working on it. It seems to slow down aging. Lamplighter may live indefinitely."

"What about him?" Ally asked at last, pointing to August, his eyes focused inward on those silvered slopes.

"He is, I think, going back home," said Avery kindly. "He has a number of nervous disorders, as perhaps you've noticed. Vitiligo makes him look like a mushroom and gives him a certain dampness."

"I'll say," said Angel. "That reminds me, Philbrick Weevol thinks that people are descended from plants, and we figured if that's true, August is a fungus."

"Could be," Avery answered with his smile.

"But what about that?" Ally asked, nodding at the latex dummy.

"Oh, that. Just a little joke," said Avery. "Nothing important."

"No," said Kay, "nothing important."

Avery continued, "I haven't had so much fun since I was nine years old and my electric goat ate Mother's Persian carpet."

He stood up and offered his hand to Kay. She accepted it and she stood up.

"Ho ho ho," laughed the Degenerate White Dwarf.

47 / The Grape of Joy

As THE DWARF CHUCKLED, "Ho ho ho," the bony father, sputtering with righteous rage, stepped from the elevator and barreled into Marty Huggins.

"Who are you?" Marty asked.

The irate father didn't respond but with one punch flattened Marty Huggins into the bottom of the ninth with the score tied, the bases loaded and two outs, and far away the coach called *bunt!* for God's sake.

In his pain, Marty suspected the man must be Avery as he struggled to his feet from those terrible depths and started up the helical stair after the man who had decked him. When they emerged, one behind the other, into the blare of sax and dulcimer, drum and bass and electric flute, they both stopped short as the smells of humus and flowers, the sounds of that silly but strangely affecting song and something else, an indefinable motion in the crowds, washed heavily over them, a *tsunami* of staggering power. The father's eyes darted restlessly, distracted, distraught, their whites shining in the rosy glow.

Then he located the person he'd been seeking and plunged up the aisle toward the podium. "Aaaaarrrgh!" he yelled, his hands arching up, two claws tearing at the air before him.

His yell was lost in the din of music, but in the first row, seated in Dudee's lap, red tongue lolling, Philadelphia raised his hideous head and low in his squat throat joined his own *Aaaaarrrgh* to that of the frantic man. Philadelphia's *Aaaaarrrgh* was enough to attract China's attention from rubbing Philbrick's knee as it flexed with the mounting rhythm of his song while her right hand slid with increasing speed up and down his inner thigh.

When she glanced up and saw the angry man, face contorted and claw-hands flailing, she jumped to her feet. "Daddy," she exclaimed, and this time the father's inarticulate yell penetrated everyone's musical trance, and the fumy effects of *Amanita muscaria* were chased from the room by a rush of fear and violence. Seven hundred and sixty-seven people scrambled to their feet.

"Child molester!" the father shouted. "Corrupter of little girls! Degenerate! Commie! Pervert!"

"Oh, Daddy, fuck off," China started to say, but, as her father approached the stage, Philadelphia, handicapped by a devolved brain, in a terrible confusion of instincts, leaped from Dudee's lap, seized the man's right leg in the powerful grip of his jaws and front legs, and began, with a mechanical, metronomic motion, to hump China's daddy's ankle.

The music on stage faltered, lost the beat. The drummer, her round breasts jogging in syncopation, observed the dog furiously raping the man's ankle and picked up that rhythm, and the song, which had slid between verses, gathered itself into a new and perhaps more basic beat, subtly altered by the spectacle near the stage. The 769 standing were joined by the rest of the fifteen thousand, who strained to see and stayed to sway to this rhythm.

China's father, now flat on his face, vigorously shaking his ankle to dislodge the dog, was carried from the room by Virge Moses and two other officers to accompany Puta Lum in that limbo of police. Marty Huggins followed the troop out, still thinking that this was Avery. Later, Marty received credit for the arrest and thus was saved from disgrace.

The song continued.

O gooey Yin and throbbing Yang.

In Ulan Bator over twelve thousand simultaneous orgasms imparted a curious blue orgone glow to the air.

The light show started, small lights popping in the air around the band, white and blue, sparks and catherine wheels, pinwheels and Roman candles, O children of paradise, Order, Family and Genus. The lights drifted out over the masses of people all pulsing with the beat, clasping hands spontaneously as the sequined outline of Philbrick's lingam began to glow in the blacklight. And as he sang, "A universe of Steady State and Big Bang," behind him, in the air, wavering at first and indistinct, the image of a maroon fence formed; on the fence, etched in perfect lines, the image of a man's profile, the profile of the ex-President who disappeared the day of Avery's launch.

No one noticed the profile through the popping lights and spinning fireworks, the ultraviolet and the noise, the fresh earth smells and heady flower fragrances, the insinuating rhythms.

But in the back of the room, Buck Sweeney noticed. "That goddam face is a national monument!" he muttered, and the profile on the fence lowered to blend with Philbrick Weevol's ecstatic singing face, and the two faces, projected profile and singing star, blended in perfect harmony.

"Philbrick Weevol's the missing President!" Buck shouted, but no one heard him.

The audience overflowed into the aisles and danced with growing intensity. Greeks and Turks, Arabs and Israelis, Protestants and Catholics, Irish and English, Russians and Chinese and Japanese businessmen and African diplomats, all danced with each other. Buck could not have made his way to the front of the hall to announce his discovery if he had wanted to.

Marty crowed into his walkie-talkie that he'd nabbed Avery, but Sweeney knew that slob wasn't Avery. Sweeney's brain was drenched with his particular brand of adrenaline and rage, his own lusts and weird currents, his own desert winds blowing through the empty spaces of his life. He drew his gun and headed for the stairs.

The song went on without him, improvising verses and variations, the naked band weaving the huge feedback resonance of the crowd's movements into its melodies. A tremendous event occurred, an event that lasted all night. A musical marathon, an endless dance began, a chain of hands, a monumental liberation that stayed with everyone there forever, after the music had played itself out, after the mushroom high was forgotten, after Avery disappeared again (though some say they saw the dwarf, dressed as a frog, hopping and croaking around the pink dome amid popping, flashing lights), after the news of the former President was released, discussed, explained and forgotten, after the baby boom that resulted from this night was over. There was a change in the world, it seemed. Statistics measured new trends.

That night, only one person failed to respond to the music. Along about two in the morning, while the party was still going strong, Joseph Harbin in his painful truss crawled around the floor searching for clues beside the stage, for in his mind hammered the relentless call of duty. He chanced across Puta Lum's plastic machete, and he marveled at the Albanian cunning that had contrived such a device. As he turned it over in his hands, he accidently triggered the hidden catch, and the machete vanished with a snicker into a deck of dirty cards.

They found him at dawn, red-eyed, haggard, fixated on the cards, an expression of intolerable pain on his face, for the pictures (hand-picked by Puta Lum from a vast Chinese storehouse of such subversive illustrations) had blasted their way straight to his shattered groin and there established such a vicious cycle of lust and agony that shock therapy was required to end his suffering.

During the evening, Jonathon Harker met a pretty young woman from Brasov in the Transylvanian Alps and sent in his resignation. He was never seen again, and although his hand would always be a little stiff, he found love.

"Eddie," said Betsy Sue, gazing at her tanned husband with a shining, Reformed Baptist smile. "Isn't it wonderful?" And Ed, his rhythm matching hers, answered, "Yes." They danced on into furniture heaven, where all the chairs have wings, and along with many others they danced their way to their room. Once in their room, they danced on through a thousand mornings, afternoons and nights of AkleyLoungers buzzing and humming through dreaming and waking, through cities and towns and isolated farms. Ed never did have to deliver his speech on furniture, for the tenth annual AKA convention lasted only one night. The next day's events were canceled because no one showed up, not even Sigismund Sparrow and Ambrose Merkin.

Ed never saw A. K. Akley again. When he returned to Milpitas he found that he was now president of Akley Republican Furniture, which had assets of over seventy-five million copies of *Reader's Digest* in warehouses all over the country.

48 / Breakfast in Bed

BUCK SWEENEY, .38 drawn and ready, tiptoed down the spiral staircase away from the noisy confusion and activity of compacted orgones, down the spiral staircase to the whispering silence of the hotel air conditioning and empty halls. Some uncanny instinct sent him to the elevator, where he waited in a humming frenzy while visions of sugar bums danced in his head.

Outside, the storm tamed itself into a giant pussy cat that lay down on Chicago and began to purr.

The elevator yawned, and Buck, waving his gun, entered, pushed the button for 100, an even number, leaned against the wall, and sighed. When the doors opened he wavered through the halls, a phantom waif lost in all that fleshy pink. He halted outside Suite 1001 at the dictate of a higher law. His gun felt hard and cold in his hand, and somewhere in his head a mocking *Ho ho ho* urged him on to fury.

The door was ajar, and Buck glimpsed through the slight opening the pressed pants and elegant shoes that belonged to Avery Krupp Augenblaue, blue-eyed bastard and source of all his problems. Fairfax Sweeney recognized in that minute what he had to do.

He took a deep breath. He flexed his knees: once, twice, three times. He rose onto the balls of his feet and bounced there. He wound the spring tightly, lifted his heavy pistol into an unwavering aim, opened his eyes wide, took one more deep breath, and crashed through the partially opened door of the room.

One huge bound, a bounce on those springy feet, a somersault to lower his profile, and flat on the floor, prone, gun aimed at Avery's heart even before the door banged against the wall, Buck Sweeney squeezed off his six rounds into Avery's calm chest, *bang bang bang bang bang bang,* with a terrible yell of hate and rage.

Sweeney was a terrific shot. He had consistently won first honors at the shooting range and had a shelf full of trophies at home to prove it. Besides his fantasies of discipline, which were always dominated by the stern image of his father, General George Armstrong Sweeney, whose crepe-draped photo hung on Buck's office wall; besides those fantasies, the thing Buck loved best was shooting. Shooting at the outlines of evildoers wearing little glowing red hearts on their chests. Sweeney always hit those little red hearts. He could empty his .38 into those little red hearts in under two seconds and make them disappear.

Oh, yes, Buck Sweeney loved to shoot.

From the prone position he emptied his gun in under two seconds, right into Avery's evil heart, and as his revolver spurted its last round right into Avery's little red heart the door swung silently shut behind him, rebounding from the violence of his entry.

There was a deafened silence as the terrible noise of the gun died away. Smoke curled up from the barrel in a small and wistful wisp, and the smell of cordite permeated the room.

"My, my, my," said Avery.

Buck shook his head. Something was wrong. He could've sworn he heard Avery say, "My, my, my."

"My, my, my," Avery repeated. Then Buck noticed that the man he had just shot six times through the little red heart already had a hatchet buried in his forehead.

Buck was on top of a vast ocean, floating, the water warm and soothing, rocked by gentle waves. Onshore the palm trees swayed their fronds, a sound so soft and gentle and sweet he was cradled in it. The sky above his head was blue, unblemished, kind, as blue and kind as the sea he floated upon. Bright fish darted here and there, small lights winking yellow and red and electric blue in the placid depths. Buck felt very sleepy and happy, rocked there on the breast of the vast maternal ocean.

But somewhere, deep in the sea, very far away, so far that Buck barely heard it, or rather felt it, someone pulled a plug out of that ocean's drain. A thin whine, a tinny roar, and Buck sensed more clearly the beginnings of a huge whirlpool forming around his floating body, a whirlpool that collected him into its relentless arms and, gently at first but with growing strength, gravitated him into a descending spiral with no end, no bottom, no ceasing. Round and round, faster and faster, Buck swirled down the biggest drain of all.

"My, my, my," Avery repeated, glancing at Buck's sleeping form. "He certainly is a violent man, isn't he?"

No one answered, but August, his mind recalled from his Transylvanian wilderness, blinked.

As his eyes focused he saw, seated before him, Avery's shattered latex dummy, oozing from its chest what appeared to be some kind of oleomargarine, a goopy substance that trickled down the dummy's shirtfront. When he saw that, and the ax handle protruding from the dummy's forehead like the horn of a unicorn, his focus widened to include Buck Sweeney lying face down on the floor, his head tilted slightly to one side, a sweet, strangely innocent smile visible on his dreaming face. August blinked again, and the moonlight in his head shredded away. The black tossing trees became faint and wispy and vanished, his ancestral memories receding to the darkness of the past, and August, once more the perfect butler, bowed to Avery.

"Welcome home, Mr. Augenblaue," he said.

"Thank you, August," Avery answered. "Nice to be back, though it will only be for a short time, I'm afraid. I hope, August, that when I leave again, you will take very good care of Mrs. Augenblaue. Mrs. Augenblaue is feeling very much better about things, but she will need someone."

"Yes, sir," said August, bowing again.

"Avery!" Kay said, aghast. "Avery, you don't mean it. You can't desert me again. You can't." Her hair, her odd orange hair, lay smooth and shiny and meek on her head.

"Ah, but I must, I'm sorry to say. There will be a reaction, of course, to what has happened here tonight. Not from the delegates or the television viewers but from those in authority. They will be searching for me and will not be pleasant about it." He nudged Buck's beefy cheek with the toe of his shoe. "It will be difficult for you, I fear, so the less you know the better. Don't worry about me. Besides, you'll have August. He really does love you, you know. He's very devoted and has suffered much, too."

Angel and Ally, stunned by Buck's assassination attempt, seemed to wake up. "Daddy," Angel said, sadness and love mingled in his voice, "Daddy."

"Don't worry, Angel. I'll be in touch with you. When the time comes. I'm not finished yet." Smiling, he placed Kay's hand, which he was still holding, on August's forearm.

"Show Mrs. Augenblaue to your room, August. It's very late,

and we all need some rest, some peace, some love." August bowed, turned to Kay and smiled. His smile seemed less damp, less moldy, less buried. He still smelled faintly of mushrooms, but the odor was no longer unpleasant, and already his skin disease appeared to be fading.

Kay paused on the threshold. Avery nodded and smiled, and she disappeared down the hall.

"Well, kids," Avery said, "I'd better be going, too. Take care of your mother. I realize it's been hard for you, but she's better now. Everyone is better now."

He hugged the two of them hard, one on each side, and departed.

The Degenerate White Dwarf said, "Ho ho ho," clapped them both on the back, smiled at them from the doorway, did a sudden and elegant back flip into the hall, and likewise vanished.

"What'll we do about him?" Ally asked, pointing to Buck's snoozing form lying at the foot of the ruined latex dummy.

"Nothing," Angel responded. "He's out of bullets. Ho ho ho."

Ally grinned, and arms about each other, they ambled into the bedroom of Suite 1001 and shut the door behind them.

On the roof, in the dome, the dancing went on until the couples dispersed and Phil sang himself hoarse. William Lamplighter and Nurse Thinger put on a joyous show that no one watched. Ed and Betsy Sue went to bed early. Outside the Countess's hotel room, Connie Hubble folded into a fetal ball and slept the sleep of innocence.

The rain, clouds and violent sunspots moved on, leaving behind a starry night of the most dazzling crispness. As Labor Day dawned over the Midwest, the eastern sky lightened, stars faded, a deep blue replaced the black, and was in turn replaced by light, blue light, *The* Blue Light. The sun came up, painting with its ninety-three-million-mile-long paintbrush the blue-green planet Earth with its wide swatch of sunspot orgone paint. The little planet rotated on through a bubbling bath of those pesky little devils that just wouldn't leave it alone, ever again.

Philbrick Weevol, crazed ex-President and deluded psychiatrist, lousy artist, sculptor and poet, rock star and patron saint of the AKA Clubs, now on their way to oblivion as its fifteen thousand delegates scattered into the morning to spread their special news, Philbrick lay down on the humus-covered stage amid the litter and debris of his band's tender couplings and, fifty-seven years old, made tired love to his seventeen-year-old girlfriend China and fell sound asleep.

Bunny Darlitch and Reba Hare joined them in happy copulation, and the sun rose rosy pink in the geodesic dome.

All over the hotel, all over the country — the world, in fact — *forniculotermes brevis*, tiny termites, munched their way to the surface of whatever Akley furniture they happened to be in.

"Oh, Dudee," said Sig Sparrow, one of the last to leave, rising to his feet from his chair in the front row. "Dudee, Dudee, I'm very tired. It has been a trying day indeed."

And Dudee, Dudee of the velvet ropes and velvet hands, led her Uncle Sig to his ropy heaven.

Electronic Epilogue

Concerning this a man once said, Why such reluctance? If you only followed the parables you yourselves would become parables and with that rid of all your daily cares.

Another said: I bet that's also a parable.

The first said: You have won.

The second said: But unfortunately only in parable.

The first said: No, in reality: in parable you have lost.

– Franz Kafka, *On Parables*

49 / A Mint

"TELL ME about Avery."

"Avery Krupp Augenblaue, also known as Arthur Kadel Accacia, also known as A. K. Akley, also known as Aldrich K. Ague, also known as Anton Armbruster, nickname 'Keb,' born September 2, 19 — "

"Not that. I know all that now."

"Multitalented scientist. Best known as a religious reformer, follower of Wilhelm Reich —"

"Not that either."

"What, then?"

"Where is he?"

"Beep."

"How can we locate him?"

"Beep."

"Where has he gone?"

"He's missing, presumed dead. He disappeared the night of September 1 or morning of September 2, Labor Day. The tenth annual AKA Club convention. He has not been seen since."

"His wife. Does she have any idea where he is?"

"Kay Augenblaue has remarried. She has been questioned repeatedly and finally won an injunction against any further government 'harrassment.' It is assumed she knows nothing."

"Kids?"

"They live quietly. It is assumed they know nothing."

"His company, Augenblaue AeroSpace. Surely the people there are not totally in the dark as to his whereabouts!"

"Beep."

"No answer?"

"That was a statement, not a question."

"Do his employees, this Dr. Merkin, for example, have any pertinent information?"

"Dr. Ambrose Merkin has become president of Augenblaue AeroSpace. He, too, has been repeatedly questioned. Avery's will designates Dr. Merkin as president of the company. He's in complete charge. Despite extensive surveillance of Dr. Merkin, no contact appears likely between him and Avery Augenblaue. Avery is missing, presumed dead. His will has been executed."

"What about the dwarf?"

"Classified as the Degenerate White Dwarf. Now acknowledged to be a clone of Avery and a partial failure as such. The dwarf also has disappeared. Missing, presumed dead."

"No sign of him at all?"

"Rumors only. Some witnesses, considered marginally reliable, have reported a dwarf dressed as a frog hopping around the Argo Palace Hotel. Sightings are reported occasionally and are always investigated. Investigation always negative. They are assumed to be hoaxes."

"Anything else?"

"One thing. A small company in Squash, Idaho, has manufactured and marketed an item called the Electric Goat. It's advertised as affectionate, friendly, good with kids. Looks just like the real thing."

"What's it for?"

"It eats trash. Garbage. It's a waste disposal system. There is no evidence, but it's not impossible that Avery is connected with this company."

"Oh, God. Anything else?"

"Nothing."

"All right. Terminate program."

"Program shitsuckfuckgoddamshitSHUTUP terminated. Good night, Mr. Director."

OLAF STAPLEDON

Last and First Men

Olaf Stapledon describes the evolution of mankind through the ages, reaching the very heights of civilization at one point, descending to the depths of near-extinction at the next, surviving onslaughts from other planets and overcoming the waning of solar energy, but always developing new thoughts, new abilities and new means of survival. The enormous scope of this great classic makes it one of the finest future histories ever written, a true master work of science fiction.

Last Men In London

The sequel to LAST AND FIRST MEN, Olaf Stapledon's great classic work of science fiction.

In LAST MEN IN LONDON the author follows up the themes of his earlier masterpiece in presenting a Neptunian 'last man's' views on our twentieth-century world, views informed by the huge dimensions of space and time which separate him from our tiny contemporary world. Once again, Olaf Stapledon has been totally successful in creating a work of such stunning imagination and brilliance that it has taken its place amongst the classics of science fiction.

JOHN BRUNNER

The Wrong End of Time

America in the future is a fortress ruled by fear. Through its massive defence works is smuggled a young Russian with a terrifying message. An alien ship has entered the solar system. Its threat – to boil the Earth's entire mass into raw energy!

'Alarming and persuasive' – *The Times*

Traveller in Black

The time was the unguessably remote past – or perhaps the distant future. Throughout the universe, Chaos ruled. Scientific laws of cause and effect held no force; men could not know from one day to the next what to expect from their labours, and even hope seemed foolish. In this universe there was one man to whom had been entrusted the task of bringing reason and order out of Chaos. He was a quiet man dressed in black who carried a staff made of light, and wherever he went the powers of Chaos swirled around him, buffeted him, tested him. He fought them, and little by little he drove them back. But the Traveller in Black himself belonged to the anti-science universe. If he succeeded in his task of changing the order of the cosmos, could he continue to live?

CLIFFORD D. SIMAK

Way Station

As keeper of the way station, Enoch Wallace was the only human privileged to communicate with the rest of the galaxy. He looked like any other man on Earth, except that he was 124 years old and showed no signs of aging. And his house seemed like any other, though mysteriously impregnable. All was quiet around Enoch's isolated farm – until someone raided the family graveyard and discovered an unknown horror.

A Choice of Gods

The Earth's population was more than eight billion. One day they were there, the next they were gone – all except the guests at a family birthday party, a small tribe of American Indians, and, of course, the robots.

Technology disintegrated, the Indians went back to nature, and the rest developed new and extraordinary powers. As for the robots, some went to live with the remnants of humanity, others gathered in their own community and commenced work on the Project, work which was baffling in all its fantastic complexity.

Then one day a traveller returned from the stars – and the idyllic existence of the last of the Earth's humans was threatened.

ANDREW J. OFFUTT

Messenger of Zhuvastou

In hot pursuit of his beautiful 'fiancée',
Earthborn playboy Moris Keniston arrives on the
mysterious and hostile planet Sovold. Before he
can sample its violent lifestyle and bizarre terrain,
or combat the amoral whims of its courts (and
blue-haired courtesans) he needs to adopt a
suitable disguise.

So with shaved head and skin dyed beige, he dons
the yellow-crested helmet and green cloak of a
Messenger of the mighty empire of Zhuvastou.
Armed only with a heavy sword he is ready to set
out on his urgent quest . . .

Clansman of Andor

Reborn in a warrior king's body, he fought to
control an alien planet.

On Earth Robert Cleve was a misfit, a man of
action who had no place in an advanced
technological civilisation. But a lust for adventure
drove him to accept a dangerous assignment on
distant Andor.

Taking on the bodily form of Doralan Andrah,
Cleve became a warrior chief in a barbaric
corner of the universe, forced to face dangers
darker and more terrifying than the worst
nightmares of his native Earth . . .

DAMON KNIGHT

Off Centre

Eight brilliantly inventive gems of science fiction
by Damon Knight.

Meet:
Michael Kronski, an ordinary human being who
can bend the past to his will
Pete the Dolphin who learns to talk to man
Kip Morgan who finds his body invaded by little
blue men
The Martian who comes to visit Earth
God's Nose
Dulcie and Decorum

In Deep

Take a step forward and fall suddenly into a
creeping blob of protoplasm, then discover that
your three companions have fallen with you and
you and your bodies have been digested by the
'Thing'.

Watch a man searching on a beach, and feel your
blood run cold when he tells you what he is
searching for. A doorway that will take you
anywhere – except back to Earth.

In Deep is a bizarre and brilliant volume of stories
from the imagination of Damon Knight.

More top science fiction available from Magnum Books

These and other Magnum Books are available at your bookshop or newsagent. In case of difficulties orders may be sent to:

Magnum Books
Cash Sales Department
P.O. Box 11
Falmouth
Cornwall TR10 10gEN

Please send cheque or postal order, no currency, for purchase price quoted and allow the following for postage and packing:

UK — 19p for the first book plus 9p per copy for each additional book ordered to a maximum of 73p.

BFPO & Eire — 19p for the first book plus 9p per copy for the next 6 books, thereafter 3p per book.

Overseas customers — 20p for the first book and 10p per copy for each additional book.

While every effort is made to keep prices low, it is sometimes necessary to increase prices at short notice. Magnum Books reserve the right to show new retail prices on covers which may differ from those previously advertised in the text or elsewhere.